Snow Swept
Book One in the Snow Swept Trilogy

Also By Derrick Hibbard
This Side of Eden
The Double Stroller Hand Grenade
Impish
Snow Swept
Snow Falling
Snow Pyre

Non-Fiction
College Fast Track
Law School Fast Track

Snow Swept
Book One in the Snow Swept Trilogy

Derrick Hibbard

Second Edition, June 2015

Copyright © 2014 by Derrick Hibbard
All rights reserved under International and Pan-American copyright conventions.

Published in the United States by Sail Away Press.

This book is a work of fiction. Names, characters, businesses, organizations, places, events, and incidents either are products of the author's imagination or are used fictitiously. Any resemblance to actual persons, living or dead, events, or locals is entirely coincidental.

ISBN-13: 978-1495988578
ISBN-10: 1495988570
FIRST EDITION

Cover Art by Melissa Goodman
Interior Design by Scott Brand

For more information visit:
https://www.facebook.com/derrickhibbard.author
derrickhibbard.blogspot.com
twitter.com/derrickhibbard
http://derrickhibbard.tumblr.com/

Acknowledgements

As always, a very special thanks to Linda Anderson, who wields her red editing pencil like a magic wand and works wonders.

Thanks to my wife, Amanda, for allowing me to constantly bounce ideas off her. I'm not sure she knew what she was getting herself into when she said yes.

Thanks also to Nina and Landon Finter, Seth Welner, and Monique Malachi, for being the first to read this book and for offering edits and suggestions.

Thanks to my brothers, Mitchell, Brady, and Peter, and too many friends to list here (among them: Joe Bowden, Adam Richards, Alex Perez, Tania Gomez, and Colton Hickman) for listening to me tell this story over and over again.

Most of all, my warmest thanks to you, dear reader. The best part of creating worlds is sharing them with you.

For Readers

Be sure to visit Derrick Hibbard on his blog, Facebook and Twitter for the free, private newsletter and get instant access to
exclusive extras and treats, including novels, novellas, stories, and more.

https://www.facebook.com/derrickhibbard.author
derrickhibbard.blogspot.com
twitter.com/derrickhibbard
http://derrickhibbard.tumblr.com/

It would be a good idea for you not to
trust
in your own reality,
the one you breathe and feel today within yourself
because—like that of yesterday—
it is destined to reveal itself as an illusion
tomorrow.
-Pirandello

When I have seen such interchange of state,
Or state itself confounded to decay;
Ruin hath taught me thus to ruminate,
That Time will come and take my love away.
--Shakespeare (Sonnet 64)

Part One
The Floating Forest

Chapter One

The young terrorist fled into the icy forest as the men who hunted her followed. Mae Edwards was very pretty. Her hair was long and blonde, her eyes the color of Caribbean surf, and her skin was smooth, and except for some light freckles on the bridge of her nose and cheeks, almost flawless. Today was her birthday, exactly six years since she'd first become a killer, a terrorist.

Now, she ran into the forest, into shadows and ice, and they followed.

Mae ignored the flashing pain in her ankle and the sinking guilt in her stomach. Her lungs burned, her muscles screamed in agony, but she kept running. It was the only thing she could think of to do. Mae had to get to a safe place, to escape the cabin and the woods, and either she escaped, or she died. It was that simple. Escape, or die.

The trees, with their enormous black trunks and snarly limbs, looked like the skeletons of giants from a forgotten fairytale, lumbering in the dark. Frozen branches creaked and groaned under the weight of ice and snow, blown by the cold winter wind. Layers of packed snow and powder blanketed the forest floor, with drifts piled high at the base of the trees.

Mae passed into a moonlit clearing and saw that the dark forest from where she'd come was nothing compared to the blackness of the forest beyond. It loomed like the cavernous mouth of a monster.

If she wasn't about to die, Mae would have stopped at the edge of the clearing, before the forest and the dark really began, but she didn't miss a beat. She kept running, ducking the low hanging branches, sliding on the ice, and breathing heavily as she thought about the dark stretches of forest, and everything unknown, beyond.

A flash of memory—she thought of her dad sitting on the edge of her bed, reading Little Red Riding Hood, his voice low and inflecting with the intensity of the story. She remembered being tucked snuggly into the patchwork quilt her mom had made her for her sixth birthday. The quilt was made up of all her baby clothes, soft and warm, each patch from a different pajama shirt, or sundress, or coveralls, each patch a memory.

As her dad read from the story of the little girl in the red cloak, on her way to Grandma's house through the woods, she remembered pulling the covers up to her chin and shutting her eyes when it came to the part about the wolf in the forest. The thought of a little girl in the woods, all alone and stalked by a giant animal with long and shiny teeth (the better to eat you with, my dear), was enough to terrify her. She imagined its cold yellow eyes staring at her, unblinking, its rancid breath misting the cold night air. The wolf was a childhood horror that constantly lurked in the shadows of her imagination.

Her mom had warned her dad against reading stories like that to her, because of her active imagination, and it was a warning that she wished her dad had heeded. Because of the wolf, she was terrified of the forest, especially at night. She would even avoid looking out her bedroom window at the trees that surrounded their home and property, afraid that she'd see a wolf just beyond the manicured grass, standing on its hind legs and grinning at her with its wide and gaping maw. It was a fear that had stayed with her, that grey wolf with its long snout and yellow eyes, always on its haunches, waiting for her.

Even now, she had to force herself to not think about the wolf. The darkness shifted all around her, moving in sync with the winter wind and the creaking movements of the forest. The persistent fear that the long, grey wolf was always around the next tree, in the shadows and waiting for her, was silly, and she knew it.

At the moment, the fear was especially silly because she was about to die anyway, despite her fears. And it wasn't the wolf she had to worry about.

A bullet tore into a tree trunk inches from her face, spraying the air with bits of wood and ice. She slid to her knees as two more bullets whizzed by overhead, barely missing her. She stayed on the ground, holding her breath and waiting for more bullets. Her lungs felt like they would explode with her sudden refusal to breathe, and she could feel her heart beat exploding in her ears. Dropping to her stomach, she slid her body behind a pile of rocks and ice, waiting for more gunshots, and searching for any sign of the shooter. Bits of snow crept up underneath her shirt and pressed against her stomach, cold and hard, and she fought the urge to jump up and brush it out.

When several seconds passed with no more shots and no movement that she could see, she got into a crouching position and crawled out from behind pile of rocks and snow. Mae scanned the forest and the outline of the cabin, looking for any movement.

A shadow shifted on the roof of the cabin, and she knew it was Eddie. She couldn't see more than the outline of his body, but even that was enough to see that his rifle was still shouldered and pointed in her direction. She shifted lower on the ground, trying to blend into the forest, and watched Eddie scan the area with the scope of his rifle. She'd seen the rifle in the room just moments before, propped up against an old dresser, and it was big enough to do some damage.

After nearly a minute, Eddie lowered the gun and slung it on a shoulder strap. He walked gingerly across the roof to a tree that reached out over the shingles and provided an easy path to climb to the ground. Mae watched closely, knowing that there was a particularly thick patch of ice on the roof, right beneath the branch, and she hoped that Eddie would slip on that patch. If she was lucky, he'd fall from the roof and break his neck without another shot, giving her more time to slip away into the darkness without being pursued.

Eddie did slip, but he caught himself on the tree branch before falling. She saw his shoulders rise and fall as he took a deep breath, and could hear his muttered curses. He moved more carefully as he began to climb down the tree. Its branches were positioned almost perfectly for climbing, and it wouldn't take long for him to be on the ground, his rifle in hand again.

As he climbed, he turned his back toward her, giving Mae a window of opportunity, and she used it. She jumped to her feet and tore through the woods. Her eyes were more adjusted to the darkness now, and the moon shone brilliantly overhead, cutting through the snarling, skeletal branches and gleaming on the icy forest floor. Once on the ground, it would take him only a fraction of a second to pull his rifle to his shoulder, find her in his sights and pull the trigger.

Even then, a shot to the back of her head would be a better end than the one that had waited for her. At least if she was dead, they couldn't take her back to the tank. As she ran, she counted off the seconds in her mind, estimating that she had no more than six seconds to get away before Eddie reached the ground, turned and saw her running.

One...

She leapt over a fallen branch and almost lost her footing on a patch of ice. Luckily, her feet gained traction on a pile of leftover autumn leaves that poked through the surface of the ice. She ran hard.

Two...

Her backpack bounced on her back as she dodged a large boulder and ducked a low-hanging branch. She ripped the bag from her shoulders and held it close to her chest to avoid making any more noise than was necessary.

Three...

Mae's heart thudded in her chest and pounded in her ears. The cold air burned her lungs. She was in good shape, but the all-out sprint in the freezing dead of winter was a shock to her body. Her cheeks stung, and her eyes watered.

Four...

She heard the rifle crack, and the whisper of a bullet whizzing to her left. She dropped to the ground, rolling with her forward momentum. The bullet hit something close by, but far enough away that she breathed a sigh of relief. Another two shots exploded in the night, but she couldn't hear the bullets hit anything, so she assumed he was shooting randomly in the direction she'd run.

Time to change directions. She glanced to her right and then to her left, trying to decide which way she would go. To her left, the forest seemed darker than on the right. To her right, she could hear the faint sound of gurgling water. If there was a river, or a stream, she would be trapped, or have to find a place to cross. The thought of falling into the water and getting wet—even just one of her feet—was enough to send her body into a shivering fit and then hypothermia and death. It was smarter to stay away from the water, she knew. It was smarter to go left.

But to her left, the dark forest loomed and she couldn't shake the image of the long wolf, standing on it haunches and waiting for her. Snow flakes drifted lazily from above and disappeared into the shadows, where anything could be waiting.

Mae turned back to the sound of water and started crawling. As she went, she looked over her shoulder and strained her ears for any sign that her pursuers were getting close, but the forest was silent. If they were following her, they were coming quietly, and they would overtake her quickly.

Mae took a deep breath, then jumped to her feet and started running again. Instantly, two bullets were fired in her direction, the first hitting a tree behind her, and the second tearing through the hood of her jacket. Tiny down feathers exploded from the coat, mixing serenely with the falling snow.

"She's over here!" Eddie called, and even then, she could hear his Brooklyn accent loud and clear. He was so close, and gaining on her! A few more bullets were fired, but they all missed.

Not like the movies. The movies make it seem easy to hit a moving target in a darkened forest—something she knew was close to impossible, especially while giving chase.

"She's headed toward the river!" Eddie called again, "Oskar, cut her off before she crosses!"

He yelled something else about shooting her in the legs, to maim and not kill, but she didn't catch it over the pounding pulsing in her ears. Mae's heart was going full steam ahead, and her lungs felt as though they'd explode. She darted around a large elm tree, but took the curve too close. Her hand caught on a snarled piece of broken bark, cutting the skin. She gritted her teeth and kept running.

It was hopeless. She knew she would never get away from them, but she had to run. She thought of her mom, and how she would have run if she'd been able to. Even her dad, before all this had happened, would have tried to escape, would have died fighting. But there was no choice between fight or flight with these people. Always flight, to the ends of the earth. To fight is death.

The dying screams in the cabin, loud and fresh in her mind, seemed to be on repeat.

To fight was a slow death in the tank. In the tank where there was nothing.

She ran faster, the trees now a blur. Gunshots pierced the night air, and bullets smashed into trees and rocks, spraying wood and ice into the air. Her adrenaline was peaking, the pain in her lungs and heart no longer slowing her down, but giving her reason to push on. With the explosion of adrenaline came the dizzying rush in her mind and body, and she felt like the split second at the beginning of a fall from a very high place. She gave into the feeling, knowing that it was a mistake that would save her life.

Another bullet pierced her jacket, right above her waist. She jerked to the side and smashed headlong into a tree. She almost fell, but caught her balance and ran.

They were gaining. Mae could hear the hard breathing behind her, and knew that her pursuers were only seconds from catching her. Mae stumbled upon a path that cut through the ice to the trodden earth below. A game trail, she decided quickly, which probably led to the river. She could hear the gurgling water more clearly now, and knew that she was getting close. A split second later, she heard Eddie crash through some brush to the path as well. He was right behind her.

The mental rush grew stronger, and she felt light and airy, despite her screaming muscles. She struggled to get enough air into her lungs, but at the same time, felt strangely at peace.

The path suddenly turned to the left, running along a tall ridge that stuck out of the ground like a wall and bordered the end of a small clearing. The ridge was maybe twenty feet high and was rife with boulders and dirt. It had large, mature trees growing from the top, some of their roots exposed between the rocks, and some reaching the full twenty feet from the top of the ridge to the ground.

The moon was in a perfect position to cast its light on the clearing and the face of the ridge. Had the moonlight not been as bright as it was in that moment, Mae would never have seen it, and she wouldn't have stopped running from Eddie. But when she saw the rock, about four inches in diameter, a dark, charcoal grey, she skidded to a stop.

The rock hung in the air perhaps 30 inches from the ground, rotating slowly in the freezing winter night, the hard surface shining in the moonlight. The rock rolled around and around in the air.

Eddie skidded to a stop behind Mae, his gun raised to his shoulder, and pointed at her back.

"Turn around!" Eddie shouted, but Mae didn't move. She stared at the rock, still feeling the peace and calm and numbness that had accompanied the rush of adrenaline. Even as she stood, she felt the adrenaline withdraw from her mind and body.

"Mae, get your hands up in the air, and maybe we can work something out," Eddie said, but in his voice was a sneering bloodlust. He was taunting her, wanting her to turn around and face her fate. Maybe it wouldn't be death; she was still too valuable for that—but whatever Eddie had in store for her would be worse than death. Mae had seen it in his eyes at the cabin, in the way that he'd looked at her. Before, he'd shown restraint because he had to. But now, after what had happened in the cabin, there was nothing to work out, and there would be no restraint. They were alone in the forest, alone and away from the other two men, and there would be no mercy.

"There's nothing to work out," Mae said, her eyes never leaving the floating rock. Eddie shifted from one foot to another, the ice crunching underfoot. He moved slightly to Mae's left, to get a better look at what she was staring at.

When Eddie saw the rock, he lowered the gun slowly, confused. His eyebrows arched, and he almost asked her if it was some kind of trick, but he never spoke. Eddie's entire body was frozen in place, watching the rock. It began to tremble slightly, vibrating faster and faster as it floated above the ground.

"Paper and ink," Mae said, but knew it was hopeless. The end was already here.

Chapter Two

A few minutes before she saw the floating rock in the middle of the forest, Mae was sitting on a rotting mattress in a dark room on the second level of the decrepit old cabin. The mattress smelled of mold and whatever animal had made its nest there, and the wood-paneled walls were covered with a thin layer of greenish mildew, dead now that the temperature was so cold. The only light in the room came from an LED lantern that sat on a chair with only three legs.

A framed poster hung lopsidedly on one wall, the faded picture depicting an old horror movie from the 50s with a title that Mae couldn't make out, and a picture that she didn't recognize. Something to do with a man-sized rodent carrying an unconscious lady in a bikini. In giant green letters across the poster, it read: IT LIVES!

Of course it lives, Mae thought, and of course it's a helpless lady with no clothes, who's about to be eaten by the gerbil monster. Mae didn't like movies like this because it was almost always a girl in distress—and not just in the old movies where women were depicted as helpless victims, only to be saved by the big strong men—but even in modern movies, where the victims, and those needing to be saved, were almost always women. It was sickening to her, and secretly, she hoped the gerbil monster would eat the bikini chick for being so stupid as to be caught.

But then again, Mae was currently being held captive. Even though the situation hadn't been her fault, and her captor wasn't a gerbil monster, Mae still felt humiliated to be sitting there. She wondered how the hunters had found them, and how they'd learned about her mom's contact with the journalist.

Mae studied the rest of the room, her eyes falling on the window on the opposite side of the room. The glass was broken, and several large boards crisscrossed over the opening. The window wasn't especially large, but would be big enough to climb through, given the chance. She shifted slightly on the bed, the rusted springs squeaking. Mae wasn't sure, but it seemed that the window opened onto part of the roof. It was dark but she thought she remembered seeing a large tree by the roof.

"I hope you don't get any crazy ideas," the man said from his seat by the door, his voice thick with a Brooklyn accent. He nodded toward the window and smiled.

"And that would be a bad idea, hate to break it to you." He was leaning back against the wall, the front two legs of his chair propped up into the air. Mae didn't respond at first, but instead studied the man who was her captor, looking for any weaknesses that she could exploit.

His name was Eddie. She knew this not because he'd told her, but because one of the two men on the bottom level of the cabin had called him by name right after Eddie had kicked her to the ground, his foot raised to send his boot into her face. Eddie was afraid of her, even before they'd barged into the cabin, and his first goal had apparently been to put Mae out of commission. To her surprise, the guy who seemed like the leader of their little outfit, smaller than the other two, had stopped Eddie from finishing his kick to her teeth.

"Take her upstairs," the man had said. He knelt beside Mae and stroked her hair. "Little miss April Showers, May Flowers."

He stood.

"Give us some time with her mom. We need to find out what she's said to the reporter."

And now they stared at each other. Eddie was still afraid, his eyes flitting from the door to his rifle, which was propped on the wall next to his chair. He was wearing black leather boots, scuffed and dirty from the trek through the dirt and snow to get from their car to the cabin. The boots matched his leather jacket, which was studded with silver inlets and buttons. The butt of a small pistol stuck out from his jacket pocket.

So two guns, Mae thought. The rifle was a .30-06, a powerful weapon with good range and a powerful kick. If she was going to escape, she'd have to run far to be out of range.

The butt of his pistol was a matte black, and probably a 9 mm, but she couldn't tell for sure.

She continued to study Eddie, taking in every detail about him. He was thin, but not scrawny, and seemed to be in good physical condition. He wore a silver crucifix around his neck, a stark contrast to the charcoal-colored polo he wore beneath his black jacket. Mae thought that the guy was trying too hard to look like an assassin from any one of a dozen action movies, and Mae would have laughed at him for such an obvious attempt to appear menacing and scary.

But Mae didn't laugh. She wanted to seem like a helpless victim who was too afraid to laugh. Like the girl being carried away by the gerbil monster, she thought, and then had to fight an even stronger urge to chuckle.

Eddie might have been handsome too, under different circumstances, with his jet-black hair, long and parted in the middle. He had more than a day's growth of beard on his face, and the overall effect made him look, aside from the clichéd assassin, like a rugged Italian in a cologne commercial.

Her thoughts turned back to her mom, who was downstairs with the other two guys. She felt sick to her stomach at the thought of her mom, all alone down there, facing whatever kind of torture they had in mind to find out what her mom had said to the reporter.

Mae and her mom had known that this day was coming, ever since they'd fled Miami. They'd known that they would be found eventually, especially after her mom had started contacting that reporter. They'd known, but Mae never thought it would end like this, out in the woods, alone and cold. If she could get the rifle and then get downstairs to her mom, they might be able to get away. It would be just as before, the two of them, on the run.

"So, you're the girl, huh?" he interrupted her thoughts. "You're the girl of the century. The girl who's caused way more trouble than she's worth." He said this with mocking grandiose. When he grinned, he revealed a set of nearly perfect teeth. She just stared at him, and didn't say anything.

"Needless to say, I've heard a whole lot about you."

Again, she didn't open her mouth, but instead glanced at the window. Mae couldn't see clearly through the glass, but she thought she saw the dark, scraggily branches of a tree, very close to the roof and the window. If she could get out to the roof, she could probably get away. Of course, the rifle was a problem, and what to do when she reached the ground was another.

She needed her bag, which was on the floor of the car that they'd driven to the cabin. She hoped that their attackers had not searched the car and found the bag, but she thought that they hadn't. If they'd recovered that, the evening would have gone much differently. Her mom would already be dead, and Mae would be in their trunk, hooded and cuffed.

So they probably didn't have the device, and her mom was being interrogated. If Mae got the gun, she thought that she'd be able to at least distract them long enough for her mother to escape.

But that wasn't the plan. If she varied from the plan, and they were both caught or killed, then all of their work would be for nothing.

Mae had to get away, even if that meant ...

"You get somewhere safe," her mom would say, "you get there, because they will always be hunting, and they will never stop."

Mae had to escape. At the very least, she had to find the reporter and give him the few details he needed to connect the dots. Her mother whimpered from down below, the sound of her crying carrying through the rotted floor boards.

I'm sorry, Mamma, she thought.

"What?" Eddie pulled her from her thoughts. He seemed annoyed that she hadn't responded to him. "Do you even know who you're talking to?"

Mae looked at him for several seconds and then shook her head.

"I don't care who I'm talking to," she said. "You're the monster."

"The monster." He snickered. "Well, little missy, maybe if you cared a little more about who's on your tail, we wouldn't be in this predicament, now would we?"

He said 'predicament' slowly, emphasizing each syllable as if to taunt her.

"I don't care who you are," she said again.

"You should."

"Well, I don't," Mae said with the hint of a sneer. She had to remind herself not to antagonize the man too much, especially with the possibility of the situation—or predicament, as he'd referred to it—turning sour very quickly. She didn't know what, exactly, was happening downstairs, but it wasn't good. The situation up here could just as easily and quickly turn just as bad, if she wasn't careful.

She felt the tinges of fear again, creeping in her stomach and insides, felt the first hints of panic, but knew that if she gave into those feelings, things would only get worse. She needed to be alert, and ready to escape with only a second's notice.

Mae slid her hands over the fetid mattress, and her fingers touched a long strand of material that had been ripped away from the mattress cover. Slowly, she began to pull on the strand of cloth, measuring its length in her head as she bunched the material into a ball in her fist. The material was soft and pulled away from the mattress easily, hardly a sound.

She kept her eyes on Eddie, who either didn't notice her movement, or didn't care. It was dark in the room, the lantern's light only illuminating so much, and she thought that maybe her motions were masked by the shadows.

"Is it true, what they say?" Eddie said, breaking the silence. "That you killed your dad?"

Mae glared at him, but didn't answer. With that question *I heard you killed your dad?* she felt as though she were in a large cavern, lit only by a single candle flickering before her, keeping the darkness at bay.

The shadows danced in the corners and on the walls, threatening to close in and swallow up all the light.

"Paper and ink," she said, with barely any sound at all. It was a habit now, to think about the paper and ink when she was upset or nervous. A little trick she'd learned from her dad, to imagine a world that wasn't as bad as this one, where she was in control. *Paper and ink*, and in her mind, the world in her mind would open and she would escape.

But she gritted her teeth and shook her head slightly. She couldn't escape now, couldn't withdraw. Not now.

He stared at her with his eyebrow cocked, but continued.

"I heard that when you were done with him, his body was in so many pieces, they couldn't find—"

"Shut up." The darkness in the large cavern grew around her, as if sentient and aware.

Eddie smiled, leaning forward in his chair, the legs of which seemed to bow under his weight. He was pleased to have gotten this reaction out of her.

"So you're still a little sensitive about that, which is different than what I heard. I heard that your heart was cold, and that you could care less about your old man."

She looked away, pulling at the length of material from the mattress. The strand caught on something, and she pulled harder, but it wouldn't budge.

"Too bad your mom's going to die too, if she doesn't talk." His eyes drifted to the closed door, and her gaze followed. She felt that sinking feeling in the pit of her stomach again, and this time, no amount of forcing herself to feel otherwise helped.

"We don't know anything," Mae said.

"That's how it always is, isn't it," Eddie ran his hand through his hair, which had a nice sheen despite the poor lighting in the room. He looked up at the ceiling when he spoke, his tone sounding more like a college professor's than the thug he was trying so hard to be.

"I talk to people about what they know and what they don't know all the time—part of the job, you know. And without fail, people always claim ignorance in the beginning. It just takes a little ... prodding, and before long, they're experts on the matter. Take a little sandpaper and vinegar to the skin, you know that area between your fingers, or better yet, get a little intimate with that sandpaper and a douse of vinegar, and you'd be surprised how much a person can know. It won't take long, don't you worry."

Mae felt her heart beat faster in her chest, and she hated this man. He sat there in his chair, leaning against the wall nonchalantly, staring at her with that half smile on his lips, eyes wandering over her body, and she felt sick to her stomach.

"Of course," he continued, "you could save your mom a whole lot of heartache if you'd just tell us where it is—"

"We told you downstairs. We don't know!" Mae interrupted, but he continued, unfazed.

"—that is, unless you don't mind having her blood on your hands too. Think of it, the girl who off-ed both her parents. That'd be a story to send shock waves around the world, if the media ever got hold of it. Of course, not many people outside this cabin will ever know just how cold you are."

The strand of mattress material suddenly loosened. She slid her hands along its length, and found that it was snagged on a broken spring. She touched the rusted and spiraled piece of metal, and ran her fingers around it until reaching the end, which broke off in a sharp point. Eddie watched her, his eyes narrowing at her faint movements. She kept her eyes on his.

"I didn't kill my dad," she said.

"Oh?" His eyebrows raised, and his half smile grew wider. "How do you figure?"

"My dad was—" A scream suddenly broke the silence from below. Both Mae and Eddie startled toward the sound, which startled them both, but Mae had been waiting for any distraction at all.

She leapt to her feet and rushed Eddie. He turned back toward her, his eyes wide and confused. But he recovered quickly, his eyes narrowed and his muscles tensed. As she came at him, he snatched the gun from where it lay against the wall and raised it to his shoulder, much faster than she'd expected. As he swung the barrel toward her, Eddie thumbed the hammer of the big gun.

I'm going to die, she thought, and Eddie pulled the trigger.

Chapter Three

Mae slid to the ground like a baseball player sliding into second, right as the room filled with an echoing BOOM from the rifle. The bullet smashed through the ceiling,

She kicked the leg of the chair, and Eddie toppled to the ground with a crash. His head hit the ground with a solid and crunching THUNK, and his look of shock and surprise suddenly went momentarily blank. He was dazed, and Mae used that fraction of a second, knowing that the guys from downstairs would be up here in short order to see what was going on.

Another scream pierced the cold night air in the cabin, but she ignored it. In a fraction of a second, she straddled Eddie's body and wrapped the strand of mattress around his neck until the jagged piece of spring was pressed into the tender skin beneath his chin. She rolled off him and quickly wound the strand around the bed frame, finishing it off with a tight knot.

She rolled back around and snatched the pistol from his jacket, but she didn't get hold of the rifle before he grabbed it.

He thrashed and rocked his body on the floor, reaching for her. Eddie tried to scream, but gasped at the tightening piece of material around his neck instead. She jumped to her feet and kicked him in the groin, hard. She felt something burst when her foot connected with his body, and he was instantly cradling himself in a fetal position. This time, his scream came through, ragged and hoarse.

Mae stepped over him again and pressed her knee into the mattress spring, which stuck in his neck. She stayed there, hovering over him without pressing too hard on the spring. Even then, the tip pierced his skin and a trickle of blood ran down and round his neck, dripping to the floor.

"If you move, if you call for help, if you try and knock me off you, I'll stick this all the way in. I'll twist it into your neck so deep that you'll lose a whole lot more blood than just this trickle," she whispered.

From down below, the screams were fading—but she couldn't think of that now. She was no use to her mother if she were dead. And if Eddie got free, she was dead. No matter what the men were looking for, no matter what they needed from her, Eddie would kill her if he got loose, she was sure of it.

But the gunshot—the two men downstairs would have undoubtedly heard the gunshot, and would likely come to investigate. If they did, she was dead, unless she could get out onto the roof and down the tree fast enough.

As if to answer her thoughts and spoil her plans, one of the men called up. His accent was thick and hard to understand, and she pegged him as the largest of the men—a behemoth compared to the smaller leader of the pack.

"Eddie, you okay up there?"

Mae leaned so close to Eddie's face that she could smell the spearmint gum he was chewing to mask the underlying stench of whiskey.

"If you call for help, so much as a peep, I'll open your neck." She was surprised at the intensity in her own voice. "If your friend comes into this room, you're dead."

Eddie hesitated only a moment before yelling, "All's good, man."

"'Cause if you're gettin' beat up by the girl, I could always give you hand," the big man called up.

Eddie glowered.

"Under control!" Eddie said, seething. Mae smiled at him sweetly, and pulled away from him.

She stayed in that hovering position and pulled the strand of mattress material tight around the bed post, and then made sure it was snug against his neck. Mae held Eddie's pistol up to the light and examined the barrel before shoving it into her own pocket. She leaned close enough to smell his cologne and the tobacco on his breath. He stared up at her with wide, hateful eyes, and kept his lips mashed together in rage. His breathing was hard, and his chest heaved with each breath.

"I didn't kill my dad," she whispered. "But I could kill you right now."

He opened his mouth to say something, his whole body seething with rage.

"Don't," she said, leaning harder on the rusted mattress spring. The jagged point sunk a quarter of an inch into his neck, and that did the trick. He clenched his jaw, but didn't say anything.

Mae groped down his body, until she came to his belt buckle. She undid the belt, never taking her eyes off him. She pulled the belt out from his pants, made a loop through the buckle. The whole time, they kept their eyes locked, his afraid and full of rage, and hers just full of rage.

She swiveled her weight off the rusty spring, and looped the belt over one of his feet, cinching it tight. She stood up and pulled on the belt, dragging his body an inch at a time until the strand of mattress material was taut, the metal spring on the verge of sliding deeper into his neck. She lifted a corner of the rotting dresser and slid the end of his leather strap beneath its frame. When she was done, she stood up and admired her contraption.

At the same time, Eddie seemed to get a better idea of his predicament. If he moved away from the bed without untangling his neck from the strand of mattress, the spiraled spring would slit his jugular. Even with his hands free, it would take him several moments to untangle himself, so as not to accidently end his own life.

She pulled the strand of mattress tighter around the tender skin beneath his jaw, careful not to stick him harder with the metal spring. She pulled the material tight, until it cut off his oxygen. His eyes bulged as he tried to inhale, but couldn't get enough air into his lungs. He thrashed his arms, but she kept her body weight on his chest and shoulders, and his range of motion was limited.

He opened his mouth to inhale, a last ditch effort, and Mae knew that darkness was clawing its way into his vision. She leaned closer again, until her nose was almost touching his ear.

"I didn't kill my dad," she said again, and pulled the strand tighter. He gasped, thrashing about on the floor, and she watched the conscious awareness drift from his eyes. He stared up at her, and she back at him until his eyes closed. She waited a few seconds and then loosed the material around his neck. She stood up, watching his chest and waiting for the oxygen to drift its way back into his lungs, sparking the instinct to draw breath. When she saw the faint rise and fall on his charcoal sweater, she darted to the other end of the room. He was still unconscious, but not for long. When he woke, it would not take long before he loosened the band around his neck. Mae didn't think he would call for help, at least not right away. If he called for help, the others would know that she'd bested him—that the girl of the century would keep right on being that girl.

Mae snatched the rifle from the floor and darted to the window at the other end of the room. She kicked the boards that crossed over the opening. Luckily for her, the wood was just as rotten as most of the cabin, and the boards broke away easily. In just a few seconds, she had cleared a space large enough to climb through.

Eddie stirred behind her, and she glanced over her shoulder. He was moving, but was still groggy and his eyes were only half-opened. She paused long enough to listen to the noises from down below. She heard talking, and was relieved that there weren't any more screams. If they were talking, her mom must still be alive.

But she had to move. Mae thrust her body through the rotted wood and wriggled out of the room and onto the icy roof. She gasped when her bare hands plunged into a drift of snow and ice, chunks of it cutting into her palms and wrists. The moon shone brightly in the cloudy sky, illuminating the dark, wooden shingles and the sheets of ice that covered the roof. Down below, the ground was frozen. If she fell, it would hurt, and may even break bones.

She was on her chest and stomach, pulling her legs through when he grabbed her foot. She screamed, more startled than anything, and kicked hard with her other foot, connecting with Eddie's jaw—at least she assumed it was Eddie, but how had he gotten free so quickly?

He let go of her foot for a split second and she yanked her legs through the window.

A piece of rotted wood snagged the rifle, and she tugged, but it wouldn't break free. Eddie reappeared in the window, reaching for her, his fingers inches from her legs and feet. She slid down the roof, pulling her body along the shingles toward the tree. She'd have to leave the gun, which meant that she had only seconds now, before he had it in his hands and ready to fire.

The tree was only a few feet away, but the ice enveloped the roof. She couldn't stop from sliding toward the edge. No matter what she grabbed, she kept sliding with both of her hands outstretched in front of her, and the other clawing at the ice and trying to slow her descent. Suddenly, the hand below her struck the steel gutter and stopped her slide. Her body came to rest at the edge, close enough to see the ground below, which was only dirt, gravel, and ice. She winced at the thought of falling, closed her eyes and exhaled.

The sound she heard was distinct and familiar. Eddie had cocked the rifle, and though she couldn't see him, she knew it was pulled to his shoulder and aimed at her back.

"Don't move," he said through clenched teeth, his voice hoarse from nearly being strangled.

Mae gripped the gutter and flung her body into the cold night air. The rifle cracked, and splinters of wood and ice exploded from the roof, but Mae was falling towards the ground. It happened too fast to be completely prepared, the moonlit ground coming at her with lightning speed.

Hit and roll! She thought as she fell, but the angle at which she fell was too awkward.

When Mae struck the frozen ground, her outstretched arms took the brunt of the fall and buckled, her shoulder and the side of her head hitting next, the rest of her body collapsing in on top of itself. Pain exploded in her head and shoulder, a flash of light so bright that she almost passed out. When her vision cleared, stars hung around her. She was dazed and rattled, but pushed to her hands and knees. She couldn't feel any broken bones as she crawled to all fours and got as close to the house, and as far out of Eddie's sight, as she could. Mae stood up on her knees with her back pressed against the outside of the cabin and breathed deeply.

The voices inside had stopped. The men inside had no doubt heard the gunshot and the struggle on the roof, and were listening. Mae could only imagine her mother there, alone with the two men, listening for her daughter as well, hoping against hope that the bullet had missed.

"Eddie?" one of them called, but got no response. Mae was not alone, she was sure that Eddie was watching for any movement on which to train his gun. She held her breath and inched along the wall toward the window that opened into the front room. A gnarly bush, covered in tiny buds of ice, snagged at her coat; she slid behind it and peered into the window. Her mother was kneeling in the center of the room next to a florescent lantern on a woven rug that was tattered and motheaten. The two men had their backs to the window, one of them staring up the stairs while the other stood close to her mother. Both men carried guns in their hands, pointed at the ground, their fingers on the triggers. Mae turned away and looked at the dirty snow. She felt a lump rising in her throat. If she went through the front door, one of them would surely shoot her. Maybe not a killing shot, but it would be enough to take her down, and then there would be no stopping them.

But how had they found them here at the cabin in the first place? Mae thought of everything they'd done to keep their trail cold, to stay two steps ahead of those who pursued them, those that hunted them.

"They're everywhere, and they will never stop," her mom would always say. Even when she was a little girl, as far back as she could remember, she would lie in her bed with her head cradled in her mom's lap, and her mom would brush and braid her hair while telling her about the people in the shadows. Together, they would read from an old and tattered copy of Grimm's Fairytales, but always, her mother would talk about those people without faces and names. They read stories of princes and princesses, of fantastical lands, talking animals, hunters and prey.

"They will hunt you," her mom would say, "and you must never let them find you, because if they do, they will end you. They'll put you back in the tank, and they won't ever let you go."

And then her mother would whisper goodnight, and kiss her on the forehead or cheek, and whisper in Mae's ear that she loved her.

"I love you, Mama," Mae whispered, her breath misting the dirty window pane. The men inside were shouting to one another, and Mae realized that her mom was right. These people were hunters tracking their prey, hounds with a scent to follow and an insatiable blood lust, and they would never stop. The cabin was in the middle of nowhere, and they should never have found them out here—it defied all logic, yet here they were.

And her mom was caught, her arms tied behind her back, her hair matted with blood. Her piercing blue-grey eyes were swollen, her cheeks bruised.

Mae peered through the dirty window to the room where her mother knelt. She allowed the tears to come, but stuck her fist in her mouth to stifle the cries. She could see that her mom's eyes were wet too, and Mae wanted to let her know that she was okay, that everything would be okay. Mae wanted to knock on the window, to tap the glass with her fingernail just enough to get her attention, but she knew that if she did that, and the men heard, everything her and her mom had done to escape would be for naught. Seconds ticked by, the chance of her getting away growing slimmer. But she couldn't look away, she couldn't leave her mom here to die without knowing that her daughter was safe.

Finally, she tapped, just enough to make a sound, and hoped that the men inside would not notice the faint tapping. They didn't, but her mom's eyes instantly went to the window, searching the darkness beyond.

When their eyes connected that last time, Mae felt a flood of emotion and cried harder. Her mom straightened up, her hands tied behind her back, with the rope looped around her neck, her shoulders jutting proudly forward. She smiled at Mae, and in that smile was hope and relief and more love than Mae could comprehend. They stared at each other for only a few seconds, but for Mae, no matter how long they looked at each other, tears streaming down their cheeks in ruddy lines, it would never be enough.

"Go," her mom mouthed, and then, "I love you."

Mae whispered it back, and touched the icy glass with the tips of her fingers, longing to hold her mom and be held by her, longing to be cradled in her arms.

The man at the stairs turned back to her mom, so their eyes stayed locked for only a split second longer. The smile on her mom's face transformed into a determined grin, and when the man was close enough, she rolled to ground and kicked out with her feet toward the man.

"Run!" her mom shouted. It might be the last thing she ever said to Mae, and Mae ran. She bolted from under the awning of the house and around the back side, to where Eddie would have no clear shot. She ran to the car that she and her mother had driven to the cabin. It was parked in the clearing, just behind the cabin, in the shadows. Because the car was parked in the dark, the men had missed her bag when they'd searched the car. And she was lucky, because the bag had her entire life inside, and if she was to survive the night, she needed everything in that bag.

Mae threw open the rear passenger door and snatched the backpack from the floor. It was wedged up underneath the seat, and the color was a dirty grey, blending with the color of the old carpet in the car. With the shadows and the night, the bag was almost impossible to see, and anyone looking for it would have needed a flashlight, unless they happened to feel the bag while searching on the floor. Either way, she was lucky—

The roar of a rifle behind her and the instant shattering of glass that followed caught her off guard, and she screamed, falling to her knees. She scrambled around the back side of the car as two more bullets were fired into the side of the car.

Where was Eddie? Or was it one of the other two men from downstairs? She didn't think that there was more than one rifle among them, but she couldn't remember exactly— Eddie's kick to the gut had pretty much fogged up her memory of those few moments when she'd seen all three of them together.

She had to get out of the clearing and away from the house. It was her only chance to stay alive, and if she remained in the clearing, she'd not only be in Eddie's sights, but the other two men would be out here looking for her as soon as her mom was taken care of. Her heart ached at the thought of her mom, but they'd rehearsed this scenario so many times that it was almost second nature. If anything like this ever happened, and they couldn't immediately escape together, they'd split up and be on their own. All that they had done would be wasted if they both died, or were captured. Of course, Mae and her mom hadn't discussed the practical, emotional side of leaving the other behind. They hadn't talked about how hard—impossible even—their plan would be to follow. They'd never discussed the pain and the guilt that came when leaving the other behind. They'd been together all Mae's life, always running, always dodging the hunters.

A bullet struck the frozen ground to her left, cracking the ice and spraying dirt and grit. She glanced up and saw the flash of gunfire from a window opposite the side of the cabin from which she'd climbed. Eddie had seen her move out of his sights, so he'd crossed to the other side of the cabin, opting not to follow her to the ground, but to stay on the second floor where he would have a higher ground and a better view of where she was hiding. Another flash, and the crack of the bullet, when it bullet struck the side of the car with a metallic PING!

She rolled to her side and began crawling to the cover of the forest beyond. Bullets sprayed in a random pattern all around, opening up black holes in the sheet of ice that covered the ground. She was glad that he was firing blindly and didn't have a good idea of where she was.

Ahead of her, the clearing abruptly ended against a thick snarl of trees, underbrush and drifted snow. She looked for a small area that she could climb through, a hole in the wall of blackness into which she could disappear, but she couldn't see anything that would allow her to pass. A tangled web of branches blocked her escape.

Mae froze as she realized that the bullets had stopped firing. She looked over her shoulder at the cabin. She couldn't see the window where she thought Eddie was perched, but she was sure he was there, somewhere, watching and waiting for her.

Probably waiting for her to make the move to the forest, she thought. From where he was sitting, he likely had a better idea of just how impregnable the tree line actually was, and when she made a run for it, it'd be like shooting fish in a barrel.

She lay on the ground, the cold seeping through her clothes and onto her skin, and she wished that she was on a sunny beach, away from this mess.

Mae and her mom had often talked about going to a beach—any beach would have been perfect—but the beach she wanted most to visit was in the south of France. She'd never been to France, but she could almost smell the faint aroma of orange blossoms on the salty breeze, away from guns and knives and men who wanted to use her and kill her.

But she was here and now.

In the cold.

Sounds came from inside the cabin, screams and scuffles and struggling, but Mae knew it was only a matter of time before the two men overpowered her mom. She didn't know if her mom would be killed or bound tightly for enhanced interrogation later, but it didn't matter. The two men were larger than her, and she didn't stand a chance.

Mae had only seconds to get away from the cabin, seconds before the men would come barging out the front door, seconds before Eddie got sick of waiting on the roof and came down to find her. If he trapped her here, nothing else would matter. There was nowhere to run, at least not on this side of the cabin.

She swiveled on her belly and pulled herself along the ground, back toward the car. To her left was a small shed with stacks of old wood piled neatly beside it. The shed was only a few meters from the cabin, and the space between was at an angle that would make it difficult for Eddie to get a clean shot.

But the space between the car and the wood shed was wide open and would be directly in Eddie's sights. He was waiting for her to go to the edge of the clearing, so his gun probably wouldn't be trained on the short distance between the car and the woodshed, but she wasn't sure. He could just as easily be waiting for her to make a run for it, his finger on the trigger, just waiting.

Enough time had passed, that he might be wondering if she was having second thoughts about the clearing, and he may be trying to figure her next move. Going to the woodshed was the obvious choice, and in reality, it was her only choice.

Mae raised to her knees and surveyed the scene. They expect you to roll over and play dead, her mom would always say, but you defy them when you fight back. You win the fight when you're two steps ahead.

She needed a distraction, something to draw his searching eyes away from where she intended to go. Her fingers brushed against some loose gravel and ice beside the tire, and grabbed a handful. She sighed and looked around for anything else that she could use as a distraction. Throwing rocks would divert Eddie's attention for only a second, and she needed more than that. But the ground around her was bare, and to reach inside the car again would let Eddie know exactly where she was.

Mae closed her fingers around the handful of rocks, dirt, and chunks of ice and paused, breathing slowly and waiting for the silence of the moment to fully settle in. She could imagine his concentration, the butt of his rifle against his shoulder and cheek, his eye squinting through the scope and waiting for any movement, his breathing slow and methodic, misting the night air.

Now or never, she thought. If she didn't act soon, she'd be caught in the open. Mae dug her toes into the ground and crouched forward, like a sprinter on her mark, ready to go. She took a deep breath and exhaled slowly, her eyes closed and concentrating. She flung the handful of gravel to her left and it skittered along the ground. Bullets smacked the ground and the instantaneous boom of the rifle cracked the night air, but Mae was already running full speed to the wood shed.

Not even a second passed before Eddie realized her ruse and fired the rifle in her direction—one bullet—which punctured the aluminum siding on the shed. Mae ducked instinctively but kept running around the shed, to the side of the cabin. She heard Eddie curse from somewhere above and behind her, and she fled into the darkness of the forest.

She fled, and they followed.

Chapter Four

The vibrations in the floating rock seemed to be coming from within the stone, like tiny ripples in a pond, expanding outward. The rock hovered and rotated, vibrating more and more rapidly. Twigs and smaller stones began to rise around it, like a wave expanding outward, the smaller objects lifted into the air. The effect of the rising objects amidst the falling snow was surreal and beautiful, reminding Mae of dancers in a winter ballet.

"What is this?" Eddie said, his voice trailing off, the lust for blood completely gone. All that was left in his voice and on his face was the same wonder and amazement of a kid at a magic show.

"No," Mae said, shaking her head but unable to tear her gaze away from the scene unfolding before her.

"No, what?" Eddie said with an undertone of fear and disbelieve in his voice. He wanted to believe it was just a trick, a sleight of hand, or a puzzle that just needed figuring. On the other hand, he could see that there was no smoke and mirrors, nothing to explain the phenomena, and his mind was reeling, afraid of the possibility that it was all very real.

Mae looked past the stone to the wall of dirt, rock and tree roots beyond, searching for a way out of the small clearing. The gushing of water sounded close, and the last thing she needed was to be stuck between the rushing water and the men who would kill her. If she turned and ran, Eddie would snap out of his awestruck trance and follow her, opting to again pursue the girl rather than attempt to wrap his mind around something so inconceivable as a floating forest.

"We need to get out of here," she said. "We need to leave before—"

A tremendous crack filled the air, and the roots of a tree ripped from the wall, shooting boulders and giant chunks of frozen earth into the air, where they hung like lifeless marionettes swaying in the breeze.

"What *is* this?" Eddie muttered, his voice trembling with terror now, the childlike wonder completely gone. Mae glanced over her shoulder and saw Eddie as she never would have expected. His jaw was slack, his eyes wide, and his face instantly drained of all color as he watched more trees, their huge trunks and branches like a monster's claws against the night sky. He watched the trees lift from the ground, rip from the earth, and fall in a slow motion toward them.

Eddie screamed, not just out of fear anymore, but with the onset of insanity lurking in the timbre of his cries. Another tree lifted from the ground, and the boulders rolled away, hovering above the ground, dirt and branches in the air like an asteroid field in space. The massive trunk of the first tree was almost horizontal now, floating above the place where Eddie and Mae stood. The forest cracked and groaned all around as the branches on the floating tree ripped into the trees that still stood tall and reached toward the sky. The snow fell in sheets now, causing the massive trees and rocks to appear as shadows.

For some reason, the image of the grey wolf, standing on its haunches and grinning with its otherworldly snout and shiny teeth, skittered across Mae's mind.

In the distance, Mae heard the voices of the other men that were hunting her. She had to leave now, knowing that they would be on her in seconds, because despite the spectacle of floating rocks and trees and branches and earth, they would have guns and knives, and they wouldn't allow her to escape.

She rushed forward, dodging a chunk of earth, stone and ice that looked like a giant wedge, with roots and branches hanging about. Her shoulder brushed into it, sending a shockwave of pain throughout her body.

"Wait, stop!" Eddie screamed, hysteria and panic now in full force. "You're doing this, stop doing this! It's a trick, just a trick!"

He was babbling now, but as Mae glanced back at the man and saw his rifle raised, his finger on the trigger, she knew that he'd lost all grasp on reality. The rifle roared as he pulled the trigger and bullets shot, the muzzle flashing its bright explosions of light. Mae dropped to the ground and rolled beneath another floating wedge of dirt. There was just enough space for her to squeeze under it, the roots pulling at her cloths and hair, and she prayed that all of floating things would not, at that instant, relent to gravity's pull and crush her beneath. She wiggled under until there was enough room for her to get onto her hands and knees and crawl.

She was in the middle of it all now, the roots and rocks all around, vibrating and rolling on some unseen wave of force. Behind her, she could hear Eddie's screams of rage and hysteria.

Another gunshot blasted through the night. Mae slipped as she ducked, almost falling. She didn't know if he would follow, but she sensed that whatever was happening with these trees and rocks would not continue indefinitely. At some point they would fall, the chase would resume, and she could either stay put or get some distance between her and those who would see her dead.

Her path was blocked by floating chunks of earth and ice, so thick that they hung in a tangled mess with no space to get through. Mae looked up and saw the flakes of snow falling toward her through the snarl of hanging roots, and she began to climb. She used the roots and scampered up to the base of the tree that floated horizontally, her weight and movements barely causing any reaction on the floating objects. She climbed higher to another one that floated toward the top of the forest, using rocks to scramble up and over the hanging earth, and it all reminded her of when she was a child, climbing the trees in her backyard on summer days. The feeling brought a sense of comfort and excitement, enough to mask the fear of certain death if she didn't get clear of the boulders and trees before they rushed back to the ground where they belonged.

The sounds of Eddie's screams and the gunshots were fading as she climbed, and the sound of the rushing river was close. She moved toward the sound, dodging another tree that soared over her head like an island in space. She scrambled along the trunk of the tree and leapt. Below her, she thought she caught a glimpse of the river, the icy surface reflecting briefly through the heavy snowfall.

She felt the warm air seconds before the gentle vibrations that seemed to come from within her body and mind. The contrast of the warm air against the winter winds was so drastic that it took her breath away. She felt the vibrations within her, like butterflies in her stomach, expanding out through her muscles and limbs, and the vibrations were followed by a feeling of weightlessness.

All around, the floating trees and rocks seemed to vibrate faster, the wood in the tree trunks cracking and whining under the strain, the soaring islands of ice and dirt breaking apart, exploding with the force of the vibrations, and Mae climbed faster. She jumped to another boulder, twisting and spinning with a tangle of broken roots, and then to an island of earth that was splitting down the center, an expanding crack that rumbled. Mae slipped on a rock that gave way, and she nearly tumbled. She reached out and snagged an icy branch, catching herself from falling. The river was definitely there, right below her, its icy tendrils twisting through and along the forest floor. The entire river seemed to be covered with a layer of ice, lined with thick mounds of drifted snow along the banks.

The branch she was holding snapped away from the base of the tree, and her foot slipped out from under her. She tumbled a few feet and smacked into a rising boulder that twisted with her momentum. She fell to one side and grabbed a protruding root that had wrapped itself around the boulder, which kept her from falling into the river, but it caused the boulder to start spinning in the direction of her fall. The backpack slipped from her back and she barely caught it by the straps before it fell.

The warm air seemed to be swirling all around now, whistling in and out of the trees and rocks. The snow that fell from the black sky above instantly turned to rain, and the wavelike vibrations grew in intensity. To her, it felt like standing in the ocean as water was pulled into an oncoming wave. The power and force of the energy took her breath away.

The root that supported her weight suddenly began to break away from the rock and she slipped further down toward the river. She screamed as it kept pulling, finally catching on a small crack in the rock. She hung there, feeling the intensity of the swirling, gathering dark energy, the warm air and the rain pattering her skin and hair.

By now, her muscles and mind felt numb and somehow disassociated from her body. She was moving faster now, over the floating forest debris. She glanced behind her and saw that she was alone.

Well, probably alone.

She didn't think that she'd been followed through the floating forest, or even could have been followed. Eddie was either in the throes of chaos while watching all this insanity unfold above him, or he was trying to find his way through the branches and roots and boulders to chase Mae. Either way, she'd lost him, and she was now alone.

Got to get clear of this, her mind screamed, just waiting for the entire, dream-like forest scene to right itself with the laws of physics.

As if in response to this thought, there was a sudden shift as the rocks and trees and islands of earth slid sideways, and a rumbling crack filled the air. An explosion of energy pushed out and away from the slide, like a static wind, with the faint metallic smell of lightning, and it burst outward, no longer a ripple in a pond, but a pounding, relentless wave of energy. The push was followed almost simultaneously by a low rumble that grew with intensity.

Everything that hung in the air suddenly fell, as if gravity had finally found its grasp and the floating forest clicked back into reality. The entire forest fell, a total rush of movement downward, like a hammer pounding from above, and Mae was thrust down toward the river.

A split second before her head and shoulders struck the ice, Mae had the fleeting thought that if the ice didn't crack and allow her into the water, cold as it may be, she'd likely break her neck or be crushed by the falling forest above. An image of her body beneath the rocks and floating islands, speared by the gnarly branches and roots, sent a split second of panic through her body as the icy river rushed to meet her.

Chapter Five

When she was just a girl, Mae's father taught her a way to escape her fears, to escape dark times or loneliness. A trick to escape.

"Paper and ink," he had said, tapping her forehead and smiling. She giggle in that way only little girls can laugh with their fathers.

"Imagine a blank piece of paper in you mind, white, clean, full of possibility."

"Okay," she said and closed her eyes.

"So you have the paper, it's in your mind. Take a pen and draw a line down the middle of the page. And there you have the ink. Whatever color you want, and in your mind, the world will open and be whatever you want it to be. "

***

As he fell toward the icy water, and after she lunged beneath the surface, her mind immediately reverted to that old trick. Paper and ink, in her mind. Paper and ink, to escape. Paper and ink, and the world opens, and her mind opens, and her heart opens. Here and now, her heart slowing to a steady and imperceptible pulse. Imperceptible, like everything else in her world, where the only feeling came from what her heart imagined and her mind forced into reality with paper and drawn ink.

Her heart thudded quickly, the only reminder that she was still alive. All thought and feeling seemed to melt away and combine with the world around her, until she felt as though she didn't exist, that only her consciousness remained.

Paper and ink, here and now, and her world becomes real.

The feel of white paper, so clean and empty, beneath her hands, the pen pressed between her fingers. The smell of a coffee shop, so hard to forget, yet her mind struggles to wrap around the smell. She raises the paper cup to her lips and sips the Americano, espresso with hot water, no sugar, no cream, her drink.

The door opens behind her, and she turns, and hears the jingle of the bell and the shuffling and wet footsteps as someone comes in out of the storm. A shiver through her body follows the gust of wind and flakes of snow that sweep through the tiny café as the door swings shut behind the new arrivals. She can hear a man, his voice deep and his words drawled, give an order to the attentive, twenty-something barista, and the ding of the cash register, and the tinkle of coins changing hands, and the whirr of grinding beans, and the bubbling of heated water.

The tip of the fountain pen gleams with the fresh ink, and she studies the blank page before her. She places the tip of the pen on the white paper, then brings the tip toward her slowly and deliberately. And the world opens, with the smells and the chill of winter wind, and a feeling of love, however contrived, that tethers her sanity to reality.

A single line, from top to bottom, like a dark river seen from far above, cutting through the white and rolling plains. Another line, and the smell of their kiss is so real, and their bodies are close and touching. Pale light from above, flickering in the falling, wind-swept snow and sleet, their scarves—one orange and blue, the other dark green, floating in the wind, as if reaching for times gone by. He is wearing a backpack over his shoulders, his initials, JWH, stenciled to a square of leather, barely visible in the sleet and rain and wind, and his bag slips off his shoulder as their arms intertwine.

More lines appear on the paper, dark cuts against the white, and the feeling of butterfly wings fluttering as the couple embraces in the storm that screams all around. But together they hold fast, their arms ensnared, their hearts beating in sync beneath their heavy coats, their bodies sharing warmth against the night. The cold whirls around them, burning their exposed skin, and the smell of her breath, and the smell of his lips, and the feel of their noses as they touch lightly at first, but he presses harder and she presses harder, and their lips and their skin and their breathing are one.

Ink on paper and the couple is real, the lines mesh into reality, the lamp post above, shining its yellow glare, and the wind whirling, and the snow pelting their bodies, and the cold stinging their noses, but the warmth of their touch, and the smells of her perfume and his cologne, and the feel of his cheek on hers, and their kisses.

"You'll take care of me?" she whispers, her voice barely rising above the howl of the wind and the screech of the storm. She cries, tears escaping her eyes but mixing with flakes of melted snow on her face, and the smell of her silk hair that carries in the wind, blonde in real life, but a dark brown here and now, wrapping around his face, enclosing them both, and the snow at their feet, drifting against their legs. They don't feel the cold, because her eyes are so green and deep, and his pale eyes so blue, and she feels a burning within, and he holds her close, they are one against the storm.

"Always," he says, and she almost believes. She cries and her tears run streams down her face, and on his face, but she has never been happier. Right here and now, on this very page, with ink and paper, they are one.

Chapter Six

Mae struck the ice and plunged into the icy-black water. The shock was instant and debilitating. For several seconds, she could do nothing but allow the current to pull her through the inky water.

This is the end, she thought, her body numb and her mind struggling with consciousness. She tried the paper and ink, tried to escape into another realm, but everything was blocked by the freezing water. The cold darkness of the river swallowed her, extinguishing the flame that was her life.

"I'll always love you." This time it was her father's voice, just before he died.

Then her mother was whispering, "You gotta move, baby girl, before the devil gets you."

And strangely, a memory that she thought was long lost, resurfaced. The feel of her first kiss, the brush of his lips on hers, and the taste of the kiss, and the autumn mountains blanketed with mist.

You gotta move—

Mae kicked toward the surface, struggling against the current to reach up to the air above the water, so tantalizingly close to her face yet separated by a layer of ice. She pounded against the ice and screamed, the last of the air from her lungs forming into bubbles and bouncing along the underside of the frozen water. Her lungs burned and her body ached. Mae slammed into a large rock and slipped around it with the current. Her arm hit a branch, sending her body spiraling along the riverbed, and her head collided with another rock. The shock of the collision didn't drive away consciousness, but she stopped fighting the river. The will to live, so intense and vibrant only seconds before, quickly drained from her body as the cold numbed her and the lack of oxygen slackened her grip on reality. She floated along the bottom of the river, bouncing into rocks and fallen tree trunks.

Her foot suddenly snagged a branch, ripping her body from the current and pulling her closer to a gnarl of roots along the riverbank where the ice was still thin. She pushed up hard against the icy surface, even as her lungs felt as though they would explode. She burst from the dark water with a gasp, chunks of ice and river debris floating in the water next to her.

She kept breathing hard, gulping and relishing each breath, and then her body was forcing short breaths despite her need for oxygen, hypothermia setting in. Mae climbed from the water and slowly squirmed out of her wet clothes, knowing that she had mere minutes to warm her body before hypothermia would claim her. Once the outer layer of clothes was a sopping bundle on the frozen earth, she peeled her bra and panties from her body, the material already stiffening as the moisture mixed with the bitter temperatures and began to freeze. She was naked in the cold, night air, vulnerable.

Mae ran her fingers over her numbing skin, and her body felt hard and frozen. Her muscles convulsed rapidly, rattling her bones and teeth, and sending waves of dull pain to her fingertips. She lay on the ground and curled into a ball on the forest floor, no longer noticing the biting cold or the frozen twigs and branches that stuck into her skin like icy needles. She fought the urge to just fall asleep and let her mind and body go to a place where it was warm, to a place where she didn't have to fight for survival, where she couldn't cry or scream or run. She was tired of running, and tired of outpacing death, which always seemed to be just a few steps behind.

She was just plain old tired, and the fight was gone.

The warm blanket of darkness called to her, and she closed her eyes for just a moment, allowing the warmth of oblivion to take control of her mind and body.

I'll sleep for just two seconds, she thought, but she wasn't really thinking at this point. Her body was methodically shutting down, and she welcomed the nothingness that swept over her, simply because it was warm. The darkness came upon her and wrapped its comforting coils around her body, slithering into her throat and around her neck.

The violent shaking in her body slowed, and the dull, but raging ache seemed to fade away. As she lay dying, she opened her eyes and stared at the black sky overhead. The moon shone behind the clouds, illuminating the tufts of winter storm with a faint glow.

She almost closed her eyes again, and it really would have been over had her eyelids finally slid shut, but the clouds parted for a moment, and the sky caught her gaze.

The stars twinkled—tiny bits of contrast in the black emptiness of the universe. She thought about a time when she was a child, looking up at the sky from her trampoline, her mom and dad laying on either side of her on top of a patchwork quilt that was soft and thick, watching the big sky unfold. It'd been summer then, and the air was warm and spiked with the scents of lilac and honeysuckle. They'd eaten popcorn from a big metal bowl perched between them and sucked on red strands of licorice. It was one of those endless nights, caught in memory on repeat, a moment when she'd been happy, when she'd wanted to live.

And her thoughts drifted to another time and place where she'd studied the stars, laying in a mountain meadow on that same patchwork quilt, listening to the crickets and cicadas, and his breathing beside her, his hand closed around hers.

Mae, frozen and dying, felt a spark of life within her nearly lifeless body, a remnant of that the spark she'd felt, both with her parents on the trampoline as a little girl, and then again with the boy she'd first loved.

"I've got to get up," she mumbled in a voice so soft and strained that it sounded alien, even to herself. "I've got to get up."

Mae uncurled her fingers, the muscles and bones creaking and trembling as they straightened. She flexed the muscles in her hands, slowly at first, and then more quickly, forcing the sluggish blood to circulate.

She forced herself to roll over onto her knees, her entire body in a seizure of cold, and she straightened up into a kneeling position, vigorously rubbing her bare skin. She reached toward her drenched knapsack and unzipped the top pocket, pulling out a plastic shopping bag. As she unfolded the bag, she prayed that the contents inside had not gotten wet. Tiny puddles of water had pooled in the creases of the bag, and her heart sank when she felt the clothes inside.

The extra pair of clothes was protected to some extent by the shopping bag, but was by no means dry. She pulled the damp bundle from the bag, set it on the ground, and ignored for a moment longer the fact that she was naked and freezing to death. Mae unfolded the pair of blue jeans that had been wrapped around her sweater, which was in turn wrapped around a t-shirt and a pair of underwear. At the very center of the bundle was a small, black iPod, one of the older models, wrapped in a pair of equally antiquated headphones. With the music player was a small notebook containing mostly blank pages, but with a few sketches toward the front. She made sure the notebook was dry and then put it aside, focusing her attention on the iPod. She turned it over in her hands and examined it closely. Her hands shook and it took a great deal of concentration to keep from dropping it. The casing was intact, but it was slippery with moisture.

The iPod had obviously been protected first by the plastic bag, and then by her clothes, but not saved completely from getting wet. Mae examined the 32-pin docking bay for the connecting wire and made sure that no moisture had found its way inside. The docking bay seemed to be dry, but she blew inside for good measure. She held it between the palms of her hands and brought it close to her face. She kissed the hard, cold surface, and gently placed it again inside the shopping bag with her notebook. She wrapped the plastic tightly around the little bundle and returned it to the knapsack.

Her body shook violently and her teeth clicked as she pulled the underwear and clothing onto her body. Even damp, the clothes provided some degree of cover from the winter air.

She moved jerkily, the blood pumping slowly through her body like a trickling stream. She stood and pulled the jeans up and over her petite hips, buttoning the front and zipping the fly. She squeezed water from her boots and pulled them over her feet.

Mae gathered her wet clothes and rolled them into a ball before shoving them into a hole beneath the twisted roots of a tree, then brushed dead leaves and twigs over the hole until the clothes were completely covered. She didn't know if Eddie and the guys from the cabin would come looking for her body tonight, or during daylight, but she couldn't risk having her clothes found, as they would know that she'd survived the river.

Mae stood, her body aching and screaming for some relief from the cold. She had to move quickly, knowing that slowing her movements would only quicken death's grasp on her. She picked up her knapsack, slung it over both shoulders, and pushed forward into the dark forest beyond.

Part Two
Route B, Michigan Ave.

Chapter Seven

Paul Fremont remembered the heat hitting him like a sledgehammer to the face, as he walked out of the airport. The air was thick and wet, and smelled like a salty swamp. The taste and smell of the air, and the never-ending heat always came with his thoughts of Ground Zero at Miami, as did the general discomfort of the weather, the running stream of Spanish spoken with a Cuban staccato accent, constantly in the background as he walked through the steel beams and broken concrete.

It came at him in flashes. The yellow police tape, the groups of men and women, some crying, others standing with their hands shoved deep into their pockets, all of them looking lost and helpless, standing in front of the temporary chain link fence that was erected around Ground Zero. The fence plastered with pictures of loved ones lost in the explosion that wasn't an explosion, victims of the bomb that wasn't a bomb. The broken sidewalk, littered with glass and debris, bouquets of flowers, and flickering candles to the Saints.

The press zone was a small area blocked off from the rest of the world, allowing reporters a glimpse of the building beyond, but no cameras were allowed. The press zone was filled with bodies, all of them sweating in the South Florida heat and humidity. The reporters and journalists, those sharks and snakes, their arms extended with microphones, or Dictaphones, or cell phones, recording every word of fluff dished out by the police, and only one thing stuck in his mind.

No evidence of a bomb, no evidence of an explosion.

Tell that to the building that looked like it'd been turned inside out before being crushed.

Paul took a deep breath and tried to push the memories of the attack in Miami from his mind. He unwrapped a piece of spicy cinnamon candy and placed it on the center of his tongue. He closed his mouth around the candy, ignoring the flashes of destruction. Ignoring the images of crying moms and dads, of the skeletal remains of buildings, Paul focused instead on the initial tingling sensation of the candy.

Paul loved Atomic Fireballs, and when he was stressed or nervous, he constantly popped them into his mouth. At the moment, Paul was more stressed than he ever remembered, probably more nervous and upset than he'd been even during the last few months of his marriage. Already, he was sucking on two pieces, and that third piece of cinnamon flavored candy was about all he could handle.

Paul savored the initial burst of cinnamon spice, moving the candies around the inside of his mouth and feeling nostalgia and comfort. The taste reminded him of scorching summers when he was a child in a small western town in the foothills of the Rocky Mountains. Every morning during that magical summertime between school years, he would work hard to finish up his chores around the house early in the morning, not just so he could run and play outside for the rest of the day, but so he could earn a dollar or two to spend at the little town store.

He would take the money and ride his bike to the store, a building not much bigger than a two-car garage. He would prop his bike on the wooden porch and when he went inside, the dark and cool interior would always be a welcome relief against the dry mountain heat. Always, he would use the money to buy a cold bottle of Sprite and a handful of Atomic Fireballs. Paul would then sit on the wooden steps, watching cars drive by while sipping the soda pop and relishing the cinnamon candy. The taste of the candy as an adult somehow brought it all back, even the dusty summer air, the sweat on his forehead, and the cool bite of the carbonation on his dry throat.

The cinnamon spice turned to fire as it stung his tongue and the insides of his cheeks. He opened his mouth and inhaled deeply, the air rushing into his mouth and throat and cooling the nerve endings, while delivering a healthy dose of spiced air to his lungs. He held onto the breath for a moment, like a smoker savoring that first lungful of tar and tobacco.

As he exhaled slowly through his nose, Paul crinkled the wrapper into his pocket and leaned forward until his forehead touched the frosty glass of the window.

The city spread out before him like an explosion of light—beautiful and vibrant on the surface, but cold and dark and dirty within. He squinted, trying to make out Lake Michigan behind the sprawl of concrete and people, to no avail. Even if it hadn't been snowing a full gale blizzard, and even if the moon hadn't been covered with thick clouds, he doubted that he'd be able to see the lake anyway at night, because the city lights were just too bright.

Paul focused again on the city, the high rises and office buildings, the lighted windows, and the cars driving slowly through the streets. Several blocks away, flashing red and blue lights burst to life and pulled an unsuspecting driver to the side of the road.

The sidewalks were sparsely populated this time of night, especially with the temperatures diving below freezing and the snow falling faster and faster. What few people were brave enough to face the elements had coats pulled tightly to their bodies, scarves blowing in the frigid wind from the lake.

Paul stepped away from the window and paced the small room as he took another piece of candy from his pocket and squeezed it between his fingers.

He stopped for a moment in front of the coffee table where loose papers bulged from a stack of manila folders. He considered rifling through the pages for the millionth time, but knew that he wouldn't be able to sit still for longer than a few seconds. He glanced at his watch, the second hand seeming to tick by in slow motion. He wanted to sip a finger of Wild

Turkey to calm his nerves, but thought better of it. He needed a clear mind.

It was almost time.

Months of negotiating with this woman had led to this, and he was minutes away from meeting the woman who would change his life. He hoped, and she promised, that her information would answer the questions that'd plagued him for years.

A bomb that wasn't a bomb.

The world had moved on from the disaster in Miami, but Paul had not moved on. The officials had explained away the disaster as a combination of faulty engineering and trembling of the earth's tectonic plates, an accident.

No matter how ridiculous it seemed, no matter how sure Paul was that a building could not lift up out of the ground and implode in on itself because of engineering errors, he couldn't prove his theories. He had no answers, no evidence, and without the evidence, he was just a crackpot conspiracy theorist.

But now the woman promised to answer those questions, to shed light on his theories, and for that he was nervous and excited. In the years that had followed the Miami attack, his life had slowly unraveled, one piece at a time. He'd become obsessed with finding answers to the disaster, pouring through engineering specs, blueprints, geological surveys and reports for the day of the tragedy. The more he read, the more he was certain that the incident could not have happened by accident.

Despite the lack of evidence of a bomb, he became increasingly sure that the attack had been planned and executed. It could not have been an accident.

The woman promised to explain it all, to give him the evidence he needed to prove that his obsession wasn't some crazy conspiracy.

He walked to the door and stared out the small peep hole, looking through the concave lens to the hallway beyond. He saw nothing and, and hadn't expected to see anything. He was nervous about the meeting, and he wasn't thinking so much as acting to quell the anxiety.

He turned back to the room, crossing again to the window while squeezing his fingers around the hard ball of candy in its wrapper.

Paul glanced at his watch again… and it was time to go. He took his coat from where it lay on the bed and slung it over his shoulders. He considered his knit winter cap, but decided against it. Even though his ears would freeze, the cap made him look like a thug, and he wanted to avoid that appearance if at all possible. He wanted the woman to trust him, and already that would be something of an uphill battle. He'd spoken to her a few times, and while she seemed to open up a little more with each telephone conversation, she remained suspicious and guarded, as if their conversations were being recorded and her location traced. Her carefully chosen words and half-references were seeped in paranoia, and while Paul understood that what they were talking about was serious business, he never quite understood why she was so scared, why it had taken months of sporadic calls to finally convince her to meet in person. As much as she wanted to avoid her face being associated with the information she had, Paul needed to know that she wasn't a hack.

On his way out of the room, he picked up a thin stack of documents and a legal pad. He didn't know how long he would be on the bus, waiting for the woman, but it wouldn't hurt to go over his plan of attack.

Paul was alone on the elevator to the lobby, so he checked his appearance in the mirrors that lined the walls. He wasn't especially good looking, but he figured that attractive or ugly people drew more attention to themselves, and what he really wanted was to blend in with the crowd, to be someone that no one ever really saw. He wanted to be a fly on the wall, always observing but never seen.

His thinning blond hair was combed into place, and the shadow of his beard gave him the distinguished look of a man hard at work—or so he hoped.

The elevator door dinged open, and he stepped into a well-lit and cheerful lobby of the Hotel Monoco. A man and woman were getting onto the elevator, both dressed as if they'd come from a cocktail party, and walking like they'd had a few too many cocktails. The man nodded at him, and grinned the sloppy grin of a drunk about to get lucky.

Paul nodded as he walked past and debated briefly about stopping at the little café in the lobby for a cup of coffee to take with him on the bus. He steered toward the café which sat opposite the hotel bar, but decided against the coffee when he saw the line at the counter.

Shoulda left earlier, he thought as he pulled out his cell phone and dialed. After two rings, Paul heard the click as the phone on the other end was picked up.

"On your way?" It was Dennis Johnson, his assistant. Dennis didn't like to be called an assistant because he found that word too similar in meaning to "secretary," and Dennis was firm that he was not a secretary. He preferred to be called an associate

"Yeah, walking to the bus stop now. Michigan Ave, right?" Paul asked. He paused at the revolving doors and threw his coat over his shoulders. The wind gusted swirls of snow outside, and he shivered despite the warm comfort of the lobby.

"Yeah," Dennis said, sounding annoyed and tired. "Route B, remember, and it will be there in just a few minutes, if the bus is running on time."

A taxi pulled up to the curb and a man in a suit climbed out. He was instantly hit with a gale of winter wind. His suit and hair were blanketed with big flakes of snow. He wrapped his arms around his body and ran to the front door, slipping on some ice as he ran and almost losing his balance. When he came into the hotel lobby, he looked as if he'd been rolling in the snow, his suit blanketed with snowflakes and already melting.

"It's going to be cold out there. Hard to believe the buses are still running tonight," Paul said, more to himself than to

Dennis. "The snow has got to be more than 12 inches deep, it's crazy."

"You're telling me," Dennis said. "I'm looking out my window at the parking lot, and my car is buried. Not going to be fun digging that baby out."

"Hold off on the digging and stay close to the phone for now," Paul said. "Still not sure how all this will go down."

"This whole thing is a little weird," Dennis said. Paul heard some hesitation in his voice, like he wanted to say something that he knew they were both thinking. The woman claimed to have information about a terrorist group operating within the government, and she was too afraid to meet in a conventional locale, for fear that that she would be found. She wouldn't talk more than a few minutes on the phone, and she always called from pay phones or pre-paid cell phones. As much as Paul wanted to get his hopes up, all signs pointed to this woman being a full-on nut job. The only thing that kept him from writing the woman off completely was that when a lucid person, or someone who seemed to be lucid, was as paranoid as this woman was, then maybe there was something to it. She was either telling the truth and playing around with something better left undisturbed, or she was a paranoid wacko.

"Yeah. I'll call you if anything happens. If you don't hear from me in an hour, then you call me." Paul said.

"You got it, boss." Dennis hung up. Paul stuck his phone into the inside pocket of his jacket and zipped up the front. He took a deep breath, buried his head and face into his jacket, like a turtle in his shell, and pushed through the revolving doors to the freezing night beyond.

He glanced up the street in the direction that the bus would be coming, and sure enough, it pulled around the corner and came towards the bus stop, which was a few hundred feet from the entrance to the Monoco. The yellow headlights flickered in the falling snow, the shadows from the yellow lights dancing out over the snow swept street.

It was cold, and Paul could feel the wintery tendrils breaching his coat and clothes, could feel it snaking its way under his skin. Not even five minutes outside, and already his muscles were starting to ache. He hurried faster to get under what little shelter the bus stop provided.

Paul was surprised to see other people huddled there beneath the short outcropping. A lady sat on the bench, her jacket pulled tightly around her body, and her scarf wrapped around her ears and face. From what little Paul could see of her face, he could tell that she was miserable. She had several grocery bags on the seat next to her and an old leather purse clutched tightly to her side. She stared straight ahead, and if she'd noticed Paul, she gave no indication.

The other two people were standing, one of them doing a little jig to keep warm, both of his hands shoved deep into the pockets of his dress pants. Paul stared at them for a moment, unable to look away. They weren't much older than teenagers, 25 at the absolute maximum. One of them was taller than the other, and he had a cool handsomeness about him that was striking, even in the middle of a blizzard. He stood there, one hand in his pocket, the other holding an iPhone and swiping through screens like he couldn't be bothered to be cold. He stood with an obvious assurance of himself, and seemed to be completely enthralled with whatever he was studying on the screen of his phone.

The shorter one, the guy hopping from foot to foot to stay warm, was nice looking too, though not to the same extent. His features were more plain and ordinary, like Paul's own, whereas the other could have been mistaken for a young Brad Pitt, if Pitt's hair had been dark and cut short.

But it wasn't their youth, or how they looked, or even how the shorter guy danced from foot to foot that was strange—it was how they were dressed. Both guys were in full-on tuxedos. Paul was no expert on fashion and design, but the tuxedos were sophisticated and impeccably tailored to fit the young men perfectly.

The taller wore a vest beneath his jacket, and his cufflinks sparked in the light from a street lamp. The shorter wore a cummerbund, a matte black that was equally impressive. The buttons on their shirts were black onyx inlaid in silver settings that glinted in the faint street light, and the shirts screamed sophistication, perfectly fit and expertly starched. Both looked as though they had stepped out from an exclusive black-tie party in Chicago's financial district. But Paul didn't think that anyone in such attire would want to ride the city bus, especially in this weather.

Aside from their tuxedo jackets, they had no coats, and must have been freezing. Not to mention, the weather was doing a number on such fine clothing. Already, their shoes were covered with dirt, and the cloudy scuffs from street salt. Even the cuffs of their pants were dirty and wet.

They had to be on their way to a party, Paul mused, or maybe they were just thrown out of a party?

The taller of the two looked up from his phone and caught Paul staring at him. For a moment, the two held each other's gaze, before Paul looked away. He stood there, feeling awkward and foolish because he had nowhere to go, and nothing to do but stand there under the boy's scrutiny. It suddenly became very uncomfortable for Paul, and if the bus hadn't been right up the street, and if his meeting with the woman not so important, Paul would have walked away. Normally, he was confident and cool, but there was something about the boy that he couldn't place, something he didn't like.

Something about the guy's eyes.

It didn't matter, Paul thought. The bus neared, the blue florescent light of the interior filtering through the large windows. Paul looked through the windows and searched the faces of the passengers he could see, looking for anyone who might be his contact. He saw a young man and woman, their heads locked together in a kissing embrace. He saw an elderly man looking out the window at the falling snowflakes, his face serene and contemplative. There was a young family toward the front, dressed warmly in thick coats, knit caps and scarves. The little girl couldn't have been more than six years old, and her eyes were bright with excitement. Her curly black hair was pulled into little braids on her head, with colored beads on the end of each braid. Her smile was wide, and she reminded Paul of someone you'd see on the beach in the Caribbean, not in the dead of a mid-western winter.

From where he stood, looking through the windows of the bus, no one looked like they could be the woman he was planning to meet. His shoulders dropped, and he sighed. He'd been a journalist for more than two decades, reporting his countless investigations to whoever would read his work. There had been many sources who'd bailed on him over the years, and even more that had actually shown up, but with bogus information. He really hoped that wasn't the case here. No conspiracies; this was the most important story of his life.

He could feel it.

As the bus grumbled to a stop, dirty sleet sprayed up from the gutter and splattered the newly fallen powder. Paul took a deep breath and waited for the doors to open.

Chapter Eight

The brakes on the bus squeaked as it slowed to a stop, its big black tires crunching in the newly fallen snow. ROUTE B MICHIGAN AVE. flashed on the digital display at the top of the bus.

Ryan Coffee stuck his phone in the pocket of his tuxedo jacket, and looked away from the man who'd just joined them under the bus shelter. Ryan caught Sam's eye, and he jerked his head toward the newcomer. Sam kept his body moving like a puppy needing to go outside, and it drove Ryan crazy— he couldn't figure out why Sam didn't just bring a coat if he was going to act so ridiculous.

Sam followed Ryan's gaze to the newcomer and looked him over. After a few seconds, he shook his head, still dancing like a buffoon.

Good, Ryan thought. At least the guy wasn't a cop. It was weird that the man was standing here at the bus stop. He didn't look like the type to be riding public transportation in the middle of a blizzard. But then again, neither did he or Sam. He tugged at his left coat sleeve and adjusted the platinum cufflink in left sleeve. The cufflinks were from Cartier, a gift from his father.

Assuming he survived the night, the cufflinks would go into the little cedar box toward the back of his sock drawer. They'd be right at home with the other little trinkets that were bought for Ryan from the highest-end stores in lieu of any show of affection from either of his parents. From his father, he got cufflinks, and tie clips from Harry Winston and Tiffany's and Cartier, with diamonds or other jewels embedded in the center, and genuine Italian shoes that glistened with the sweat and tears of child labor. From his mother, it was always video games and electronics that he'd never really been interested in, but that she thought he liked, even at the ripe old age of 23. With every gift, his parents beamed, as though the gifts were actual hugs and kisses, and then the moment would be done, and the little show of affection over. Each of them would move on with their lives until the next occasion to show affection presented itself.

Ryan didn't care, didn't need the affection—especially on nights like tonight. His heart beat loudly in his chest, and he felt nervous and shaky anticipation build up within him. He allowed himself a few seconds with his eyes closed, to imagine the grip of the steering wheel in his hands, to hear the roar of its engine, and the quiet thrumming that flowed through the metal. He saw flashes of light, extended into glowing trails of reds and yellows and blues, the speed warping the reality around it.

When he opened his eyes, he realized that he'd also been holding his breath, and he exhaled slow and long, the smoke of his breath rising toward the falling snow.

The night of the dragon, he thought. Lit dragons. Ryan felt a surge of adrenaline, and couldn't help but smile.

A gust of freezing wind smacked him in the face, and he stopped smiling. The weather was bitingly cold, and Ryan had a lot on his mind. The map, for one, was difficult this evening, and he didn't know how it would work in this weather. He tried to remember the last time he'd led the dragons in winter conditions, and he was sure that it had been more than a year. Ice and snow changed everything.

The door to the bus slid open, and Ryan stepped away from the curb to allow the old lady and the newcomer to board first. Again, he was surprised to see these people out in weather like this. Ryan didn't pride himself on his knowledge of the behavior of others, didn't care really, but thought most people would have stayed inside on a night like tonight. They all formed a line behind the old lady, who struggled to climb the big, wet steps into the bus.

"That guy ahead of us?" Sam whispered.

"Yeah."

"I think he's got to be some sort of reporter or something." Sam said, gnawing on the nail of his little finger.

"That's really gross you know," Ryan said. "Do you realize how much dirt and crap gets up under there?"

"Sorry." Sam spit a bit of fingernail into the mud and snow on the sidewalk and continued, "So he's got some sort of file folder, with a bunch of papers. Who carries around stuff like that, especially in a full-blown, hold-your-hat snowstorm? Businessmen and lawyers, that's who, but he doesn't look like a business guy, and certainly not a lawyer. A night like tonight, and the lawyers are lining up in the hospital to wait for ambulances."

"Sam, if he's not a cop, it doesn't matter," Paul said. It was their turn to board the bus. Ryan went first, nodding to the big man at the helm, and dropping some coins into the payment collector. The man driving the bus was black, with his salt and pepper hair cut short and his eyes framed with deep laughing lines. He nodded back at Ryan with a smile that was genuinely friendly, a playful twinkle in his eyes.

Ryan walked along the aisle, past a young girl with black braids and fluffy pink coat, past the guy who'd been staring him down at the bus stop. The guy was now buried in the papers of his file, reviewing what appeared to be handwritten notes.

The floor of the bus was wet and dirty, streaked with muddy foot prints and small puddles. The air smelled liked dust burning in the heating vents. When Ryan sat down, he felt moisture on the seat, and he sighed. He hated the weather in Chicago during the winter. It was just so cold and wet and miserable, and it reminded him too much of home.

Sam sat next to him on the seat, his legs still fidgeting in an effort to stay warm.

"Can you stop that, please?"

"What?" Sam asked. The tip of his nose and cheeks were bright red from the cold, and his eyes had that glazy look of someone just trying to survive.

"Moving your legs like that," Ryan nodded at the constant movement of Sam's legs. "It's annoying."

"I'm cold."

"There's a heater on this bus." Ryan said. Sam shrugged. He stopped moving for a few minutes, but then he started again.

"Sorry."

Ryan shook his head and pulled out his phone. He tapped an icon that featured a dragon drawn with what appeared to be neon bulbs, and a map appeared. He swiped through the screens and settled once again on a map. He studied the line that marked the route, tried to picture the curves and the angles of the road. He saw a grayed area that looked to be a bridge, or an overpass. Ryan pored over the details, memorizing as much as he could.

They rode in silence for a few moments, then Sam started chattering away again.

"I gotta talk, man, 'cause it's cold, and I've got to move, and I'm a little nervous about the rundown tonight."

"Why are you nervous?" Ryan asked. He swiped at the screen on his phone, and the names of the other players appeared. Most of the names were unfamiliar, but he recognized a few.

"Because it's icy," Sam said after a few seconds hesitation. He sighed, as if admitting defeat. "The black ice scares me, okay? You can't see it, especially with it snowing like this and covering up the road.

"I'll take care of it." Ryan smiled and gave his friend a sideways glance.

"I'm sure, but it's been awhile, and I've got a kid to think about now. And Dani, jeeze-man, I hope she doesn't wake up while I'm gone. We've never really talked about this stuff, but if she'd seen me leaving with the tux and all, she'd be asking questions, and she wouldn't like the answers."

"You know the rules," Ryan put away his phone.

"I know the rules, and that's why I'm nervous, that's all, and being nervous and cold as balls, makes me want to talk."

Sam paused, waiting for Ryan to say something. Ryan made a twirling gesture with his fingers.

"So talk then."

"I'm going to," Sam said, but hesitated. "But now I feel like you're annoyed, and you don't want me to talk. It's uncomfortable."

"For the love, Sam," Ryan said under his breath, "good thing you married early, because if she has to deal with this BS, she's going to divorce you for sure, and you'll at least have some time while you're still young to find someone else."

"You don't know Dani and me," Sam said, then blew warm breath into his cupped hands.

"We're good together, and holy crap it's still freezing in here, even with the heater."

"I'm sure you guys are good," Ryan said. His phone vibrated from the pocket of his tux, and they both heard it, glancing toward the sound. Ryan pulled it out, and a tiny red circle began to flash on the surface of the map, instantly followed by a cyan-colored line that led from the red circle to a solid green circle.

"We're here," Paul said, and the adrenaline was back. He could feel it in his bones, could feel the cool rush of blood to his head.

"The guy has a pencil too, and he's chewing on the eraser. You don't get that in non-reporter types, and again, no way that guy is a lawyer."

"What are you talking about?"

"The guy we came on the bus with," Sam said. Ryan looked over the seat at the guy and shrugged. If he wasn't a cop, it didn't much matter. He reached up and pulled the cable that drooped above the windows. A sign that read STOP REQUESTED flashed at the front of the bus, followed by a loud ding. Both Ryan and Sam stood as the bus slowed. The man who was probably a reporter, not a lawyer, glanced up at them as they walked out of the bus.

"Have a good night, gentlemen," the bus driver said in a thick Chicago accent. His eyebrows were raised with concern as he looked through the windshield of the bus at the nasty weather and rough section of town.

"Later," Ryan said as he passed by and exited the bus. Sam smiled at the man and followed Ryan into the snow.

As the bus pulled away from the curb and the snow pounded down on them, Sam and Ryan looked around at the street that could have been mistaken for an abandoned ghost town out west, except for the swirling snow and the cars parked along the sidewalk. One of the street lights, close to where they stood, had burned out, and the area around it was dark. Although small brick houses lined one side of the street, the area consisted mostly of large storage facilities and warehouses.

"Sure this is the right spot?" Sam asked.

Ryan wiped away some snowflakes that had fallen onto the touch screen of his phone and studied the flashing red bulb on the map. He nodded.

"I'm sure," he said, and pointed to the entrance of an alley about halfway down the block.

"I bet it's right over there."

"Think an SUV this time?"

"Sedan," Ryan said. Of course he didn't know for sure, but the SUVs seemed to be fading out of style. And besides, SUVs weren't good for their line of work, as the bulk of the vehicle was more of a benefit than the performance.

"You've got the keys?" Ryan asked as he trudged through the snow. The cold seeped into his socks.

"FedEx came yesterday," Sam said, "right on schedule. Dani almost opened it, and that would have been bad."

"Have you ever had to explain the money?"

Sam shook his head as they rounded the corner and peered into the darkness. A few meters away, they could barely see the sleek outline of a car. Sam punched the button on the key fob in his pocket. Red lights flashed, and the car beeped as the doors unlocked and the alarm was disengaged.

"After you," Sam said, and Ryan crossed to the driver's side. As he walked, he ran his hand over the smooth cold surface of the car, his hand getting wet from the fallen snow. The car was black, and was indeed a sedan, although like always, any indication as to the make and model had been removed from the car's body.

The car was anonymous.

He opened the door and smelled new leather. It reminded him of the first car he'd received from his father, on his sixteenth birthday. That car had been a Mercedes S600 Sedan, with a 5.5L twin-turbo V-12 engine and 510 horsepower. The leather in that car had smelled like power, much like the leather in this car. Of course, he was too young and naive for a car like that, but his father had been completely oblivious to that fact and had beamed on their first, and only, ride together.

Ryan slid into the seat and adjusted his coat and neck tie in the mirror. He flexed his hands on the steering wheel and pressed the ignition button. The car roared to life, a guttural rumble that echoed off the walls of the alley and shook the windows in the nearby buildings. Sam sat in the seat next to him and smiled.

"Nice ride, this one," Sam ran his fingers over the woodgrain in the dashboard. "I hope it comes with a good seat warmer, cause my butt is freezing."

"Ready?" Ryan asked, setting his phone into a cradle atop the dashboard. The blue line extended out from the flashing red bulb, cutting straight through the alley.

"System connected, standby," A sweet, melodic voice said through the car's speakers. Ryan always liked the sound of her voice and hoped that one day, he'd be able to meet woman behind the voice. Although that too was against the rules.

Ryan gripped the steering wheel and pumped the accelerator ever so slightly. The engine revved with an explosion of power and raw energy.

"Welcome to Lit Dragons," the woman said. "Emergency personnel are standing by."

"Well, that's good." Sam said. Ryan could tell that he was nervous, but the nervousness was mixed with an adrenaline rush that was difficult to explain. It felt like surfing, at the exact moment before the wave caught you. That moment when the sheer force of nature pummeled against your body, threatening to either send you below the surface in a shattering current or thrust you and your board across the water.

Sam pulled a picture from the pocket of his tuxedo jacket and stared at it. Ryan saw that it was his wife, a pretty girl that he'd met only once. She had dark brown hair that was long and smooth. In the picture, she was still pregnant, and she glowed. Beside her, Sam also glowed, that stupid grin on his face, his arm wrapped around his wife's shoulders.

"You know the—" Ryan started, but Sam interrupted.

"The rules, I know," Sam said. He lowered the window a crack and shoved the picture out into the snowy storm.

"On my mark," the woman's voice said.

Ryan revved the engine harder this time. He flipped on the car's headlights, and the alley was lit in a yellow glow. Sam gripped the arm rest, his knuckles turning white.

"Lit Dragons initiated," the woman said. Ryan dropped the car into first gear and jammed the accelerator down. The engine boomed as the car shot forward through the alley, the rear wheels skidding to the left in the snow. He corrected the wheel carefully, finessing the brakes ever so slightly. Once righted, he stepped hard on the accelerator, and they were off.

Chapter Nine

A blue dot appeared on the map on her computer screen, indicating that the team had found the car and was online. She pulled her chair close to the computer, typed several commands that accessed the car's operating system. Her heart beat faster in her chest as she activated the microphone on her computer and leaned close.

"Welcome to Lit Dragons," the woman known in the digital world as ANONX^17. "Emergency personnel are standing by."

She sat at her computer and studied a map that depicted the streets of Chicago and the surrounding area. She ran a diagnostics on the car and communications system, and they came back clear. She glanced at another monitor that showed the city's grid of traffic lights. Along the bottom of the screen were the controls she used to control the traffic lights.

"On my mark," ANONX^17 said. She opened a window on her screen which showed the location of police cruisers around the city. The are was clean, at least for the moment. If the started now, their paths would intersect with a cop, who was driving slowly a few streets away.

That could be fun, she smiled. She took a deep breath. The blue dot stayed still, and would until she gave the go ahead. She leaned forward so that her lips nearly touched the microphone.

"Lit Dragons initiated," the woman said. The blue dot shot forward through the alley as the players began the game. ANONX^17 watched, holding her breath.

Of course, her real name wasn't ANONX^17. That combination of letters, numbers and symbols was the mask she wore every day. Some people chose to be imaginary people on the internet, but she thought the character combination packed more of a punch. A faceless entity to be reckoned with. Her real name was Heather Gardner, and the people who knew her as Heather had no idea of her life indoors. To them, she was a pretty girl with unrealized beauty, who was fun to be around when she wasn't keeping to herself. Heather had dark, shoulder-length hair which she always wore in a loose ponytail. She hardly ever wore makeup, and she carried some extra weight, but didn't mind. The extra weight made for a fuller figure and sleek curves that her friends were envious of. Not to mention, she jogged three times a week and hit the gym enough to feel like her body was in good shape.

Heather didn't date much, and on the rare occasion that she did, the guys she went out with were ones that she met on campus where she taught advanced computer programming twice a week. That's not to say that she wasn't asked out regularly; she simply didn't have an interest in long term relationships, at least in the physical sense of a relationship.

Mostly, her relationships were online with people she'd never seen. She liked it that way. Safer.

To most people who knew her, she was a well-mannered, brainy woman who was focused primarily on her career. But inside her apartment and online she was an elite hacker to be reckoned with. There was virtually no system she couldn't enter, no firewall she couldn't bypass. To Heather, the digital world was like a wilderness to be explored, a wealth of untapped information and data that flowed beneath the external world like a great unknown river.

When she started out as a neophyte, or a newbie hacker, it was mostly for fun. The language of code came easily to her, and before long, she was entering secure networks to see if she could. In college, she hooked up with some programmers who introduced her to the world of Blue Hat hacking, where outside consultants would exploit a system for weaknesses prior to launch. When Heather felt she was good enough to run with the wolves, she broke into the network of a security firm that touted itself as the best in the business. She introduced herself by sending an email to the CEO from the CEO's email account, listing the details of his personal bank account and a detailed summary of the places he'd visited in the previous 48 hours. Of course, his phone had been secured and the connection encrypted, but once she lifted the number from his personal computer, she traced the connection through the phone company and bypassed all the encryptions. Once she had access to his phone, it was cake to track his whereabouts—

mostly to places of no import, restaurants and coffee shops. There was only one location he visited that would raise any eyebrows, and although she didn't know for sure, Heather figured his wife of 13 years hadn't accompanied him.

He'd given her a job as a security consultant immediately, and she began to pick up projects when she had the time. Of course, the firm only knew her as ANONX^17, and paid her with untraceable deposits to an account in Zurich. It paid very well, was challenging, and most importantly, it was relaxing. She would crank the stereo (anarcho-punk rock, always) and treat her work like a puzzle to be solved.

And on the other hand, she had the games. For brief moments of time, her life became vivid and real as the lives of her players hung in a balance.

The microwave beeped and Heather pulled a steaming cup of water from within. She dropped two tea bags into the water and held it close to her nose, inhaling the subtle aroma of kava and anise. She closed her eyes and tried to slow her racing heart. In a few moments, when the tea bags had sufficiently seeped, the kava would do wonders to calm her nerves, but for now, she had to rely on just the steam.

Although it was probably just her imagination—and she fully accepted that—the steam from the kava tea did calm and slow her racing heart. She breathed deeply, allowing the stress and anxiety of the evening to dissipate with each breath.

Heather had been running the games for more than a year now, but each time it was played, the anxiety was overwhelming. It wasn't just the risk of hacking into the networks for the departments of transportation, police departments, and phone services, although there was a certain risk there. It was the risk that the game would result in death.

As much as her work was relaxing to her, the games made her anxious. She figured that what she did online was virtually harmless, mostly because she wasn't a malicious hacker, but in the games, real people died and the most she could do was watch. Heather hated it when people were killed in the games. She hated to think about the friends and family left behind by the adrenaline junkie who took the game a little too far. But she had to remind herself that the people playing the games had chosen to play. She chose to play herself, although in a different capacity, because the thrills were real.

Of course the families of the departed were compensated and taken care of (from an anonymous and untraceable deposit into their bank accounts), but it was more than that. She couldn't help but think about the player's life and the little details and quirks that made up each day, the people and relationships, the habits and feelings of happiness and sadness and love. It all disappeared when the player died. Maybe there was something after this life, she didn't know, but she did know that one minute, the player was alive and breathing and laughing or crying and loving and enjoying the sunlight or the newly fallen snow, and the next minute the player was gone. Dead. Leaving behind a fading memory.

She sipped the tea, still weak, and tried not to think about death and dying and memories. It was time to play.

Chapter Ten

The black sedan shot from the alley, tearing down the street with a frightening jolt of speed. Ryan felt a similar jolt of excitement that punched through his gut. He was breathless and excited, the sound and feel of the powerful engine, rumbling through his body and mind.

In his mirrors, he saw the snow shoot out from the rear tires in great weaving fans of powder and ice, and he had to concentrate to maintain control of the car.

"Ever done a snow drive before this one?" Sam asked.

"Never snow, so this will be fun." Ryan took a turn in the road sharper than needed, and the car slid sideways into the turn, like graceful dancing. He punched the accelerator, correcting the slide into the straight road ahead. The lights at each intersection were blinking yellow now and the roads were empty.

Perfect. Ryan dropped the car into the third gear and sped forward, the revolutions per minute climbing above five thousand, six thousand, seven thousand, and still the car wasn't close to redlining. They sped along the street, yellow street lamps whisking in flashes, the snowflakes in their headlights reminding Ryan of how the stars looked when the Millennium Falcon was traveling at light speed. He shifted to fourth, and they were gliding over the streets as the car's suspension absorbed the bumps in the road.

Ryan was driving at close to 110 miles per hour and approaching an intersection when they saw headlights approaching the intersection perpendicularly.

"Whoa, boy!" Sam shouted.

"I see it," Ryan said and pressed harder on the accelerator, his left foot hovering above the clutch. "We can make it."

Two seconds before crossing the intersection, Ryan dropped gears and stomped the accelerator in almost the same instant. The engine boomed as the revolutions per minute redlined, and the car increased its speed with incredible power.

"You feel that?" Ryan screamed and laughed as they hit a dip in the road at the beginning of the intersection, and the car was airborne. They rocketed past the oncoming headlights. Red and blue flashing lights suddenly lit up their rear window.

"Oh, guess we've got some company," Sam said.

"Out on the evening patrol!" Ryan slowed the car, allowing the police officer to get within a reasonable distance. The officer would have been close enough to read the license plate, but it didn't much matter, as the license plates were fake.

"Reports of police activity," the woman said through the speakers, as emotionless as ever. "Please adjust accordingly."

"And adjust we will!" Ryan said and saluted the dashboard. Up ahead, he saw an alley street that cut between two large brick buildings. They jumped the curb at the last moment, the wheels spinning and sliding, their speed not allowing traction, and they were sliding along the sidewalk, smashing into a street sign before their wheels finally caught and they raced down the street. The police car tried to follow, but his tires didn't catch traction in time. The side of the car smashed into the corner of the brick building in a burst of sparks, folding inward at the corner, then bouncing off like a pinball and smashing into the building on the opposite side of the alley.

"Whoa!" Sam said, turned in his seat. "You think the cop's okay?"

"I'm sure," Ryan said. The alley was mostly free of snow, which allowed for better traction and maneuverability, which was helpful to Ryan as he dodged metal dumpsters and piles of wooden pallets.

"There'll be more cops coming—"

"And we'll be gone," Ryan said.

Chapter Eleven

"You going to get off?" the bus driver asked from his seat at the front of the bus. Paul looked up from his notes and caught the driver's gaze in the big rectangular mirror.

"Don't think so," Paul said. "One more time around, I guess."

The driver hesitated and then said, "I've got to have you pay the fare again, Mister, and I'm truly sorry to have you do that, but I have rules to follow, you know."

"Completely understand," Paul said. He rose and walked to the front of the bus, where he deposited $1.25 in the payment collector. The bus was empty now. Everyone who'd been on the bus when Paul had gotten on were all long gone, and another round of people had come and gone as well.

The winter storm increased in its intensity, and Paul wondered how many times around the driver would go on his route, before calling it quits for the night. They hadn't picked up another passenger for more than 20 minutes, and from the looks of it, they wouldn't be picking up any more for the rest of the night. The town outside the bus was empty, not a person in sight.

"You waitin' for someone?" the driver asked, looking over at Paul with a cautious smile. It was a smile that conveyed experience in the city, which was big and harsh enough to chew people up and spit them out.

"Yeah, but doesn't look like she's going to show." Paul said, a little bitterly.

"Date?"

Paul laughed at this and shook his head. "No, Mr.—"

"Ambrose, Nick Ambrose."

"Mr. Ambrose, I haven't been on a date for years. Not since the wife took everything, including the desire to ever love again."

Ambrose laughed, a big bellowing sound with nothing held back. The laugh was contagious, and Paul found himself chuckling, despite his contact's no show.

"Well, I've got two more rounds on this route, and then I'm hanging up the driving cap," Nick said when his laughter died down.

"I think one more round should do it for me then," Paul said, returning to his seat. It pained him to say this, but he knew that any more time on the bus would be foolish. The woman wasn't going to show, maybe was never going to show, and it made him angry to think that he'd been played a fool.

But she had called him, and there wasn't a reason for this woman to set up this meeting if they weren't going to go through with it.

For the thousandth time, he looked over his notes from their last phone call, but like every other time he'd studied through the pages of college ruled paper filled with his scraggily handwriting, there were no other clues. He was in the right spot at the right time, and she hadn't shown up. It was as simple as that. Paul sighed and then leaned his forehead against the cold window, watching the fat snowflakes flutter past.

Paul breathed slowly through his nose, despite the feeling that he wasn't getting enough air. It was a trick his therapist had taught him to help with his nervous hyperventilating—which was an unwelcome side effect of his divorce a few years before. Of course, when he'd developed the quick breathing and rapid heartbeat, it usually accompanied the anger that was so prevalent throughout that time in his life. Most of the anger came from his growing obsession with the attack in Miami and his frustration that no one seemed to see the holes in the official account of what had happened. His obsession led him to retreat into himself, to mull over the facts again and again, to withdraw from his wife and children. He could see it happening to him, as if he were a third party observer, and even though he knew the consequences of his obsession and anger, he couldn't stop himself. His wife and kids had never left him, but he'd abandoned them. He went days without seeing them during those first few months after Miami, and when he did see them, his temper was hot and his patience nil. It hadn't taken his wife long to pack up the kids and move back home to her parent's house in southern Illinois. Paul had barely noticed their departure. Weeks became months, and then months became years, and his kids were nearly grown, his wife a stranger. The anger boiled at the lost time with his children, his lost family, and the nagging obsession that would never leave. He'd lost so much, for nothing. Until the mystery woman had called out of the blue.

Paul reached into his pocket, pulled out a piece of candy, and popped it from its wrapper. He held it between his thumb and forefinger. They were driving over a bridge now, and the lights of the city twinkled through the storm as if laughing at him.

He thought about the months it'd taken him to make contact with the woman—he still didn't know her real name—and the countless hours of digging through old newspaper articles, police records and dusty documents in the city archive to verify what little information she'd given him. They had planned to meet on the bus, and now he was alone, bouncing along the frozen road. She should have gotten here already.

Paul thought back to the last time he'd spoken to her. He remembered that the fear in her voice was palpable over the phone. He had told her that she would be alright, that he didn't want to know her name, and that he wouldn't even reveal the gender of his source.

"It's going to be big," she had said and couldn't mask the fear in her voice. "And it's going to change the world."

"You can trust me." His words had sounded empty, even to him. "No one will ever know who you are."

Paul knew that it was going to be big—already it was bigger than he'd ever imagined, if she was telling the truth, that is.

"No one will believe you, and you can't protect me."

"Anonymity," he responded simply. In truth, it was the only thing he could offer her, and it was her best protection. Paul wasn't a formidable man and certainly couldn't provide her with any physical protection. He didn't own a gun and wouldn't know how to use it even if he did. He was on the shorter and paunchier side of a medium build, and what muscles he'd had over the years had long since started to sag. He could jog for nearly a mile, but any physical exercise beyond that would put him out of commission. Anonymity was really the only thing he could offer, but in this case, he was confident that it would be protection enough. You couldn't kill the rat if you didn't know who the rat was.

"They'll know, and they'll kill me," she said. The finality in the way she said that struck a chord in Paul. He'd been an investigative reporter for twenty-some-odd years and there was something about the way she was talking.

Not just fear. Fear was a normal part of talking to sources and contacts with information. They were naturally afraid that they'd be found out. Most were afraid that they would lose their jobs or friends or family, or that they would be exposed as a whistleblower, but few were afraid for their lives.

This woman was not just scared. There was something more in her voice: acceptance. As if she could sense the end coming—like a cancer victim after years of treatment, who had finally accepted death with open arms as a friend and a companion to accompany into the darkness.

If not death, then what was she afraid of?

Then it struck him. Paul started to worry that she wasn't just running late. He worried that her paranoid fears had finally caught up with her, that whatever she was afraid of had finally caught up with her.

He feared that she was dead, or that whatever was worse than death in her mind had actually happened. His heart ached for her, but he didn't kid himself—couldn't kid himself. He was worried that he would never know the information that she had promised him.

His cell phone vibrated on the hard plastic seat next to him, its tiny square screen blinking to light. He reached over and grabbed the phone, snapping it open.

"Hello?"

"Yeah, Paul?" It was Dennis. In his rush, he hadn't looked at the caller id.

"Dennis."

"Hey boss, don't sound so happy to hear my voice."

"What's going on?" Paul demanded.

"Did you make contact?" Dennis asked and Paul glanced around the bus as if hoping that the woman would materialize from nowhere.

"No," he said, not even trying to mask the disappointment he felt. "I'm going to finish up this route, and then get off back at the hotel. I'm guessing that if she was going to meet me, she'd have been here before now."

"You think she's okay? I mean, maybe she isn't the paranoid nut you thought she was," Dennis said, echoing Paul's thoughts.

"I don't know," Paul said.

"Okay, so then am I done?" Dennis asked. "The wife is at home and is getting restless. Something about how I work too hard and my boss doesn't pay me enough to put up with this crap."

"Give it another hour, follow the police scanner," Paul said, "and I'll make it up to you, I promise."

"Whatever," Dennis said and ended the call.

Paul put his phone away and stared at his notes. He wondered if asking Dennis to monitor the police scanner was a good use of time. In truth, he had no idea—and no idea what Dennis should be listening for except that he was sure if the woman he'd spoken to on the phone was about to kick the bucket, she would go out with a fight. He was sure that if there was a fight, it would generate at least some radio chatter with the police.

Then again, she may have just hedged her bets and disappeared. Paul couldn't fault someone for wanting to avoid getting killed, but he hated that it came at the expense of his story, or worse yet, at the expense of truth.

He cursed himself again for not insisting on a way to contact her instead of waiting for her to reach him. He reached into his pocket and pulled out another piece of candy.

Chapter Twelve

Ryan dropped the car into third and jammed the accelerator as he made a turn in the middle of an intersection. The rear tires skidded across dry pavement, then hit a patch of black ice, and the back of the car almost slid out from under them. On the corner of the intersection, a man stood by a small hibachi grill, holding his hands over the fire that flickered. He wore a thick coat that was tattered and worn, and his face shown an expression of shocked surprise. For a fleeting second, Sam caught the man's gaze in his own, and he burst with laughter.

"Whoa!" Sam screamed and then laughed again. "Almost lost that one and hit that guy on the corner."

Ryan smiled as the engine revved to 6,000 revolutions per minute, and in a swift motion, he shifted to 4th gear and the car shot forward, snowflakes pelting the windshield.

"Prepare for a 45 degree turn to your left in 600 meters," the woman said through the speakers.

Up ahead, the road was black and any visibility was blocked by the incessant snowstorm. Ryan looked at the control panel of the car, gauged his speed and the distance to the curve on the map of his phone. He gripped the steering wheel and peered into the darkness.

"How about some tunes?" Sam said. He pressed a few buttons on the console and heavy rock and roll blasted through the speakers. The song was unfamiliar to Ryan, except that the song was distinctively early 90s. The heavy guitar and the steady drums thudded his adrenaline into further action, and he sped up toward the curve. The digital speedometer blinked and shot up from 73 miles per hour to 86, and the snowflakes didn't hit the windshield so much as swirl in the wake of the car's speed.

They hit the curve a minute later, and the back wheels did slide out from under them. For just a moment, they both felt as though the car would spin out of control. At that speed, if they hit a patch of dry asphalt while sliding like that, the car would roll, flipping through the air until it crunched to the ground, twisting and crushing the metal. Ryan adjusted the wheel expertly, the back tires caught, and the car righted itself as they moved into the turn.

Sam whooped again as the car seemed to float over thin air, shooting through the darkness like a meteor crashing through the atmosphere.

"You feel that?" Sam screamed. "That is some quality suspension, dude!"

"You gotta stop talking so much," Ryan said, his entire focus on the feel of the slide, the angle of the curve, feeling for that moment when—

—the road straightened, and he jerked the wheel and shifted down to third gear as he jammed the accelerator. The engine bellowed and the sedan shot forward.

"Data collected," the woman said, barely audible above the smashing sounds of guitar and drums. "Bridge straight ahead in one mile, beware of ice."

"Beware of ice!" Sam screamed and laughed again. "As if, man, she probably thinks this is such a cake walk."

They shot forward, their soundtrack the heavy garage rock and the roar of the engine. A pair of headlights blinked into view, coming at them in the opposite direction.

"That a civilian?" Sam asked, but looked at Ryan's phone on the dashboard and answered his own question. No colored dots flashed on the screen just yet, so the approaching car wasn't driving with the Lit Dragons. It must have a civilian driver.

Ryan adjusted the trajectory of the car, pulling it to the right side of the road, away from the middle. He liked to drive in the night like this, because fewer cars on the road meant more room to drive, more room to flex and still dodge civilian drivers.

They shot past the other car and sped toward the bridge. Ryan massaged the leather steering wheel in the grip of his hands, as if kneading bread, his adrenaline pulsing through him.

He glanced at the screen of his phone and saw an orange dot suddenly appear. It was approaching the bridge from the opposite direction.

Lit Dragons.

The adrenaline in his body felt as though it had been shooting through a pipe or down a gorge, and then was suddenly stopped, the force of it piling against the blockage. His heart thudded hard in his chest, and his breathing quickened.

Too soon, he thought. It felt as though they'd only just gotten in the car, and it was too soon for this to be over. He looked at Sam, who'd also seen the orange dot on the screen. Blood drained from Sam's face. The look of pure joy and energy died as the paleness set in. Ryan saw Sam tensing his muscles, tightening his grip on the handle above the window.

"You ready?" Ryan asked. He consciously reminded his muscles to relax and physically forced the relaxation into his muscles.

"Yeah right. How can you ever be ready?"

"Stay loose, Sam," Ryan said. "Don't be so tensed up."

"That's kind of hard," Sam said. "The Orange Team is coming fast, and a bridge? Man, they're pushing it."

"It's what they do." A faint smile appeared on Ryan's lips.

"Increase speed on approach," the woman said over the speakers. The bridge was coming fast, and suddenly another pair of headlights peeked out from the opposite side. Ryan looked at the blinking orange dot on the screen of his phone and furrowed his brow. The orange car wouldn't have cleared the bridge just yet, and there were no other Lit Dragons on the road. The closer car was a civilian. He tapped the brakes, and the car slowed slightly.

"Increase speed on approach," the woman said again, her voice emotionless.

"There's another car! A civilian!" Ryan said, his voice more shrill than he'd intended.

"Increase speed on approach." The woman said, and the screen of Ryan's phone flashed red, indicating that their speed was too slow.

Ryan pressed down on the accelerator, and the car again jumped forward. The power in this engine was incredible, and Ryan wondered if it might be too much power. The headlights cleared the top of the bridge and began their descent toward Ryan and Sam.

"You can't hit that civilian," Sam said. "That's collateral, man."

"I know."

"Data processing," the woman said.

They both watched the orange dot start ascending the other side of the bridge.

"It's going to be too close!" Sam yelled.

Ryan didn't respond, just gritted his teeth, and the car shot forward. They rode up on the bridge just as the second pair of headlights—the orange dot—cleared the top, driving at least as fast as Ryan, and coming up on the civilian car, which was driving much slower.

What happened next, happened fast.

Very fast.

The orange dot swerved to miss the car in its path, swerved onto Ryan's side of the road. The two cars barreled toward each other, the light from their headlights meeting and melting together, becoming one, and the world seemed to slow to an almost standstill. Ryan jerked the wheel even further, dodging the civilian car—a minivan.

Snow flurried as Ryan corrected the wheel. He tried to dodge the orange car, but he dodged to the left and their front ends clipped, knocking his car into a sidewise slide. He felt the tires ripping into the snow and ice as they cleared the summit of the bridge, and then the full force of their momentum lifted the car up into a roll. In mid air, he saw for the briefest second the orange car smashing into the guardrail along the downward slope of the bridge, crashing through the concrete and metal. Ryan was turning and flipping, the roof caving in, the glass exploding outward, and he was distantly aware that Sam was no longer sitting next to him, that his seatbelt flipped loosely around as the car rolled and skidded on its roof in a shower of sparks and a swirl of snow, until it came to rest at the base of the bridge.

The world around him fell instantly quiet, his ears ringing from the explosion of sound that came from the wreckage of his car. He looked at the black ice that blanketed the ground just beyond the broken windshield, just inches from his face. Fat snowflakes, the size of cotton balls, settled in around him, and the world fell silent, black.

Chapter Thirteen

The snow swirled like ghosts on an alien planet, the flakes whirling in the wind and dusting the street. Mae stood on the side of the road, just outside the spot of yellow light shining from the street lamp above. Her wet clothes had already started to harden, the dampness turning to ice and clinging to her shivering body. She looked down the road, which seemed to extend forever into the empty and starless night. Tall, looming trees lined the road, and icy snow stood in banks along the tree line. The fresh layer of powder was lying atop the dirty mounds of ice and the black asphalt like a fresh, clean blanket.

Through the falling snow, a pair of headlights pierced the darkness, coming up over a hill and driving toward her. She watched the lights as they grew closer and tried to see what type of vehicle was approaching. The lights were low to the ground, too low for a bus. She wished she could flag the car to a stop, to climb inside the dry, warm interior and be whisked away from this place.

But she was waiting for a bus. A specific bus—Michigan Avenue Route B, she remembered. Her mom was supposed to meet a reporter on that bus tonight, but that was hours ago, and Mae doubted the reporter was still waiting. Despite the danger that they would be found (which seemed silly now, given that the men hunting her had never really lost them), the meeting was supposed to set them free. The reporter had unknowingly unearthed a conspiracy that was not just a theory, but was closer to truth than he'd ever imagined.

He was the reason they were in Chicago, to find him and bring the final pieces of the puzzle out into the open.

As the car got closer, she shrank into the shadows. Her feet crunched through the crust of hardened snow and ice as she backed away from the light and out of sight. A gust of wind whistled from the trees behind her, and she figured that if the bus didn't come soon, she would freeze to death. Already, she felt the wisps of sleep creeping in around her mind and body. Hypothermia was again fast approaching, followed by that long and endless sleep that ebbed at the corners of her consciousness.

The long sleep would be warm, she thought. A warm darkness that would envelop her and take her away from this place. The girl's body shivered with such violence that it rattled her bones and made her muscles ache. She clenched her jaw, forcing her teeth not to click together as her muscles convulsed in a vain effort to stay warm.

The car whizzed by, driving much to fast for the icy conditions of the road. She waited in the dark for several seconds after the car passed, making sure that if the driver looked in the rear-view mirror, she wouldn't be seen. The headlights disappeared over the long hill and once again she was alone in the night.

It's going to be okay, she kept telling herself, doing her best to refocus her mind on something good and hopeful. Never mind her mom's screams of terror, and never mind the writhing ball of panic that grew within her, threatening to take control of her mind and body and plunge her headlong off the cliff into the depths of insanity.

It was going to be okay. She'd done what she needed to do, and she was safe. She'd lost them.

Mae shuddered, as much from dread as from the cold. She peered into the darkness and strained her ears for the sounds of the bus that she knew would be along soon.

She lifted her arm closer to her face and pulled aside her flannel shirt. The scratched and battered Timex read 9:03 PM, and she shivered harder. The watch had been a gift from her father when she was 12, and she held onto it not because it was fashionable, with its pink and green band and its slightly childish design, but because it reminded her of a time before all of this.

Before the bad things. Before the evil.

The wind died, and she suddenly caught a wisp of a sound—the blast of a large engine roaring up hills and churning through the falling snow. She looked down the hill toward the sound, and saw headlights cutting through the darkness. A few feet above the headlights were the words: ROUTE B MICHIGAN AVENUE BRIDGE.

A branch snapped somewhere behind her, and she whirled around to peer into the dark woods beyond.

"Oh, please no," she whispered when she saw the dark form a few hundred meters into the woods. Hunched, the figure was running over the drifts and snow, dodging dark trees and low hanging branches. It was Eddie, the hunting rifle held tightly to his chest, his head low.

She heard another branch snap and heavy breathing to her right. Another lurking form was coming through the woods towards her in the opposite direction. She stepped out of the light from the street lamp, but knew that it was probably too late. They had seen her, and there were at least two of them.

She turned toward the bus—still a couple of miles away and coming too slowly.

Why, oh why couldn't you just let me be dead? Why couldn't you just assume that I drowned? But she knew that being swept away under the ice of a raging river was not enough.

They needed her body, cold and lifeless, to be sure. And if not dead, they needed her alive.

The sound of footsteps and large bodies coming through the forest were getting louder. She thought about running, but knew that it would be no use. Her body was too cold and stiff to move quickly.

Her only hope was the bus. It was now less than a mile away, and she fidgeted nervously.

"Come on, come on ..." she whispered.

The thin whisper of a silenced gunshot pierced the air, and the bullet whistled just inches from her head. She screamed and ducked, the bullet smashing into the trunk of a tree a few feet away, splinters of frozen wood bursting with a crack.

Had to move now. Mae shuffled toward the bus, forcing her body into an awkward and painful jog.

Another gunshot and the bullet skinned into her shoulder. She felt a thick oozing of warmth over her freezing skin. Two more gunshots hissed in the night as she jogged down the hill. Her atrophied muscles raged, but she could see the driver now. He was a big black man, a look of deep concentration splayed on his face as he drove through the falling snow.

She raised her arms and started running in the middle of the road, directly in front of the bus. For several very long seconds, it seemed as though the bus wouldn't stop in time, that it would slam on its brakes at the last moment and slide right into her.

The driver's eyes widened and she saw his body shift as his foot dropped on the brake peddle. The tires skidded slightly over a patch of black ice, but the bus slowed. She ran forward and toward the bus and slammed the open palm of her hand on the door.

The driver, scared and confused, opened the door, and she fell inside, scrambling up the wet steps into the bus.

"Go!" she shouted.

Three bullets smashed through the windshield, barely missing the driver and leaving behind tiny holes and vein-like cracks running several inches into the shatterproof glass. The bullets hit the roof of the bus, one of them lodging into the metal ceiling and the other two bouncing and ricocheting. Mae screamed, and the driver grunted loudly as he pulled the door closed in a hurry. He jammed on the accelerator, and the bus lurched forward. Eddie's lone figure stood just inside the tree line, his hulking shadow watching as the bus drove away. The driver also saw Eddie standing there, his rifle raised and smoking, and he did a double take at the bullet holes in the window.

"What the devil?" the driver shouted as the bus's speed climbed. He grabbed hold of his radio and screamed, "I've got some thugs shootin' up my bus! I need cops out on route—"

"No!" she yelled, her voice cracking. "No police. Don't call anyone."

The driver froze, his mouth hanging open. He looked at the girl as if she were crazy.

And she was crazy, by the looks of it. Her hair was a mess with tangles of leaves and twigs and dirt, her clothes were wet and freezing to her body, and her cheeks pallid and cold. She looked like that girl who was raised with wolves, just barely re-entering civilization, but there was something more. Sorrow and dread had long ago washed away the innocence on her face. Her eyes pled with him as he held the radio close to his quivering lips, his finger still pressing the "call" button. He hesitated for a second longer, examining that sorrowful pleading in her eyes, then returned his radio to the cradle.

The driver grunted with a more-serious-than-death look on his face as he switched off his radio altogether. He looked up at the holes in his windshield and shook his head, pursing his lips together tightly and whistling.

Mae clamored to her feet, her skin tingling as the heater blasted warm air from the vents in the floor of the bus. She looked over the empty rows of seats and breathed a sigh of relief. At this time of night, and this far from the city, there were no other passengers. She turned back to the driver and saw that he was breathing fast and heavy, and soundlessly mouthing words that looked like a prayer. He closed his eyes for a second, shaking his head as if to drive away the fear, and at the same time, let his foot off the accelerator. The bus slowed quickly.

"Please don't stop the bus," she said. The driver jerked, startled, pounded his foot on the accelerator, and the bus roared forward.

She watched the place in the road where she'd stood only moments before, grow smaller and smaller in the back window, erased by the flurries of snow.

Always moving, she thought. Always running.

They would not be far behind.

Chapter Fourteen

Robert Morales burst through the trees right as Eddie fired his rifle into the bus's large front window. He cringed at the sight of the bullet holes in the glass and felt the boiling rage within him churn as he watched the bus disappear over the hill. On most days, his anger was a like a constant humming in his ears, a steady and purple throbbing in his gut, but now it was a thriving cauldron of bubbling mass. His ears were hot, and his fingers numb. Rage, the color of dried blood, edged his vision.

He tightened his grip on the handle of his .50 caliber Desert Eagle, flexing the muscles in his fingers and hand until they ached against the metal grip. The bus was gone, but he could still hear the engine cutting through the night, moving away from him and toward the city and the people and the safety in numbers.

Morales took a deep breath of the cold, winter air and swore as he exhaled through his nose in small billows of mist. He'd been waiting too long for a moment with this girl, and that moment was now botched. Since Miami, the girl and her mom been on the run, and since Miami he'd followed like a bloodhound. Morales was a finder, a tracker, a hunter, and yet despite the many people he'd found and taken as prey, Mae and her mother had evaded him every step of the way. Like a squirming pup, little Mae was now once again out of his reach.

Eddie.

Eddie had let her escape, and in the forest, he had once again let her slip through his fingers. The thick, crimson rage welled.

Morales tried not to think about the consequences of her escape, but still, the thoughts nagged at his brain. He wasn't afraid—no, it wasn't fear he felt, he was much too important in the organization to feel much fear anymore—it was a sense of disquiet, that all he'd been working for these many months was coming unraveled at the seams. So much sacrifice and death had led him here, to cross paths with this girl. Not that he minded the death and sacrifice—it wasn't his sacrifice.

He thought about the body in the cabin and flexed his raw knuckles, feeling a small bit of relief from the anger.

He hadn't realized that he was holding his breath in those last few moments, but he began to feel dizzy and light. He pushed aside the purple and black thoughts, and exhaled slowly through his nostrils. When his lungs emptied, he inhaled slowly and methodically, concentrating on putting aside the mounting rage. The flood of oxygen to his body relaxed his tense muscles and he could feel the anger slowly subside. He focused on the smell of the winter night around him, the evergreen trees, the falling snow on the frozen asphalt.

Morales walked to the street lamp that stood near the bus stop, wondering how it had all gone so wrong. First in the cabin, then the woods, and now this. The girl had been two steps ahead of them for the entire night, and he didn't think that it was anything other than dumb luck. And the stupidity of his comrades.

He heard footsteps and chuffing behind him and he turned slowly. Despite everything he wanted to do, needed to do, to relieve the anxiety he felt, he turned with serene calmness, his breathing steady and his face placid. Two men approached him from the woods, their breathing quick and heavy.

"You okay, boss?" Eddie said. Morales turned and studied him. Eddie's black clothes and slicked hair really pissed Morales off. Eddie was an enforcer for local methamphetamine dealers, and a good one at that. He was deadly, but he didn't appear to be any more dangerous than a run-of-the-mill neighbor walking his dog at twilight, just another blue collar shmoe trying to make it in this city. It was this unique combination of unremarkable ordinariness and lethality that drew Morales to him.

Oskar Svensson, on the other hand, looked more like a slick version of Frankenstein's monster. A transplant from Sweden, he had an exaggerated square jaw and a large, flat forehead. He was slightly more than six and a half feet tall, his head was completely bald, and he had scars that ran down his face from his forehead to his chin. Morales had often wondered about those scars and wanted to ask the big man about them, but was more than a little apprehensive to hear Oskar's response. He thought that the injury must have been severe, and he felt sorry for whatever, or whoever, had given Oskar the scars, as the end had surely come quickly for that person or thing. And despite the scars and the sheer size of the man, he had a quality about him that screamed class and refinement. Morales wouldn't be surprised to see Oskar beating a man to a pulp, then wiping the blood and broken teeth from his hands and sitting down for tea and biscuits with his mother.

When Morales had come upon Eddie, he was blabbering about the forest floating into the air. The forest had looked ravaged, but not floating, and it made Morales think of the destruction in Miami. For a moment, he'd felt a quickening of excitement, thinking she'd been crushed by the fallen trees and rocks, but they found no sign of her. It had taken them close to an hour to conclude that she'd fallen into the river that gushed nearby, and he was sure that the girl had died.

Out of some morbid curiosity, he'd dipped three fingers into the water, up to the second knuckle, and gasped at the temperature. He'd begun to chuckle then, imagining the pure torture of being fully submerged. The thought had filled him with a strange joy, the thought of that girl being tortured. He was sorry that he hadn't been able to inflict the pain on the girl himself, but he'd been happy that her death was not entirely without agony.

After concluding that she'd been swallowed by the river, Eddie had wanted to pack up their equipment in the cabin and return to the city. Morales refused, saying that they would need the girl's body. Eddie was angry, it was his sister's birthday, and he was missing the party. But both he and Oskar obeyed Morales' order to walk along the banks of the river and search for the body.

Oskar had found an area along the river where the snow had been disturbed. After a few more minutes of searching, he found tufts of blond hair that had snagged on a low hanging branch as well as tracks leading toward the county road. He'd called to the others in his thickly accented voice, and their search through the woods resumed.

Sometime later, Oskar had been the first to spot the girl, standing under a street lamp a couple hundred meters away. They'd started running then, and for a moment, until the bus had rumbled into view and the gunshots exploded in the wintery silence, Morales had thought that everything would be fixed, that they would catch the girl and make things right. He'd wanted to hurt her badly for the pain and frustrations she'd caused him. A little payback was in order, and until the bus rumbled into view, he'd allowed himself to get excited. But the bus and the gunshots that followed had dashed those thoughts to shards.

"Boss," Eddie said, nodding toward Morales' hands and bringing him back to the moment. "You still got blood on your hands. Maybe still from the girl's mother."

Morales looked down at his hands, saw dark streaks across his skin. He reminded himself to stay calm. Eddie was still chattering away, about something completely different now. The sound of his voice was grating on Morales' nerves.

Morales turned the Desert Eagle in his hands so he was holding the barrel. He held the gun out to Eddie, who stopped talking long enough to take the gun, his eyebrows cocked with confusion. It didn't take long, though, until Eddie started talking again.

"You see what bus she got on?" Eddie asked. "Looked like one going downtown, and if we hurry and get the cars, we might be able to catch up to it and take her down. And did you see what she was wearing? Some different clothes, blue sweater, looked like, or a hoodie. Sketchy girl, that one, coming out here with a change of clothes. Who would have thought?"

Eddie was addressing Oskar, and motioning with Morales' gun as he spoke. Oskar didn't say anything, but watched the gun move back and forth in front of him with narrowed eyes. He reached out and gently pushed Eddie's hand, and the gun, until the barrel was pointing at the ground.

"Careful you don't shoot," Oskar said, his voice low and thick with accent.

"Hey, man," Eddie said, looking hurt. "I'm not going to shoot you man, and besides, the safety's on, and I've held a gun before, ya lurch."

"Quiet," Morales said. Eddie looked like he was about to argue with Morales for a moment, but saw that his boss was in no mood for bickering. Morales took several steps to a nearby mound of snow, stooped down and gently rubbed the palms of his hands against the snow. The dark red, which looked black in the meager light, mixed with the white snow and made it look muddy. Morales took a handful of snow in his hands and worked it over the skin on the back of his hands as well, washing away the dried blood. He crossed back to Eddie and wiped his wet hands on the sleeve of his jacket, a curt smile on his lips.

"Thank you, Eddie," Morales said, holding his hand out for the gun. The rage he had felt earlier had melted away, and he took a deep breath, not to calm his nerves, but to enjoy the cold and invigorating air in his lungs, to savor the moment.

"Who fired the shots?" Morales said, his breath coming out in short bursts of mist in the frozen night air. Of course he knew the answer, but he wanted to teach a lesson. Above all, Morales considered himself a teacher. He felt the calmness wash over him, and the rage completely disappear. His thoughts were as cool and targeted as hardened metal.

"The shots?" Eddie asked, his forehead scrunched.

"The gun shots at the girl, at the bus," Morales said, his tone and expression placid.

"Yeah, I shot at the girl. 'S too bad I missed, though, coulda saved us a nice evening of hunting her down."

"The bus, Eddie, who shot the bus?" Morales seethed.

Realization clicked in Eddie's eyes, and he stared at his shuffling feet. It reminded Morales of a school boy who was caught pulling a girl's pigtails.

"I shot at the girl, yeah," Eddie's voice wavered, "and I'm sorry I missed too. I think if I'd gotten that shot off right, we wouldn't be in the hot pot we're in right now."

"No, Eddie," Morales said in a voice so calm, it might have been mistaken for one belonging to a priest who's just heard a confession and is about to list the steps of repentance.

"You made this particular hot pot a bit worse. Quite a bit worse."

"But boss—" Eddie started, his face flushed and his voice rising with defensiveness. Morales stopped him with a wave of his hand.

"What happens when the bus gets back to the city?" Morales asked in his priestly tone. "What happens when the bus driver pulls into his garage and his manager sees the gun shots? What do you think then? What happens when the driver moseys on down to the police station and files a report, which is something he'll have to do if he wants to keep his job? And then the police are going to be here, this close to the cabin, sniffing around, and I know you're not so stupid as to think they won't find something if they go looking."

"But the girl won't go to the police because of who she is, and what she is, and she's gotta tell the driver not to say anything—and if it does go through to the police ..." Eddie hesitated, and then said, "well, you know."

Eddie gestured at Morales with a look that said, I know, and I'm pretty sure you know that I know, but I'm going to stop short of saying it.

"She ain't gotta do nothing,'" Morales said, mimicking Eddie's accent, "and the bus driver could do anything he wants, as soon as that girl gets off his bus. And you can bet your best button, my friend Eddie, that the bus driver will not be taking the blame for getting his bus all shot up."

"This is Chicago, man, stuff happens all the time."

"I don't care what this is, besides the fact that this is my operation and we draw no attention to ourselves. Absolutely no attention, and that means we don't go shooting up buses."

Eddie opened his mouth to say something more, but thought better of it and stayed quiet. He looked at his shoes again and shivered. The adrenaline from the chase in the woods was wearing off, and the cold was setting in.

"I'm sorry," Eddie finally said. He looked up at Morales like a puppy dog, his head still bowed, but his wide eyes seeking approval. It warmed Morales' heart to see Eddie looking like a penitent child. Eddie was finally learning that to be a part of this organization meant no mistakes.

"Good," Morales said, "apology accepted."

He raised his Desert Eagle and pulled the trigger once. There was a soft, high-pitched whir as the bullet passed through the silencer, and then a thump as it struck Eddie in the chest. Eddie, that look of sincere contrition still in his eyes, spun around with the force of the shot, falling on his face in the snow.

Morales was struck by how quiet the night seemed, the snow falling silently from the dark sky. In his death, Eddie had finally learned.

"You still have the bags?" he asked Oskar, who'd barely batted an eye at his colleague's demise. The big man didn't say anything, but nodded and pulled a bundle from within his heavy coat. The bag had been intended for the girl's body, and it was a little shorter than Eddie's corpse, but it would do.

"Bag him up quick, before too much blood gets into the snow. No bodies, remember," Morales said. "No trace."

"No bodies," Oskar mumbled, and unzipped the bag.

Morales pulled his phone from an inside pocket of his coat and dialed a number. The connection took a few extra seconds because of the storm and their current location. The phone rang only twice, followed by a click as the operator on the other end of the call picked up.

"Is it done?"

"I need a trace on a city bus, Route B Michigan Ave.," Morales said. He watched Oskar struggle with Eddie's body and smiled. Joy in the journey, he thought, but corrected himself.

Joy in the hunt.

Chapter Fifteen

The pain in Mae's body seemed to explode as her body thawed. Her head pounded and her muscles ached.

"Just don't stop the bus," she whispered.

"You bet I won't stop this bus. Not till we're a long way from here—holy shin-dig!" The driver said. His face was stark and pale.

He slowed the bus and turned its lumbering mass onto a road that led to the freeway.

"Only in Chicago you get some crazy thing like this, but not out here. I expect to get shot up in the ghetto, but not out here in the country, ya dig it?"

"Yeah, I dig it," she said, her heart still racing and her lungs aching from the blast of warm air. She felt that buzzing from within her body and mind, that warm fluttering spreading out like a wave, and she fought it.

Paper and ink. A single black line on a white page, fresh and clean, and the world opens.

"What the blazes is goin' on?" the driver asked. "What's your name? Holy mother Mary, we just got shot up in here."

She stared at her dirty fingernails. It'd been so long since she'd told anyone her name. The desire to be known by someone else, to have another person besides her mother know her real name, even a kindly bus driver, was almost too much to bear.

"Mae Edwards," she said with a wan smile. "My name is Mae."

"Yeah, well Ms. Mae, can you tell me what's goin' on here? My last route, and I'm out here in the middle of this crazy, shot-up situation out here."

Mae grinned at the way he emphasized each syllable. She took a deep breath, wondering how much she could tell him. Of course he'd want to know something—his bus had just had three bullets pounded through the windshield, and for all intents and purposes, the bus driver was in danger of being killed himself. He had the right to know, but with the information came more risk. It was enough that he'd seen her face, but if the driver knew where she'd come from and what she was doing, he'd be one dead bird.

He looked up at her, expectantly.

"There are some people after me, some very bad people."

"Is this about drugs? Are you trippin'?" the driver asked. "'Cause I don't want nothing to do with no drugs on my bus. They just as soon blow your head off as shoot the devil juice into their veins."

"No drugs," Mae said, and it was true.

The bus bounced along onto the sparsely populated freeway, and in the distance, the Chicago skyline appeared. The city lights shown up in the black sky like a halo, beckoning them to safety. The girl glanced at the speedometer and saw that they were driving too fast, but that was just fine with her.

The driver sighed heavily, as if trying to force his heart to slow its heavy beating. He flexed his fingers on the steering wheel. He was a big man, barely able to fit behind the steering wheel, even with the seat pushed all the way back. His uniform was neatly pressed, and the only thing out of place on his body was the driving cap, the rim of which pushed a little too far to the side of his head. He seemed kind, even loving, but the determination in the steely gaze of his eyes and the hardened set of his jaw told her that he'd seen much that he would probably rather forget.

"Listen, I know you're in trouble, that much I can tell on my own." The driver paused, looking her petite frame up and down. His eyes settled on her platinum blond hair, usually smooth and nicely kempt, but now gnarled with dirt and twigs.

"I can see you're upset, and that's A-Okay, because I would not be handling this here situation any better," he said. "But you gotta tell me what's goin' on, and why you don't want no police involved."

She swallowed, her throat raw from screaming. She watched the snow falling around the bus, pelting the windows and gusting in the yellow headlights. It was beautiful really, the snow and the cold, like a frozen wonderland, bathed in the sparkling yellow lamp light. Several cars passed them on the left, and the driver waited patiently for her response, but shifted in his seat nervously.

"I'm sorry," Mae said. "I can't tell you what's happening, not now."

"Honey, I don't want to get involved in this any more than you want me to be involved, but sometimes fate just pushes two people together, and that's that. You can't help the fact that I was driving this bus, and I can't help it that you was standing there in the middle of the road like an angel 'bout to be shot or run over. Now, you gotta tell me what's goin' on, and why you don't want no police involved. I gotta trust that the police would help in a situation like this one, so convince me otherwise."

Mae ran her fingers through her hair and pulled on a snarl, which was tangled with some dead leaves. The city loomed before them like a giant, and in a few minutes, it wouldn't matter that they'd seen her alive and getting on a bus. They would soon be in the city and with other buses, and other people and crowds. And the crowds were what she needed to stay alive.

Her heart was racing, and the panic swelled.

"Miss?" he asked expectantly, and she wanted to tell him everything. She didn't want to spill so much to explain the situation, but to unleash all the secrets that were pent up inside, to let go of the burden and be free. But out here, alone on this lonely bus route, she still wasn't safe. The men who hunted her could show up at any moment, like they had at the cabin.

"Miss?"

"Please," Mae said, "just give me a second."

Paper and ink.

Anxiety mounted and the panic churned, but the world faded away.

She opened her backpack—another gift from her parents, when she was much younger—and rummaged through her meager belongings. There was a time when she'd had her own room, a bed to sleep on and clothes that were not expensive by any means, but certainly fashionable. She'd lived with her mom and dad in a small, two-story home with white siding and blue trim. They had a tire swing and trampoline in the back yard, a flower garden in the front, and a white picket fence that enclosed their property. Before it had all happened, before they'd taken her away, there was even talk of a little brother or sister joining their family.

Their house was in a small town outside of Boston, nestled in rolling hills, apple orchards, and pumpkin patches.

For a split moment, she could almost smell the mulled apple cider and hear the whisper of autumn leaves in the breeze.

Mae squeezed her eyes shut and forced the thoughts from her mind. When she opened them, she was again bleeding and freezing cold, and the open bag on the green leather bus seat was all she had left in the world.

She pulled a small notebook from the bag and opened its pages, which were full of sketches and notes. The first page in the notebook was a sketch she'd drawn only a few weeks before, sitting in a coffee shop and waiting for her mom to return. She'd been sitting at a table, facing a large window that looked out onto the street. Her hands wrapped around a warm cup of coffee, and the blank notebook was open before her. Mae's heart was beating fast as she glanced at the door to the coffee shop at least once a minute, praying that her mom would walk through the door like she'd promised. She forced herself not to think about what could happen to her mom, and then what would likely happen to her if they were found out. Like she'd done so many times as a child, she focused outward to escape the fears inside. She took a black ballpoint pen into her fingers and placed the tip of the pen onto the first page of the notebook.

She heard laughter—pure laughter. Nothing cynical, or sarcastic, but the sound of actual cheeriness. She peered out the window, searching for the source of the sound. Outside, the wind and the snow were blowing hard. The streets were empty, except for the parked cars along the sidewalk. Large piles of snow had been pushed up against the parked cars, and drifts of snow covered the sidewalks, which were empty. Two people were walking hand in hand down the middle of the street, where the snow was only a thin layer of glistening powder. The larger of the two—Mae assumed it was a man, but couldn't tell for sure—pulled the other close to his body and squeezed tight. That laugh again—definitely a woman's voice. The two of them, stopped beneath a yellow street lamp and kissed, completely unaware that they were being watched by a girl in a coffee shop across the street. The wind and snow whirled passed them, blowing their scarves and coats and the woman's long hair, which Mae could see was dark brown under her green knit cap. They kissed amidst the winter storm, the two of them together and one despite the dark and cold and freezing snow.

The little mark on Mae's notebook, left there by the tip of the pen, grew larger as Mae drew. She sketched the couple standing under the light, sketched their kiss in the winter wind. As she drew, she almost lived the kiss, could almost feel the warm embrace against the cold.

The bus hit a pothole and she was jarred back to the reality of the moment. She stared at the picture, one that had filled her with such warmth at the time, but left her now feeling empty and cold. She tore out the page and crumpled it into a ball.

Mae thought about the cabin. She thought about the blood and the screams, and she started to cry. She turned toward the road, away from Nick, and wiped her face quickly. Mae wanted to tell him everything, but to tell him would be very dangerous. She hated that she'd stopped the bus in the first place, and for getting this older man involved.

"What's your name?" She asked.

"Nick Ambrose."

"Why did you stop to help me?"

"Well, I didn't have much choice." He looked fleetingly at the bullet holes, and then said, "but mostly, I didn't want you to get hurt."

She smiled at this, and for a moment, they held each other's gaze.

"I don't want you to get hurt," she said, masking the emotion in her voice. "Please understand that I am in your debt for picking me up, and just know that I'm not going to tell you anything because the less you know, the less chance you have of getting hurt."

"Well I can respect that." He eyed the bullet holes again, studying the spider-webbed cracks. "At least tell me you're one of the good guys."

She paused, watching the city grow as they neared its outskirts. She thought about the first time she'd seen Chicago—she'd been on an airplane then, flying in from Miami. It was now, as it was then, a beacon of hope. She'd been running then too, and at that time she'd had no idea of the beast she was awakening.

"I hope you're one of the good guys," he said again, his voice deep and serious. He looked at her with his large, brown eyes and she knew that he cared about her—even if in just a cursory way of someone who still had a glimmer of humanity left in him.

"I hope I'm one of the good guys too," she whispered.

Chapter Sixteen

Ryan was first aware that he was shivering, but the world around him was black and silent, so the shivering seemed out of place. And then he was coughing, and the shivering grew more violent.

Cold. He could feel the cold throughout his entire body, as it permeated every limb, every finger and toe. The cold was on his skin and in his muscles. The cold was in his lungs and felt like it was slowing his heart. Ryan wanted to go back to sleep, but realized he hadn't yet opened his eyes, that he wasn't quite awake. The world around him was black, and the cold so real that he knew that this being a dream was impossible.

Slowly, he parted his eyelids, which felt as though they'd been frozen shut, and opened his eyes.

Instantly it came back to him, and his mind and body jolted with adrenaline. The car, so beautiful only a moment before, sleek and stylish and seductive, was now crushed under its own weight, laying on its roof. All the windows had been smashed. The engine block had come partway through the dashboard, and the roof had crumpled like an accordion. Ryan was still buckled to his seat, hanging upside down, his head and neck bent so far to the side, it was a wonder that his neck hadn't snapped in the accident.

The windshield was shattered, bits of torn clothing stuck to the jagged pieces of glass. The seat next to him was empty.

Ryan vaguely remembered Sam being thrown from the car as it had rolled. The crash had happened so fast that the memory itself was a blur, a jumble of images and snapshots meshed with the screeches of the crash.

He had to find Sam.

"Collecting data," the woman said through the speakers, though her voice was filled with static and seemed very far away.

"Data, processing."

"Shut up!" Ryan yelled, knowing that she couldn't hear him. He wondered about the second car, the orange team. Had they made it? Were the guys in that car still alive?

In the distance, he could hear sirens and knew that he hadn't been unconscious for very long... but still long enough. If the sirens were from the emergency personnel on duty, then all would be well, but if the police showed up, or an ambulance who hadn't been called by his employers, then that would be bad.

Very bad.

The cops would arrive on the scene to find two unmarked luxury sedans, some people dressed for a formal event, and possibly some corpses. The scene couldn't be explained, and wouldn't be explained. Ryan's employers would make sure of that.

His fingers moved across his body, feeling for the seatbelt which had probably saved his life, and pressed the button that released him from the seat. He fell to the roof of the car, wet with melted snow and ice. He rolled onto his back in a single move, twisting so his neck straightened out and didn't break. It was sore, and would be sore for a long time. He pushed himself toward the dashboard and felt along the steering column for the flash drive. He felt it sticking out from its slot, and he sighed with relief. No payment unless the flash drive was intact. It was the car's little black box, detailing the accident and identifying which of the car's systems had worked according to design, as well as those that hadn't. The data was collected wirelessly, but the flash drive ensured that all data would be saved in the event the wireless system malfunctioned.

But the cradle that had housed his iPhone was empty, and Ryan punched the dashboard. It gave way, and his arm punched through, slicing the side of his hand on the faux wood.

"Piece of crap," he muttered, as he pulled his hand free. The cut on the side of his palm wasn't deep, and though it would bleed, he wasn't worried about it. The car had been beautiful, even if the beauty had only been skin deep, and it was a shame that it hadn't survived.

But then again, Ryan couldn't think of a car that would have survived this wreck. He had a dizzying recollection of spinning through the air, twisting, bending, tearing and crushing under the sheer speed of the crash. It was a wonder the car had stayed in as good shape as it had.

Ryan pushed against the seat and wiggled his body out of the driver's side window. He got to his knees slowly and then climbed to his feet. He wobbled, but gained his balance as he did a quick check over his body to make sure that it wasn't gushing blood, or that bones weren't magically sticking out of his skin. Everything seemed okay, except that the side of his tuxedo jacket was ripped to the shoulder.

He studied the wreckage, a trail of littered engine pieces and car parts strewn from the top of the bridge down to where they lay. He looked for Sam's body, but it wasn't there.

"Sam!" he yelled. His voice didn't carry far in the storm. The sirens were closer, and he needed to find Sam before they arrived, or he might be left for dead. It was another rule in a list of rules that made being associated with the Lit Dragons a risky proposition. Emergency personnel arrived within minutes, but also left within minutes. If you weren't at the scene of the crash, they would leave.

Ryan began to run, a jerky shuffle that would have been almost comical in other circumstances. He was so cold, and all sense of feeling in his legs and arms was fading into a thick numbness.

"Sam!" He yelled, his voice croaking, "answer me, man!"

Amidst a pile of broken glass, he saw his phone lying face down. He bent over and picked it up. The screen was shattered, but when he pressed the "Home" button, it came to life, and he exhaled with relief. He pressed the "Contacts" button, found Sam's name, and dialed. After several seconds, Ryan heard Elvis Presley rocking out in Sam's ringtone.

"Sam, you dumb idiot," Ryan said, chuckling with the relief that swept over him. The sound was muffled and soft, but it was close by. He ran toward the sound of Elvis' warbling, which led him back up the bridge and over the guard rail. He found Sam lying face down in the snow, the area around him red with blood.

"Sam!" Ryan said, sliding to the ground near him. He rolled his friend's body over and saw a wicked gash from his neck down to his belly. The cut was deep and jagged, as if someone had taken a serrated knife and cut jagged strips of skin from Sam's body. Which, considering the shards of broken glass Sam's body had passed through, wasn't too far from the mark.

Ryan ran his fingers over the gash. He didn't think the cut had severed any major blood vessels, which was good. That his friend had lost so much blood, maybe too much blood, even without slicing a large artery, was not so good.

Ryan gently shook Sam's head, whispering his name, and got no response. He pressed two fingers against Sam's neck, just below his jaw bone, and felt a pulse, although very light. After a moment, he saw Sam's chest rising and falling with shallow breaths.

The snow and ice, Ryan realized, had saved his life, slowing the bleeding from a cut that could have killed him. He held Sam close, cradling his head in his arms, and gave him a hug.

"I'm sorry to go, Sam," he whispered. "I'll call when the dust settles, and I'll call ..."

He meant to say that he'd call Dani, Sam's wife, but it was another of those rules that simply could not be broken.

The sirens were on them now, so close that he could hear the rumblings of the engines. From the sound of it, there were at least two ambulances and several tow trucks following. The clean up would be quick, and Ryan had to act fast. He had no idea how long the snow would keep Sam alive, but knew it would not stop the blood forever, not to mention the inevitable onset of hypothermia and frost bite.

He rolled Sam back onto his belly and patted him on the head.

"Hang in there buddy," he said.

Voices carried over from the other side of the bridge. Ryan jumped to his feet, his entire body shaking from the cold, and stumbled as fast as he could through the snow and back to the road.

One ambulance was parked by his overturned car, paramedics peering inside with several large flashlights. They were talking, but Ryan couldn't hear what they were saying. He called to them.

"Hey!"

They turned, surprised.

"You the driver?" one of the medics asked. He was tall and muscular, his chest one that would give a barrel a run for its money.

"Yeah," Ryan said. "Listen—"

"Let me check you out," the medic said, cutting him off with a curt wave of his hand. The medic crossed the road quickly to Ryan, and immediately began feeling along his neck and spine and checking the rest of his body.

"Listen, man," Ryan said, out of breath. "My partner's alive, over there in the snow. He was thrown from the car."

"Let's take care of you first, man," the medic said. "You should not be up walking around."

The medic prodded Ryan, feeling for broken bones, and then returned his attention to the neck and spine.

"Any soreness there?" the medic asked, feeling along the base of Ryan's skull.

"Yeah, a little." Ryan shrugged the man's fingers away.

"We had this guy once, driver like you, and he was ejected like your friend over there. This guy gets up and walks around, talking to the first responders and the other players, and he keeps saying his neck is real sore. He keeps rubbin' the back of his head, and when he bends to sit down, he just drops dead."

"Yeah?" Ryan asked.

"Yeah, just like that." The medic pulled out a small flashlight and shone the light into Ryan's eyes. "See, the guy's neck was broken, just snapped right in two, but the spinal cord hadn't been severed yet. So he's up walkin' around with a broken neck, and when he leans down, the weight of his head separates the spine along the break, and cuts the spinal cord right there and wham bam, thank you ma'am, he's a goner."

"Well, I don't think my neck's broken," Ryan said.

"Well, you're luckier than the other driver." The medic nodded to the other car, Team Orange, and Ryan felt a sinking in his stomach despite the crippling cold. As much as he loved the game, he hated it when people died.

"Dead?"

"Engine block came through the steering column and crushed his lungs. Passenger is okay, physically, but he's a mess. Gonna have a whole basket full of nightmares when this all settles down. But, man, what happened out here?"

"Collateral," Ryan said, already walking over the bridge. Flashing red and white lights could be seen over the summit, and Ryan wondered if had known the driver. He coughed and felt sick to his stomach. His foot slipped on the black ice as he cleared the bridge and saw what was left of the other car below. Except for the front seating area, the car was demolished. Bits and pieces of metal and engine and glass were strewn out over the ice, currently being covered with snow. Several men were gathering the pieces in large orange bags, and several others were hooking a winch to the largest pieces to pull them up onto the flatbed truck.

Paramedics milled around two gurneys that lay on the ground. On one, a white sheet had been pulled over the body, with just the heels of the guy's feet sticking out the bottom. Without seeing the face, he knew who the driver was, and the feeling that he was going to throw up swelled. The dead driver's name was Brian Frank, a tall guy with straight blond hair in his twenties. He was from Pennsylvania, if Ryan remembered right, and they'd driven twice together with the Lit Dragons. Ryan wondered if he'd ever broken up with and left the girl he'd been complaining about during their last drive, and for her sake, he hoped so.

"You the driver of Team Blue?"

Ryan turned and saw a clean-cut man in a suit and tie. He had a black overcoat pulled around his shoulders, and his face was frozen in a grimace.

"Yeah."

"You got it?" the man asked, holding out his hand.

"Wired?" Ryan said, reaching into his pocket. "All of it?"

"Of course."

"And you'll take care of Brian's family. The other driver."

"Of course."

Ryan pulled out the flash drive and placed it in the man's hand. As he did, he noticed the stains of red that covered his skin, a dramatic contrast with the other man's designer gloves with rabbit fur linings.

"And take care of my partner." Ryan motioned with his head back to the other side of the bridge.

The man nodded as a black town car pulled up. The driver got out of the car and opened the door for Ryan, who slid onto the plush leather seats. There was a change of clothes in the center of the seat with a white envelope balanced on top. The clothes would fit perfectly, as they always did, and the envelope contained a confirmation that the money had been wired to his account.

He reached into the seatback pocket and pulled out a thick magazine—Esquire—and started thumbing through the pages absently. He would change out of his formal wear in a moment, once his heart had slowed and his freezing limbs had warmed.

The car pulled through the wreckage and flashing lights, snow flakes falling, though not as hard and fast as before.

"Where to?" the driver asked, a slight New England accent in his voice.

"Airport."

"Headed home?"

Ryan nodded.

Chapter Seventeen

The snow was swirling as Paul trudged down the sidewalk to the entrance of the building where he worked. His feet and toes were wet, and he shivered as he walked, but he was not aware of the cold. As he walked through the drifts of snow on the sidewalk, squinting ahead to keep the frozen bits of water from his eyes, he thought about the woman who'd not shown up that evening.

She had called him. Not just once, but several times. Even after the first time they had talked, he'd known that she was not calling a random reporter, but that she'd sought him out specifically. The only reason that he could think of as to why she would seek him out was because of the series of articles he'd written about the disaster in Miami. Besides a few outspoken (and possibly insane) bloggers who'd latched onto his ideas, he was the only person that he knew of who hadn't accepted the official response to the explosion and building collapse. It was disturbing, of course, that of all the reporters who'd seen the destruction, some as seasoned as himself, or more so, he was the only one who'd seen something that could not have been an accident.

But there was no bomb, the other journalists had cried, no incendiary device, and no evidence to speak of. Paul had to admit that he was standing on shaky ground, but at the same time, he'd seen the destruction. The wrecked buildings. The bodies.

"Hey, watch your step man!" some guy said, and Paul jerked from the daze he was walking in and dodged a man who was hiking through the snow in the opposite direction.

"Sorry," Paul muttered and nodded toward the man, who carried on with his head burrowed deep into his scarf and coat, his hands shoved deep into his coat. They passed, and Paul returned almost instantly to his dazed thoughts.

The woman had called him because of what he'd written. She wasn't the first person who'd called him, although others usually wanted to join their ideas into the typical grand conspiracy that the government had been responsible, and was covering its tracks. Like JFK, like 9/11, like Benghazi. The most interesting conspiracy was passed along by one of those crazy bloggers who claimed he'd hacked the computers of a secret organization who called themselves Il Contionum. When Paul had questioned the blogger about what this supposedly secret organization did, the blogger had quickly hung up the phone, and then later sent an email with instructions on how to log into a secure VPN server. Of course, Paul had never logged on. The blogger was just one in a mass of nuts who were chopping at the bit for any way to see conspiracy in the grand scheme of things. Paul was not one of them, and neither was this woman.

In fact, each time the woman had called, it had seemed as though she was trying to determine if Paul was a conspiracy nut, or if his ideas were grounded in logic and facts. The logic was there, and what facts he'd managed to assemble over the years were there too, just no evidence. Nothing to prove that the attack in Miami had indeed been an attack.

Finally, during their last discussion on the telephone, the woman had promised the final piece to the puzzle. She had set up the meeting, giving him the specific bus route and time.

Then why didn't she show up? The questioned gnawed at his brain as he mulled the facts and his history with the woman, repeatedly going over every word that he could remember. Something must have happened to her, of that he was sure.

Paul arrived at the entrance to the building where he worked and finally started to feel the cold. He pushed through the revolving doors and nodded at the front desk security guard. The guard looked half asleep, an old black and white monster movie playing on the TV behind his desk.

Paul rode alone in the elevator to the third floor, which was leased entirely by the Gazette. The receptionist was gone for the day, but a few night owls still sat at their desks, typing away at articles due the next morning. No one noticed him as he walked through the large open room toward his office in the back.

The lights in his office were turned off, and he didn't bother turning them on when he stepped into the room and sat heavily on the old couch that ran along the wall opposite his desk. Paul wanted a couple shots from the bottle of Wild Turkey he kept in his desk, but the moment he sat on the couch, exhaustion set in. He didn't feel like moving at all, just sitting there in the soft, worn cushions and going to sleep.

"Paul?" He looked toward the door and saw his assistant. He started to smile, but it turned into a yawn.

"Tired, eh?" Dennis asked as he came into the room and sat on a chair near the couch.

"Yeah," Paul said. He couldn't mask the disappointment in his voice. "You should go on home, Dennis."

"I was planning to, just didn't expect to see you here."

Paul shrugged, and decided he did have enough energy for a shot of whiskey after all. He got up from the couch and pulled two glasses and a bottle from the drawer, setting them on the desk. He looked up at Dennis, who nodded.

"Just a little."

"You got it, pardner," Paul said and filled both glasses nearly halfway.

"Maybe she'll call tomorrow, let us know what happened tonight." Dennis took the offered glass from Paul.

"No, I think something happened tonight." Paul sipped, enjoying the warmth that cut against the winter chill. "Something permanent, I think."

"Like she's dead?"

"Not necessarily. She was always so afraid of being caught, worried that someone would find out that she'd talked to me, but I think she was a tad bit paranoid. I've decided that anyway."

Paul took another drink, gulping this time, and it burned hard.

"You decided?"

"Yeah, I don't think she was being watched, or followed, or whatever she thought. But I do think that she's done with us. Our contact set up the meeting, and that was after some serious vetting on her part. She wanted to be sure of something before she handed over any information. But the point is, she did make sure before she set up the meeting. She should have been there, and I can think of only a few things that would have stopped her from getting on that bus."

"So if not dead, then what?"

"Maybe someone stopped her," Paul said slowly, then took another sip of the whiskey. "She was intensely paranoid, and if her paranoia had any basis in reality, that is a definite possibility."

"But not what you think," Dennis said.

"No," Paul said, "her paranoia did play a part, I'm sure. I think she got scared. At the last minute, she decided that she wasn't ready to hand over the information, or that her vetting process was not as thorough as it should have been."

"Okay, so what do we do?" Dennis took a small drink from his glass and scowled at the taste. He set the glass aside, apparently done with the drink.

"All we can do is wait."

"Waiting sucks," Dennis said. He stood up and set the glass of whiskey on Paul's desk.

"I'm going to get going," he said. "Heather was pissed a couple of hours ago, but I'm sure she's fallen asleep by now, so it's probably safe to go home."

"Tell her I'm sorry I kept you here," Paul said, and then, after a few seconds, he added, "I don't know how much longer we—I—can deal with this story."

"We just wait," Dennis said. "Something will come along."

Paul nodded but didn't respond, letting his office fall silent as Dennis returned to his desk. Somewhere nearby, another night owl was typing furiously at a keyboard, but otherwise, there wasn't any noise inside the office space or out on the quiet city street.

Paul lifted the glass to his nose and inhaled the woody fumes of the drink before taking another sip. He savored the burn.

Chapter Eighteen

They were nearly back to the city, and with each second that passed, the crowds grew closer, and with the crowds, the ability to become invisible. She tried to swallow, but her throat felt like it was lined with cotton and sand. She took a deep breath, closed her eyes, and tried to calm her thudding heart, tried to regain her composure. No matter what she tried, the panic seemed to stay, pulsing under the surface.

She tried to concentrate on keeping her mind in the present, tried desperately to keep it from sliding back into the terror of the previous hours. Tears threatened to spill down her cheeks as she realized that there was no going back to the way it was—that she was on a trajectory that couldn't be stopped, and it would only lead further and further from the life she'd known and loved.

Maybe they would just forget about her, let her live her life. But she knew that they would never forget, and would never forgive what she'd done. They were hunting her, and they knew she was alive, and they would never stop.

As if in chorus with her thoughts, a flash of a car's headlight swept through the bus. Mae turned toward the back window and saw a small hatchback following the bus too closely. She leaned forward, trying to make out who was driving, but the snow was coming down to hard. She did see that the driver wasn't alone, and that at least two others were in the car, their dark forms large and hulking.

Mae sank lower in the seat as the car slowed and pulled in close behind the bus.

"Ah, Miss?" Nick gazed up at her in his rearview mirror. "You see that car back there?"

"Yeah, I see it," she said. Up ahead, there was a sign for the Chicago O'Hare International Airport. She stood up and walked to the front of the bus.

"Can you turn off up there?"

"The airport?" he asked.

"Yeah."

He hesitated, fidgeting in his seat. "Listen, Ms. Edwards, I know you've got something going on that I can't understand, and I'm fine with that. But we're being followed and I recommend that you go to the police."

"If they catch me, I'll be dead," she said, "and I don't trust the police—especially not in this city."

"Well, I guess I can see that," he said and flexed his fingers. He turned the steering wheel and the bus turned off on the exit that led to the airport.

"Alls I'm sayin' is that they're right behind us, and if you get off the bus, they're going to know where you are and they goin' getch ya."

"I know, but I think I can blend in enough with the people in the airport, and get out of here."

Nick hesitated for a moment, thinking about all the crazies that came out at night in the city. He opened his mouth to say something, but hesitated. He'd been driving the bus for more than a decade now, and he'd seen his fair share of lunatics on the streets.

"You gotta be careful out there, Ms. Mae," Nick said, breaking the silence. His voice was soft and far away. "There are lots of bad people out there, just waiting to get a bite outta you."

"I'll be careful," Mae said, and made her voice as sincere as possible. Nick meant well, but couldn't know the full extent of the mess he'd driven into that night. Mae just prayed that it would end without the driver getting hurt.

They continued in silence for a few moments. Mae looked over her shoulder and saw the car still there, following at a safe distance. She leaned her forehead against the window and watched the street lamps drift by and the snowflakes flutter past the windows like tiny tufts of silk. The cold glass of the window misted with each breath, and she remembered drawing pictures or messages in those misted portions of windows when she was a child.

She looked up at Nick and saw his kind eyes studying her in the rear view mirror. She had to tell him something, that much she knew. He'd risked his life for her, and he deserved to know something. But aside from all that, if he was ever questioned, she wanted the picture that he had of her in his mind to be that of the helpless victim. No doubt he already saw her as the victim, but she needed it cemented there, so when the question inevitably came, he would not falter in his story.

She closed her eyes and imagined that time before, like a fairy tale of places and people far away, where memories are light and sweet and airy, and then she spoke, her voice quiet and sad. Exactly how she wanted to sound.

"My dad was a wonderful father, and he really loved my mom and me. He was always there for my school plays, for the stupid graduations from each grade in elementary school. When I was little, he would always come home for dinner. He would tell me and Mom jokes around the dinner table, or stories about what happened at his work that day, and we were the perfect picture of a happy family. At night, he would sit in his special chair beside my bed and read stories that he'd loved as a kid. He would read a couple of chapters, and I would beg him to read more. Always, even when he was tired, he would read that extra chapter. That was just like him, to keep reading even when he was tired."

Mae paused and looked up at Nick, who glanced up in the mirror and nodded for her to continue. His face was calm and somber, and Mae was reminded of her dad, who would listen to her with that same focus and intensity that made her feel like he cared about everything she said. She smiled, knowing that her smile was sad and distant. Despite whatever she told Nick, at the heart of it all, her dad had taken a piece of her when he left. She longed for the time in her memory when she would wrap her arms around his neck and feel his whiskers on her face, and smell his spiced cologne. She missed his laugh and smile, and forever the memories of him would trail her like whirlwinds of autumn wind. She wanted nothing more than to hang onto those glimpses of her childhood, but try as she might, they kept slipping through her fingers like wisps of smoke.

She bit her lower lip and pushed forward, not just for her sake, but for Nick as well. If he was going to die tonight, which she hoped with all of her heart wouldn't happen, she wanted him to die seeing the good and light part of her, so he would be convinced that what he had done was good. That was one thing her dad had actually said, a small piece of truth in her story that was otherwise a lie.

"Everyone wants to be a hero," he had said. "You want to die a hero, so you'll be remembered as a hero. And if you're remembered as a hero, that's immortality."

Because that's what it really came down to, in the end, the feeling that you've done good in the world, that in some small way you died a hero—whether true or not.

"One day, and I remember the day very distinctly, because it was in the middle of winter, but the day was very warm. I remember playing outside without my coat on. I was swinging on a rope swing that my dad and I had tied to one of the high branches of an oak tree in our backyard.

"My dad came home early from work, and he looked like he hadn't slept in days, or maybe that he'd been drinking. He didn't drink much in those days, at least that I was aware of, but that's what he looked like. His hair was messed up, and his suit was wrinkled. I remember his eyes—usually so blue and beautiful like the sky on the first real day of spring, but on that day, they were bloodshot and dark. I ran up to him, like a usually did, but he walked right on by without so much as a sideways glance.

"It hurt, but only for a minute. You know how kids are, hurt one minute, and then onto something else the very next."

Nick nodded in the mirror, as if to say, "if you only knew…"

Mae saw a sign that said the airport was only a few miles away, and she felt like bursting with excitement at the news. She was so close that the excitement was nearly palpable, but even then, Mae held the excitement well. She smiled briefly up at Nick in the mirror and continued.

"I started swinging again, the branches on the oak tree creaking and groaning as I swung. And then the shouts came. It was the first time that I'd ever heard my dad shout at my mom. She was inside making dinner, or sitting beside the fire in our living room and reading a book—she loved to read, back then, and he started shouting. I stayed on the swing, not wanting to move, afraid to move. I didn't know what to do, and for the first time in my life, I felt helpless. I was just a little girl, and there was nothing I could do to help my mom.

"He shouted for maybe ten minutes, although it felt like hours, and then it was quiet. I waited for another half hour. I remember being very cold, just sitting on the swing and drifting in the winter wind, until my mom called me in for dinner.

"Everything was normal inside the house, as if the whole shouting episode hadn't happened. My dad even looked cleaned up—his hair was combed and he'd changed his clothes. His eyes still looked dark to me, like there was a secret there, but they were better. Much better than before.

"Both of my parents were smiling as if the whole wide world was just peachy keen, but under their smiles was something dark. Even as a little girl I could see it. For my dad, there was maybe a little bit of guilt, maybe panic. Knowing now what I do, I think it was mostly panic. But for my mom, it was terror. She was terrified of something.

"Over the next few weeks and months, my dad got worse. He stopped coming home every day and would show up at seemingly random times, sometimes in the middle of the night. It wasn't until six months later or so, I don't really remember much except that it was in the middle of the summer now, and that my mom told me that my dad had a gambling problem. She told me that he'd lost his job and the house, and that there might be some bad people coming to collect the money he owed.

"It was a lot for a little girl to handle, to understand. We cried, my mom and I, almost every day. I think my mom wanted to leave my dad, but for some reason she seemed afraid to leave. We moved shortly after, to start a new and fresh life, but the problems followed us. The problems never left, really. There were people who followed us, and they were always in the shadows. You'd turn your head, and there'd be someone just disappearing from view, always just outside the corner of your eye. But you knew that they were there.

"Those people you saw, the ones who were shooting at me, they were ... collectors, you could say, coming to collect on my dad's debts."

Her voice trailed off to a dramatic pause, and she almost believed the story herself. She kept her head pointed toward her lap, and didn't need to look up at the rear view mirror to know that Nick was looking at her intently. He started to say something, but the words caught in his throat. He coughed into his fist and tried again.

"And your parents?" Nick asked.

"My mom finally managed to leave my dad, but she left me too," Mae said and fought the pang of guilt that followed, seeing her mom's teary eyes in the cabin. "My dad died shortly after. They killed him, and they'll kill me too, if they catch me."

She almost winced at these last few details. If he tried, it wouldn't be hard for him to pick through her story. Thankfully, when Eddie fired the gun at the bus, it had only added to the sense of emergency and panic that she was the victim, and she hoped and prayed that Nick would take the bait, hook, line and all.

She assumed right. When Mae looked up at the mirror again, she wasn't looking at a man who doubted her, but one that pitied her. He felt sorry for her, ached for her even, and it was exactly what she needed.

"You poor girl," Nick said after several long seconds. The empathy in his voice was genuine. He hesitated for a moment longer, unsure of how to continue.

"Has your mother reached out to you since your dad died?" he finally asked.

Mae felt that guilt again, mixed with despair and hopelessness, rising in her gut and threatening to choke her poise. All the lies that had come before this one had been twisted with truth, but this lie was the worst of all. A wave of emotion hit her, and she fought back tears. If she cried now, she was apt to tell Nick everything, to spill the beans. And that would not just spell disaster for both her and Nick, but it would undo everything she and her mother had been working for. She felt like a little girl who was much too young to be feeling this weight on her shoulders, and she wanted nothing more than to curl up on a couch, her head on her mother's lap. Mae could almost feel her mother's fingers run through her hair, like they'd done a thousand times before, and this brought the sobs closer to the surface.

"No," she said. "My mom left me with my dad. I think that once she realized her marriage was over, I just reminded her of the failure, and she left. Maybe she went back home, but I doubt it. She wanted to be far away from anything that reminded her of my dad, and home would have been too much."

As she spoke, that familiar coldness came into her and replaced the longing she'd felt only moment before. The coldness that swept over her was invigorating, like stepping out of a warm house in the middle of a snowstorm. The coldness honed her senses, which was good, because she needed her senses to be sharp, especially now. The coldness was survival, and if her mom had died for anything, it was Mae's survival.

She looked out the window and saw that the bus was on the causeway that led to the DEPARTURES section of the airport. The bus was surrounded by cars going in the same direction, and she noticed another city bus just a few hundred meters in front of them.

"Why don't I take you to a hotel, or someplace safe and away from crowds?" Nick asked, and Mae was grateful for the way he cared. He seemed to genuinely want to help her.

"No," Mae said, "I need to get out of town, and away from my dad's *friends*."

She broke off, hearing the double meaning of the last word she'd spoken, even as it spilled from her lips. She glanced up at Nick, trying to hide the panic, but he hadn't noticed.

"Why are they after you to begin with?" he asked. "If they ... got your dad, why do they need you?"

She smiled furtively, as her story unraveled. "Because I know where he kept his money."

Mae hoped that he wouldn't see the sly smile, but he was watching the road ahead and nodding, as if this was just the most normal thing in the world. Of course, on nights where you pick up a girl who's freezing to death in the middle of the countryside, and then have some goon shoot up your bus, what's normal is open for discussion.

Nick pulled the bus into the DEPARTURES lane, and drove along slowly with the other cars. He slowed to a stop to allow a family with three kids to walk across the road to the entrance of the airport. Mae watched the little girl, bundled up like a little pink marshmallow. The girl pulled a miniature pink, roll-along suitcase behind her and although she looked tired, her eyes were bright with the excitement of getting on an airplane.

"Why not the police?"

She looked up at him, and the lie came easily. This time, the lie had a tinge of truth, enough to make her shiver, despite herself.

"My dad was killed in police custody," she said, and Nick stared, wide-eyed but believing.

"I hate just leaving you here," Nick said as he started the bus forward, and then looked questioningly at her in the mirror.

"You can drop me off anywhere, it's fine." she said. "I'll be okay. Much better, in fact, with all the people here."

"You be careful, and notify the police the second anything looks fishy. You got some bad people on behind you, whether you realize that or not."

"I know, and I will." Mae looked over her shoulder, through the windows that lined the back of the bus. She didn't see the hatchback that'd been following them earlier, and there weren't any other cars that stood out to her. She stood up and gathered her bag in her arms. Nick stopped the bus several feet from the nearest entrance, and put the bus in park. He undid his seatbelt and lifted his considerable body out of the seat.

"I hate this, Ms. Mae," he said, and the kindness in his voice touched her deeply. He was speaking to her as a father would speak to his daughter. Mae stepped forward and wrapped her arms around his neck in what would have been, under different circumstances, an awkward hug. She'd just met this man, but he'd saved her life.

He returned the embrace, and then took her by the shoulders.

"You be safe," he said, his big hazel eyes wide and open with concern. Mae saw that the big man was doing his best to suppress an explosion of panic and anxiety. She nodded with a tiny smile.

"I will."

"And you call me just as soon as you're safe." Nick scribbled a telephone number on the back of a crumpled receipt and handed it to her.

"I don't care if you don't want to talk to me ever again, but you call me this one time, or I'll hate myself for lettin' you go like this."

"I'll call. I promise," she said.

"Now go, and you keep movin' before the devil catches up."

Chapter Nineteen

Nick Ambrose watched Mae get off the bus and walk quickly toward the entrance of the airport. He reflected for a moment that despite the dirt and grime, she was a beautiful young woman—too beautiful and young and innocent to be dealing with whatever was going on in her life. He knew that she wasn't being completely honest, that there was something left out of her story, but it didn't change the fact that she was being chased and shot at.

Nick was scared for her, and no matter how many times he told himself that she would be all right, that if anything happened now, there would be cops and security guards around, he still felt that something was deadly wrong. Mae shot him one last look right before she disappeared through the automatic doors, and she smiled warmly at him. He smiled back at her and watched her until she was gone, feeling a pang of regret that he hadn't offered to do more.

He sat at the curb for a moment behind the wheel and wondered whether he should hop right out of the bus and tell an officer what had happened. Surely they would be able to do something to protect the girl. Whoever was after her was dangerous, but she was adamant about not involving the police.

Maybe it was the police that were after her?

But he doubted a cop would shoot at the bus. Unless, of course, the risk of losing the girl was greater than the risk of collateral damage.

It was dangerous to be caught up in business like this, and Nick felt foolish for getting even this involved in something that didn't concern him. Truth was, Mae reminded him of his own daughter, Janelle, who was in the middle of her final year of high school and seemed to love every minute of it. As it happens with most dads and their daughters, they'd grown apart over the years, he and Janelle, but no matter what, he would always see her as his little girl. He loved her, and when he made a promise to Janelle, he intended to keep it.

Just like with Janelle, Nick intended to keep his promise with Mae, no matter how strange their brief encounter had been. She had been alone and had needed help. If that had been Janelle, regardless of the reason she was in that situation, he hoped someone would have stopped for her.

As he pulled away from the curb and merged with the traffic leaving the airport, his mind wandered briefly to a place it often went—to the summer of Janelle's fifth birthday, when he'd taken his wife and daughter to the northern shores of Lake Michigan for a weekend. He'd worked overtime for six months to save for the tiny cabin they'd rented—their first real vacation as a family, and also their last.

They'd lived like kings for those two days, enjoying the cool summer breeze, the manicured grass between their toes, and spending the long afternoons fishing off the end of their own private dock.

And the tire swing. It was best part of the entire vacation for Janelle. The tire swing was tied high in the branches of a cottonwood tree, and Nick spent hours pushing his girl on the swing, while tufts of cotton floated in the breeze like pieces of sunlight. He remembered her laugh as she swung up and down, twisting and turning as he pushed her.

At that moment in his life, he felt complete. His wife looked on from a rocking chair on the porch, engrossed in a biography about some World War II pilot, or something or other. Nick felt like a man that day, happy to have provided the short, but ever-so satisfying vacation for his family. He visited that weekend in his memories often, to remember his little girl and her big grin as she swung in the waning sunlight.

As always, he couldn't think about that trip without thinking about the end of their family as they'd known it. Not long after that trip, his wife was diagnosed with stage four ovarian cancer. She'd died not long afterwards, opting to reduce the mountain of medical bills in favor of a quicker death—over Nick's strong and desperate objections. He hated watching her go, but in those final moments, when he'd laid in bed with her, their arms clasped together like they'd lain for so many years, they sang together. They sang songs from Sunday School, praising Jesus or recanting tales from the Bible. It was mostly kid stuff, but as their soft voices melded together, he'd felt that same completeness again. He was with the woman of his dreams, and when the end had finally come, it was quiet and peaceful. He'd let her go into the night. It had been a fine way to say goodbye, but he'd cried all the same.

Shortly after, Nick and Janelle packed up their house and moved in with his older brother and his wife. It hadn't taken long to become a part of their family, and despite the fact that they no longer had a place to call their own, Nick always did his best to let Janelle know that he was always there for her. That she was never alone.

Like Mae.

He sighed heavily as he switched gears and sped up with traffic. He checked his mirror and pulled into the quicker moving traffic toward the interstate. He drove in silence for a few moments, wondering when he should call the dispatcher about the bullet holes in his windshield.

As he eased the bus onto the interstate, he decided that he'd tell them that someone had shot at the bus while he was driving through West Pullman. And why was he driving through West Pullman? Why, he'd taken a wrong turn and had to detour down some side streets to get back on his main route. Nothing to it, and the service guys at the garage would be none-the-wiser. Gunshots on a bus had to have happened before.

Nick reached down and flipped on the radio to a station that played the Blues and only the Blues. He sat back a little in his chair and enjoyed driving the bus without worrying about passengers getting on and off, or getting shot at. His thoughts returned to the lake with Janelle and his wife. In this memory, they were making chocolate chip cookies. Laughing in the kitchen, splashing water, and his wife wiping a finger full of batter across his cheek.

Flashing red and blue lights suddenly lit up behind him. Nick stared into the mirror, waiting for the police officer to pass. His eyes shifted to his dashboard. He'd been driving within the speed limit, nothing out of the ordinary.

Nick slowed the bus and pulled it onto the shoulder. He was surprised to see the cop car follow suit. He parked the bus and waited, running through everything he'd done in the moments before seeing the lights. He was sure that he'd done nothing wrong—

Ah, he thought, remembering his shouts into the radio right after he'd picked up Mae. Of course they'd send someone to check up on him—he'd yelled about gunshots and then flipped off his radio. Or the cop had simply seen the bullet holes in his window and had pulled him over to check it out.

Through his mirrors, he watched the officer get out of car and walk along the bus until getting to the front doors. Nick was surprised to see the officer wearing a heavy bomber jacket, tucked neatly into his pressed khakis, but he opened the door all the same. He was clean cut, shaven, and aside from the lack of uniform, nothing was the least bit odd about him.

"'Can I do you for, officer?"

"Where'd she go?" the officer said, stepping up onto the bus.

"Who?"

"You know who."

"I'm not sure I do." Nick said. Mae's voice rang in his head: *Do not trust the cops.*

He felt a pang of panic, and the officer took another step onto the bus and glanced back at the empty rows of seats. A strand of hair fell onto his forehead, and he didn't bother brushing it away.

"Officer—"

"Morales," the man said, the hint of a smile crossing his lips.

"Officer Morales, I'm off duty, heading back to the garage."

The cop pointed to the bullet holes in the corner of the windshield and said, "Cause of your bullet holes there?"

"Well, yes," Nick stammered, but regained his poise quickly, "that's exactly why I'm headed into the garage. Got a few shots over in West Pullman, and got to get the windshield patched up."

"You're a long way from West Pullman," Officer Morales said and walked toward the back of the bus. Nick unbuckled his safety belt and pulled his substantial body from the seat. He watched Officer Morales examine each row of seats until he came to the seat where Mae had briefly sat. The policeman picked up a crumpled piece of paper and unfurled it. When he saw the scribbled image of the man and woman beneath the lamp post, snow whirling around them as they embraced, the officer smiled.

Morales held it up for Nick to see, and said, "I want the girl who drew this."

Nick saw the scrawled picture and wondered if and how Mae had dropped the drawing. Even if she had somehow dropped the drawing, how could the officer possibly know it belonged to the girl he'd rescued. He'd been driving the bus for hours now, with any number of people who could have dropped the crumpled piece of paper

"I don't know who drew that picture," Nick said, his mouth suddenly very dry. "I've had many passengers this evening, and it could have been any of them."

"You stopped your bus for a young lady not too long ago," Morales said and then nodded toward the windshield. "Right around the same time you got your pops to the windshield."

"I don't know what you're talking about. I haven't done anything wrong, and I don't see how that little drawing means anything to you," Nick said. He swallowed hard, trying to clear the dryness.

"This little drawing means more than you could know." Morales smiled and looked on the floor around where Mae had been sitting for any other clues of Mae's whereabouts. When he saw none, he folded Mae's picture and placed into his pocket.

"She got off the bus at the airport, that much we know," he said, "but we need to know where she is going."

"I'm telling you man, I don't know who you're talking about. Now please let me go home to my own little girl," Nick said. Officer Morales stared at Nick for a moment and then shrugged casually.

"I'm guessing that you don't know where she went," Officer Morales said calmly. "She knew that we would have talked to you soon after she left, so she wouldn't have told you. I understand that. But what I do not understand, is that you're trying to cover for some person you don't even know."

"Sometimes," Nick said, his voice quiet and soft, "you can just tell the good guys and the bad guys without ever really knowin'."

The officer grunted. "What if I told you that she was, without a doubt, one of the worst bad guys you could ever come across? What if I told you that she's a terrorist, responsible for the death of hundreds?"

"Then I guess I'd know that you're lyin'," Nick said and suddenly understood where this conversation was going. He looked at the wet floor of his bus, muddy tracks from the passengers he'd served that evening, and then studied his fingers in the harsh light from overhead. He thought of Janelle, probably home and doing her homework now. She was a good girl. He was sad that they hadn't talked more before she'd left for school that morning.

"It's a shame that you couldn't help more, although it wouldn't have mattered much for you." Morales casually pulled the gun from the holster on his belt and leveled it at Nick's chest.

The bus driver didn't try to run. There was no way that he would turn his back to this police officer. No way that he would die with a bullet in his back. He just stared at the officer and waited. He wondered how the night could have taken this drastic turn, but you never really expected things like this to happen. And then suddenly, a faint connection sparked in his mind. He thought about the man who'd ridden the bus several times around his route, waiting for someone to get on the bus. He wondered if there was any connection—

But it was too late now, and he didn't want to think about those things. Instead, Nick thought about pushing Janelle on the tire swing on that cool summer day, the smell of chocolate chip cookies baking inside the cabin, the sparkling sunshine. He could hear his little girl's laugh, so vibrant and full of life, could smell the long grass and the blue water. He thought about singing sweet songs with his love as they lay in their bed, holding her hand in his as she died.

"Be with you soon, baby," he whispered.

An echoing gunshot that felt a like hammer to his head, and everything was quiet.

Part Three
Hunters and Prey

Chapter Twenty

Inside the airport, the fluorescent lights shone brightly, reflecting off the black tiles. Even this late at night, the airport was crowded with people rushing about their business. The loud speakers erupted with an announcement telling people not to accept baggage from strangers, and not to leave their own bags unattended. The sound of the speakers overhead, the people and the lights were all comforting to Mae. In crowds, everything was anonymous and neutral. But it also meant that you could never be completely sure if the person standing next to you wanted to kill you. She glanced over her shoulder to be sure she wasn't being followed as she slipped into the throng of people and tried to disappear.

Mae didn't think that anyone had followed her inside, but she knew that it was just a matter of time. They would find her as they'd always found her, and she would keep running.

She prayed that Nick would ditch the bus soon, because that large, lumbering vehicle would draw her pursuers like vampires to a bleeding body. He had to get far away from the bus and disappear, but she knew that he probably wouldn't. It made her feel sick inside.

As she walked, Mae noticed a teenaged girl and her boyfriend standing in line for the ticket counter. The line didn't look like it was moving, and the girl was leaning against the boy, his arm slung casually around her shoulders. Neither of the two were paying much attention to their suitcases, which were sitting a few feet behind them.

Mae walked by them, and without skipping a beat, picked up the girl's smallest piece of luggage. She rolled it away from them without looking back, praying that no Good Samaritan onlooker would start blabbing. She walked quickly, disappearing again into the mingling crowd of people, then darted into the nearest bathroom. The last stall was open and Mae stepped inside, pulling the suitcase behind her. She waited for a few moments, making sure that no one had followed her, and then knelt beside the piece of luggage and opened it.

Mae groaned when she saw the contents—a collection of tween-style clothing. She rifled through the shirts, most of which were too small for her, and finally settled on the only one that would likely fit: a black tee-shirt that had the head of an angsty rock-star-vampire plastered on the front. The shirt was big enough to be a night gown, and Mae figured that it probably was what the girl wore to bed.

She pulled out a make-up bag and a hairbrush. As she had walked through the airport, she'd purposely not paid attention to the people around her, trying to appear as nonchalant as possible, but she was sure that she got some pretty crazy looks for looking like a zombie just-risen from the dead.

Mae also found a pair of dark gray yoga pants and a sweater. She quickly shed her dirty clothes and stuffed them into the suitcase.

"Sorry about this, girl," she muttered, wondering what the teenager was doing at that moment. Probably confused out of her mind.

She pulled the clothes on, and it felt good to be wearing something dry and clean. They even smelled good, and she thanked her luck for the first time that night. She could just as easily have grabbed the luggage for a complete slob coming back from a sweat fest with a suitcase full of dirty and unwashed clothes.

Mae worked quickly, zipping up the suitcase.

30 seconds, maybe? She shoved the brush and makeup back into her own bag, and slung it over her shoulder. She opened the door to the stall and stepped out with the suitcase. The bathroom was empty, except for two stalls down the line. She rolled the suitcase to the large trashcan near the entrance, popped off the metal casing and slid the bag into the bin. She pulled an armful of damp paper towels out from under the suitcase and piled them on top before replacing the lid. She went back to the sink and was brushing her hair when two female security guards came into the bathroom. One nodded at Mae before glancing around. The other guard started pushing on the doors to the stalls and glancing inside.

"Everything okay?" Mae asked as sweetly as she could manage.

"Just looking for a lost suitcase," one of the guards said. "Haven't seen a lone bag around, have you?"

Mae smiled and shook her head before returning to her hair, which was a royal mess. She pulled a few leaves and twigs from the tangle and dropped them into the sink. One of the guards noticed and scowled.

"Rough night?"

"Yeah, just getting back from a camping trip," Mae said. It was the first thing that came to mind, but the lie slid easily from her mouth.

"It's really cold out," the guard said skeptically.

Mae rolled her eyes, "I know, right? That's what I kept telling my boyfriend, but he insisted. I'm just glad we got back before the storm hit."

The guard lost interest and nodded absently before leaving the bathroom with her partner. Mae breathed a sigh of relief and finished brushing her hair. She opened the makeup bag and applied a little color to her eyes and lips. The color of the makeup wasn't what she would have chosen, a little too dark for her tastes, but the effect was dramatic. Most of the time, Mae didn't like looking in mirrors, because she didn't want to see the face of a young woman who'd lost everything. It was melodramatic, sure, but it was just too depressing. But now, she smiled at herself, pleased with how she looked. Maybe even pretty.

"Not half bad," she said under her breath, but continued to stare. The makeup had done a good job covering up the dark circles under her eyes, and the pale gauntness of her face.

Mae smiled once more, then pulled her backpack over her shoulder and dropped the makeup bag and brush into the trash bin on her way out. The girl she'd stolen the suitcase from was sitting on a bench near the bathroom, sobbing. Her boyfriend stood over her while an uncomfortable security guard was filling out an incident report.

Sorry about that, Mae thought as she turned and walked the other way toward the ticket counters, watching everyone carefully. She didn't see the two men who'd come into the airport after her, but she knew that someone had to be there already.

Looking for her.

Hunting her.

But she wasn't trying to spot the people hunting her, not right then. Instead, she was scanning the crowd for a different reason. She was looking for *herself*. Or as close a version of herself as she could find. She needed someone who could have passed for Mae in a passport photo. Blonde, close to her age and size, with green eyes.

Mae passed a group of teenagers with snowboarding gear, and a few families with excited, but tired-looking kids. Mostly, she saw business people, dressed in suits and carrying shoulder bags and briefcases.

Up ahead, a man carried a little girl who couldn't have been more than two years old. The girl was sound asleep on her father's shoulder, and he was struggling with some luggage and a car seat. Mae smiled at the sight, and wondered if she'd ever been held by her dad like that in a crowded airport.

She ducked into a newsstand and studied the people there. Of the woman who browsed through the magazines and stacks of books, none shared any resemblance with Mae. She heard some laughing from behind, and when she turned, Mae saw a group of boys gawking at a scantily clad actress on the cover of a magazine. No luck there.

Mae left the newsstand and stepped inside an Irish pub, which was very busy given the hour. She remained in the doorway, allowing people to walk in and out of the restaurant. A waitress tapped her on the shoulder and Mae turned, startled.

"Table for one, miss?" the waitress asked.

"Oh, no, I'm just looking," Mae said, and tried to smile. Mae stood in the entrance for a few seconds longer, but with the waitress hovering nearby, she figured she was drawing more attention than she wanted. She kept walking through the terminal, until she smelled coffee and decided that she needed some. It was called Airport Roasters and was attached to a small bookstore.

Once inside, she spotted a woman near a magazine stand, sipping a cup of coffee and reading through that month's issue of W. She was slightly shorter than Mae, and maybe 10 pounds heavier, but the hair color was virtually the same.

Mae walked past the woman to a shelf of the newest fiction. She picked up a book by John Grisham and pretended to read the words on the back cover. The woman's purse sat on top of her suitcase, and her passport and ticket stuck out of the front pocket for quick access. The trick was getting just a few seconds with the purse without the woman noticing. The last thing she wanted was to be caught stealing this woman's purse. Landing herself in a detention room with security was the last thing she wanted, and would surely draw her hunters.

Mae put the Grisham novel back on the shelf and dug around in her pocket for the last of her money, a few coins and a damp crumple of bills, before stepping up to the counter.

"Americano, small. And not too hot, please," she said, and studied the woman who looked kind of like her. Her eyes were a lighter shade of green than Mae's, but they were similar enough. Her cheekbones were set higher, but their noses were both about the same size and fairly neutral. Mae wondered for a moment where the woman was flying that night and felt sorry for her. Whether it was a trip for business or pleasure, she wouldn't be going.

"Dollar-fifty," the Barista said, and placed the small Styrofoam cup on the counter. Mae handed over two crumpled bills and took a sip of the coffee. It was still hot, but not enough to cause serious burns.

Mae took a deep breath and savored the warm and pungent mist from the coffee cup. She greedily took another sip, then turned toward the woman. Their eyes met for just a moment before the woman resumed flipping pages in her magazine.

Mae wandered close to the woman and pretended to study the departures board just a few feet away. She took another sip, enjoying the citrus notes and earthy tones of her drink, wishing that she didn't have to do what she planned. She took a few steps toward the woman and paused so as not to draw any attention. With her thumb, she pushed up on the lid of the coffee cup, hearing the faint pop as it came free and rested on the lip of the cup. Mae took a deep breath.

Here goes nothing, she thought.

Another step, and Mae tripped toward the woman, spilling the coffee as she flung forward and drenching the woman's blouse and coat. The woman shrieked and dropped her magazine, flailing her arms as if trying to keep her balance, and then took hold of the soaked fabric of her blouse and pulled it away from her chest.

"Oh!" the woman yelled, and then turned to Mae. "Why don't you watch where you're going?"

"I'm so sorry, so so sorry," Mae said quickly, over and over again. "I guess I was just looking at the departures over there, and didn't—oh, I'm so sorry."

"Fine," the woman spat as the Barista came over to offer some paper towels. He bent down between Mae and the woman, sliding the woman's luggage away from the puddle on the ground

"I'm really sorry," Mae deftly lifted the woman's wallet and passport. "Is there anything I can do?"

"You've done enough." The woman scowled at Mae and shook her head.

"I'm sorry."

The woman took the roll of paper towels offered by the Barista and stomped off to the bathroom, dragging her luggage and purse behind her. Mae turned to the Barista.

"Listen, I've made a mess here on the floor. Can I help you mop it up or something?"

"Nope," the Barista with a sarcastic smile, "it's my job. But thank you for offering."

Mae returned the smile. She turned to walk away and saw the two men from the cabin walking in her direction. Eddie wasn't with them, but she knew that he was either dead or coming from the other direction.

Mae looked the other way as she walked past the two men, attempting to block a clear look at her face, without being too obvious. She started walking with a group of tired students who were wearing hockey jerseys and making their way through security.

Mae kept her back turned to the men while pulling out the passport and wallet of the woman she'd drenched with coffee. She flipped open the passport to the first page and saw that the woman had changed her hair style and color drastically from the time she'd had her passport photo taken. If the woman in real life had shared a passing resemblance to Mae, the photo looked nothing like her. Surprisingly, the woman was older than Mae by more than a decade.

She looked at the woman's name, Gertrude Pettingale, and cringed. Unfortunate name, she thought. She decided that she would go by Gerti, which was about as good as it would get with a name like that.

Mae got into line at a ticket counter, and felt a rush of anxiety at the number of people who stood before her in line. She counted them: two women in business suits, a few passengers standing by themselves, and a family with several kids running around like banshees. The parents had apparently given up trying to maintain order. The dad was typing furiously on his phone and the mom was looking of f into space.

The person at the counter finished getting his ticket and the two businesswomen stepped up, moving the entire line forward a bit. Mae opened the Gerti's pocket book and found her credit card, hoping that there was enough credit for at least one ticket. She pulled out the credit card and put the wallet back into her bag, trying to look as bored as she could be.

Someone tapped Mae on the shoulder and her heart froze. She turned around and lost all the feeling in her legs

"Hello, Ms. Edwards," the man named Morales said. "You've been quite the pain this evening, and we'd like to talk to you a few minutes."

The other man, whom Mae had yet to hear speak, stood a few meters away and watched her through narrowed eyes. In the poor lighting of the cabin, Mae hadn't noticed the thick scars running down his face.

"Where's Eddie?" Mae glanced around, trying to keep her voice light. "Still lost in the woods?"

A glint of anger entered Morales' eyes, but as quickly as it had arrived, it was gone. He smiled and took her arm in a firm grip.

"Ah, Eddie. I'm sure you'd be happy to know that he joined your mother on the path in the sky to the great unknown." Morales suddenly pulled her close. She could feel his hot breath on her face as he spoke in a harsh whisper, "We can do this the hard way, where other people get hurt, and there's running and screaming, or we can leave this place without creating a scene. Either way, you're coming with us."

Mae's entire body was tense, and her arm ached under Morales' grip. She looked at him, her eyes wide, and felt that ball of panic squirming inside of her, so many worms and snakes. She nodded and his grip loosened. The taller man grabbed her backpack, and the three of them walked to the car.

"Where'd you think you were going to go?" Morales asked, his tone dark and mocking. They walked out the sliding doors and the taller man opened the door to a silver van that was parked in the unloading zone.

"I don't know if you can park here," Mae said quietly.

"Shut up." Morales spat.

The three of them climbed into the rear of the van, which had two bench seats facing each other. There was no driver, and Mae could only assume that the driver was still in the airport, looking for her.

The tall man sat next to Mae, keeping his large hand around the back of her neck, and Morales sat across from them. The van was cold, and Mae shivered as she sat, thinking that the warmth of the airport had been way too short lived.

Morales took his phone from his pocket and dialed a number. After a few seconds, he said, "I've got her. Rally the troops."

He put the phone into a little compartment near his armrest and clasped his hands together under his chin.

"Mae, Mae, Mae, flowers in May and showers in April, why did you run?"

She just stared at him, no expression on her face. Morales pulled the pistol from his holster and leveled it the girl. He smiled, rubbing the tip of the barrel with his thumb and middle finger.

"You know I just used this gun, not twenty minutes ago." He pulled out a box of bullets, .50 caliber hollow points, and started loading his clip.

"Used this baddy on your good friend, the ghetto bus driver. In fact, hang on …"

Morales rummaged around in his front shirt pocket and pulled out a crumpled piece of paper. He unfolded it slowly, methodically, and examined the picture she'd drawn there. He looked at her and smiled.

"Did you draw a nice picture for your ghetto driver?" he snickered, "'cause that was probably the last nice thing anyone did for him, that is, until I put one in his head."

Mae could feel the color draining from her face, could feel her stomach dropping as if in a slow motion free fall. The tall man sitting next to her chuckled—the first sound that Mae had ever heard from him—and she tried to squirm out of his grip. He tightened his clench on her neck, puller her close.

Not Nick.

She felt like she was going to vomit. All of the adrenaline and motivation that had kept her going from the dank room in the cabin, through the forest, and to the airport, drained from her. Her will to survive suddenly nose-dived.

Her dad and mom, so many others, and now Nick. A bus driver who'd done nothing other than help a lonely girl. They'd all been killed because of her. Because of what she was.

A terrorist, they said.

Click. Morales snapped the last round into his clip and shoved it back into the gun. He pointed it at her. She was about to close her eyes and give in ...

But she couldn't. She thought of the grey wolf waiting for Little Red Riding Hood, the beast on its hind legs, standing and watching for her at the edge of the forest. Its yellow eyes glinting in the moonlight, the sparkle of moist white teeth. She was the hunter, not the prey. She would not be a victim.

"Yes, the kindly old bus driver covered for you until the end," Morales said. He was smiling at the despair on her face. "I shot him right here."

He touched the barrel of his big gun to the center of his forehead, and grinned.

"And your mother, well, we weren't as nice to her, were we, Oskar?" he asked the tall man, who chuckled again.

"Please stop," Mae said in almost a whimper. "I don't want to hear any more."

"That's what happens when you run, little missy. People die. They die like your mother, like the ghetto bus driver, like in Miami. People die when you run."

Mae glowered at Morales, the hint of despair that she'd felt earlier now all but gone.

"You forgot about something," she whispered.

"Yeah?" He snapped off the gun's safety with his thumb. "And what is that, Mae flowers, April showers?"

The gun lowered, and Mae watched the barrel carefully.

"You forgot about him." She nodded to the window that ran along the door of the van. Morales followed her gaze, her bluff, for only a second, but it was long enough. Mae jutted her leg forward and kicked at the gun. Morales pulled the trigger, sending a bullet into Oskar's chest, the blast of the gun was deafening in such tight quarters. A blossom of red spouted on Oskar's shirt, and his hand tightened around Mae's neck for an agonizing second before going limp. Mae kicked at the gun again, knocking it from Morales' hand.

Morales swore as both he and Mae lunged for the weapon, but Mae sent an elbow into his face, knocking him backwards. She snatched the gun from the floor of the van, raised it and pumped two bullets into Morales' shoulder and one into his leg. He screamed in pain, clutching his arm. Blood squeezed between his fingers, and an expression of pure hatred splayed on his face. Mae leaned forward until she was just inches from his face, pressing the gun into his stomach.

"If you follow me, I'll kill you with your own gun," she said and reached for his phone with her free hand. She thought about killing him anyway, to give herself more time, but she heard her mother once again.

The hunters will never stop hunting, and you must never stop running.

"We'll find you, wherever you go." He said through clenched teeth.

"And I'll never stop running." She swung the butt of the pistol into Morales' temple, swung the gun hard, cracked it against the side of his head, and he went instantly unconscious. She sat back in her seat and took a deep breath. She checked her clothes to make sure no blood had splattered there. Mae noticed some drops of blood on her hair, the dark crimson a stark contrast to her blonde locks, and did her best to scrub it clean. She took her bag, the phone and the gun and climbed out of the van. She looked around and saw that the unloading zone of this particular gate was sparsely populated, and if anyone had heard the four shots from inside the van, no one was doing anything about it.

Mae walked back into the airport, slipping the gun and telephone into a trash can with a hollow clunk. She held back the tears as she pulled the borrowed passport and credit card from her bag.

She didn't cry until after she purchased a ticket and had gone through security. Mae didn't cry until she was at the departure gate, waiting for the plane to begin boarding. She turned away from the other people waiting for the same plane and leaned against the cold window where no one would see her face. Only then did she let the tears come.

Chapter Twenty-One

Paul dozed in a sitting position on the couch next to his desk, a manila folder opened on his lap, the same stack of papers lying on the coffee table before him. He was still in his office, not wanting to return to the empty room at the Monoco.

He jumped when his phone began to vibrate on the table. Paul rubbed his eyes and picked up the phone. It was Dennis calling. It was 1:12 AM, and he wondered if his assistant had gotten any sleep yet. Dennis was his third assistant in as many years and was shaping up to be the best of the bunch, mostly because he was as neurotic as Paul himself. Once he got onto something, he usually didn't let it go.

"Yeah?" Paul asked.

"First off, you owe me big," Dennis said while chewing something crunchy. Paul cringed at the sound.

"You gotta stop eating like that, or don't call until you're done."

"I haven't eaten since noon yesterday, and these chips are the only thing keeping me awake."

"Then go to sleep."

"I'm up 'cause of you," Dennis said, taking another bite and crunching loudly.

"Just tell me," Paul growled. His back ached from falling asleep on the couch.

"Got a strange blip on the radio." Dennis said and swallowed, "and you're gonna like this."

Paul sat up straight, stretching his back.

"Okay?"

"Well, it's kind of crazy that we were just talking about all this, because they just found an Officer Morales in the back of some van at the airport, shot three times."

"Dead?"

"Nope, the guy's still tickin', but in pretty bad shape, I'd imagine."

"Okay. What does that have to do with anything?" Paul said, hoping that he didn't sound too impatient.

"Well, I turned on the news, and this shooting is everywhere, and they—the news stations and media—are running little bios of the fallen police officer, you know, giving us all the emotional touch. Turns out this guy was a cop with the Miami PD."

The Miami connection was something, but not much. Certainly, it was too much of a leap to make any real connection, so he assumed Dennis wasn't finished. Paul hoped the punch line would come soon, as he was still feeling sleepy. He wanted to get this over with, and if what Dennis had to say wasn't that impressive, it could wait until morning.

"Do they know who did it?" Paul asked.

"No, but here's where it gets a little kooky," Dennis said, and took in another mouthful of chips. The fried potatoes crunched in Paul's ear, and he cringed.

"The same bus you were riding all night—you know, Route B Michigan Avenue—they found it a little ways from the airport, and the driver, an older gent named Nick Ambrose, was shot dead. Single bullet to the forehead."

Any sleepiness that Paul had felt a moment ago evaporated, and he felt sick about Nick. Of course, he hadn't known the bus driver before this evening, but he was a nice enough fellow. He whistled low and ran his hand through his hair.

"Any leads so far?"

"None that they're releasing to the public." Dennis took a drink of something and gulped loudly. On another occasion, Paul would have hung up on the guy, sure that Dennis was doing this just to piss him off, but he stayed on the line. After hours of riding the bus to meet the mysterious woman who'd never shown, and then spending more time going through the same stack of notes and documents that he'd gone through a thousand times before, he'd convinced himself that that something was going on, that he'd somehow stumbled into the middle of something much larger than he'd anticipated.

There was no discernible connection between the woman he was supposed to meet, the bus, and the cop from Miami, but he was sure that if he had all of the information, he would find one.

"So," Dennis said, "I'm thinking that whatever you've got up your sleeve is in full 'play' mode at the moment, and that the cop went to investigate the bus and then wound up sniffing where he should not have been sniffing. Or maybe this cop has something to do with our contact and her paranoia, I don't know, but I thought the coincidence was a little much to let slide."

"No, thanks for this. Who knows about coincidences anymore?" Paul said. He was pulling on his clothes now, a white shirt and dark slacks. "What hospital?"

"Northwestern Memorial," Dennis said, "but they won't let you see him, there's no way. Besides the fact that he is probably undergoing surgery, and is probably out like a light, he's still a cop, and they don't let just any shmoe off the streets see their downed cops."

"I'm not going to be just any shmoe off the street, Dennis." Paul was pulling his loafers on over his black socks—which socks he hadn't taken off for a day or two, and yet another thing that drove his ex-wife batty.

"I'll bet this Officer Morales has a cousin, visiting for the holidays, who is completely aghast at the fact that his favorite cousin is holed up in the hospital, all shot up, and no family at his side," Paul finished, transferring the phone from the crook of one shoulder to the other as he tied his laces. "I think I could be that cousin."

"Unless there is actually family at his side," Dennis said, "family who will know their strange cousins, I'm sure."

Paul shrugged but didn't respond. If Morales' family was at the hospital, so be it, but if not—people coming off anesthetics were the best people to gather information from. Maybe not all the information was accurate, but enough usually was to point in the right direction. He grabbed his keys and wallet and left the room.

"I'm getting into the elevator, so I'm going to sign off—" Paul said.

"Wait," Dennis said, his breathing heavy. Paul could picture him standing nervously in the center of his kitchen. "I know you don't have much to live for."

"Thanks—"

"But you've got to be careful. They killed a bus driver, for heaven's sakes. A bus driver, and they shot up a cop. Now, I'm not one to get all mushy, but I think you should tread a little softly."

"Thanks again," Paul said as the elevator dinged open. He could only wish it was so simple. He thought of the destruction in Miami, of the countless hours he'd spent obsessing over a conspiracy that he knew wasn't a theory. He thought of his marriage, of everything he'd sacrificed for answers.

"It's too late to tread softly, Dennis," Paul said.

Dennis was quiet for several seconds. The elevator doors had shut and the connection lost before he muttered, "I know."

Chapter Twenty-Two

The real Gertrude Pettingale—or Gerti, as she liked to be called, because she absolutely hated the name her parents had given her—paced in the tiny cinderblock room that was lit with bright fluorescent lights, and for what seemed like the zillionth time, checked her watch. Her blouse had dried already, although there was a large brown stain that covered a large portion of it. She crossed again to the tiny window in the metal door and looked out into the hallway which was equally bright. As was the same each time she'd looked through the window before, there was no one in the hallway.

Except for several large travel posters on the wall, the hallway was as bare as the room she was in. She looked at the posters and sighed. Each with a simple black frame, an easily recognizable landmark from around the world printed in bright colors, and large block letters announcing the name of the country. One of the posters depicted the Parthenon in Rome, which was where she was supposed to be in the morning— before all this other crummy business happened. The spilled coffee on her blouse was a rotten deal, but she could handle it—had handled much worse being spewed onto her shirt. But this...

Gerti sat down at the table and covered her face with her hands. She moved her fingers to her temple and rubbed them with slow circular movements. How could this have happened? She was supposed to be on the plane right now, sleeping away the long hours of flying over the Atlantic Ocean.

When she landed at Heathrow, she would have met up with a longtime friend who was teaching art history at a university in Paris, and together they would have traveled to Rome. She'd tried calling her friend—Claire was her name, but she liked to be called CeCe—and had left several messages trying to explain the situation. At best, she'd have her ex-husband, a loser named Simon, with whom she'd been married for close to eleven years, bring her a credit card, and she'd get to London tomorrow. Of course, Simon's credit cards were likely maxed out, but she could at least ask him, and she thought that he would lend her the money, even though he was borrowing it himself.

On the other hand, she was probably out of luck and would have to cancel the vacation altogether. The thought of cancelling the vacation was enough to make her feel sick. She'd been saving her money for months to go back to Europe, something she had frequently done with her ex. Their travelling, however, had almost always put them further and further into debt.

Once she'd cut the marriage string, she'd vowed to never use a credit card when she couldn't pay it off during the same month, which was another reason why she felt sick. When she'd called the credit card company to freeze her funds and cancel the credit cards, the polite customer service representative—who was far too cheerful for the situation, thank you very much—had told her that the thief had rung up more than $10,000 while purchasing multiple tickets at this very airport.

Gerti couldn't, for the life of her, figure out why someone would use her card to purchase five airplane tickets. Two of the tickets were domestic, and departed that night, and two more, international this time, departed the following morning. When Gerti demanded to know how a thief had rung up $10,000 within such a short period of time without the credit card company being alerted to the unusual spending, she was reminded that Gerti herself had called that morning and requested a limit increase for her cards over the next three weeks, on account of her vacation. The credit card company was now investigating Gerti for possible fraud.

"And isn't that just fabulous." Gerti muttered and put her forehead on the table in front of her. She ached for an aspirin and a glass or two or a bottle of chardonnay. Even a backrub and neck massage from Simon, clumsy as he was, would be welcome at the moment. She wanted to wake up from this nightmare and find that it was all just a product of her overactive imagination. She wanted to wake up in Rome, with a black Italian espresso and a biscotti, ready for a day of mixing with the locals and seeing the sights. She wanted—

The doorknob turned slowly, and the door was pushed open deliberately. Gerti raised her head from the table and saw the tall man standing in the doorway—no, not tall, gigantic was a better word. He looked at her with no expression on his face for several seconds, and then he smiled. He had deep scars on his face, and for some reason, the scars caught Gerti's attention more than anything about the man. Whatever had caused those scars had come close to gouging out his eyes.

"Ms.—" he said, pausing as he looked through a few pages in the manila folder he was carrying. His breathing was wet and raspy, and he favored his left shoulder as if it were injured.

"Pettingale," they both said at the same time, and Gerti burst out laughing. The man chuckled and entered the room.

"Oh, am I glad to see you," Gerti said. She stopped laughing when she heard a ring of panic and exasperation in her voice, and instead breathed a heavy sigh of relief.

"I'm sorry to have kept you waiting," he said and sat at the chair across from her. He laid out the folder and removed two small bundles of paper, stacking them neatly before him.

Yes, he was definitely favoring his left shoulder, and although he tried to mask it, he winced in pain when he moved.

"Well, I would probably be upset about waiting for so long—it's been more than an hour, you know—but the truth is, I just want to get out of here."

"Understood, ma'am," he said and rifled through one of the stacks of paper. "My name is Detective Stevenson, and I'm going to help you get on your way tonight. As you know, the airport has had quite a lot of excitement this evening, which is partly to blame for the extended wait time that you experienced, Ms. Pettingale."

"Please, it's Gerti."

"And you may call me Oskar," he said, nodding politely.

Gerti noted a distinct accent in the man's voice, despite his efforts to sound neutral. The accent was unfamiliar to Gerti, who considered herself well-traveled and well-versed in various accents from around the world.

"Another reason to blame for your waiting here is that we are in the airport, and by its very nature, you must wait in an airport."

He paused with an awkward smile on his face for several seconds before Gerti realized that this was a joke. She gave a courtesy chuckle, which seemed to make the large man very happy.

"You mentioned some trouble here at the airport," Gerti said when the chuckles had died down. "Are you referring to my stolen credit cards and passports?"

"Yes," Oskar said, his accent coming on a little thicker now. "It seems that a police officer was shot earlier this evening, in a van outside the airport, and we think that the shooter may have gotten away, possibly using your identification."

"Oh my goodness, that's horrible," Gerti said. "How did someone not notice a shooting before the shooter could get away?"

"The police van is armored, used to transport criminals. It's a double edged sword when it comes to the van—bullets won't go inside, but you can't hear anything from the inside either. They think that the shooter shot the cop, then calmly left the van."

"And you think the killer might have stolen my identification? But then it would have to be a woman, and with a cop, I don't know—"

"Shooter, not killer. The police officer, a Detective Morales, is still alive."

"Well, that's good at least, but I just don't think that the girl who stole my stuff was the shooter. It doesn't add up."

Gerti said this with a tone that she had used on Simon many times when she was sure of her superior logic and the improbability of his. The condescending tone drove Simon crazy, to the point where any discussion would more often than not escalate into a full-blown, explosive fight. But her tone seemed to have no effect on Oskar. He'd told her that he was a detective, but something was off about him. Something she couldn't quite place. Gerti suddenly grew suspicious of this man, who hadn't shown her a badge or anything for identification.

"Are you with the Chicago PD?" she asked.

The man didn't say anything, just looked at her for several long seconds. The awkward grin slowly disappeared as he studied her, from her hair to her eyes and then to her body. She squirmed in her seat and looked away.

He took a piece of paper from the stack and slid it across the table. Gerti looked at the page and saw a black and white picture printed in the center. The picture was grainy, but not so bad that she couldn't see who the woman was. She looked younger in the picture than she had tonight, with shorter hair that was darker—almost a femme fatal kind of look. She was carrying a bag over her shoulder and had a rectangular object in her hands. She was in midstride and appearing to be in a hurry, wherever she was going. The girl also appeared to be healthier, with a fuller figure and there was something about her eyes that seemed more ... bright?

"Yeah, that's the girl," Gerti said. She reached forward and tapped the picture with her forefinger and nodded. "At least, she's the one who spilled her drink all over me. I know that I had my wallet when I went into the coffee shop, and sometime between then and when I left the bathroom after cleaning up, my wallet was gone. Could have been someone in the bathroom, I don't know, but, yeah, I recognize her."

The man was silently staring at Gerti, his face expressionless, and Gerti wished he would try to make an awkward joke again. She wished Simon were there, too, and she chided herself for traveling alone.

But why is that? Her mind wondered. There isn't anything inherently dangerous about this situation, just a creepy guy who...

"Wait a second," Gerti said, that condescending tone slipping its way back into her voice. "You don't think that this girl was the one who knocked off that cop, do you? There is no way; the girl actually looks better and healthier in this picture than she did tonight. Not only was she much thinner, but she looked like she'd been through the ringer."

Oskar pulled the picture toward him and set it on top of the stack of papers. He pulled out a few more sheets and laid them in front of him. Gerti leaned forward and saw that the pages were printouts of ticket confirmations.

"What was your destination this evening, Ms. Pettingale?" Oskar asked. His raspy breathing was getting worse, and his accent was fuller now, as if he'd been trying to hide it before. That thought struck a chord in Gerti, and she suddenly wanted to be done with this man and this airport. Screw it, she just wanted to go home and forget about CeCe, and Rome, and the whole stupid vacation. This was way too weird, and it was getting weirder by the moment.

"Which is your ticket?" he said again, and the accent was strong. Scandinavian, she thought, maybe Norway or Sweden, but she wasn't overly familiar with those accents, as she'd never visited those countries.

"Uh ..." she cleared her throat, "London first, Heathrow International, and then on to Rome."

"Right," Oskar said, scanning the pages. He saw the ticket that Gerti had just identified and slid it away from the others. He then turned his attention to the remaining pages, and meticulously lined them up in a straight line on the table.

"Sir," Gerti said, and had to clear her throat again. "I don't see how I can be of any help to you right now. I'd like to just leave, if that is okay with you."

The man smiled quaintly.

"You've helped a great deal, Ms. Pettingale," he said, "because you see, this woman—" he motioned to the stack of papers—"this woman is a very dangerous psychopath who may appear weak and harmless, but has a penchant for killing innocent people, like she would have done to the police officer this evening, had she had a gun that didn't misfire. She is a ruthless monster, the epitome of a wolf in sheep's clothing, and you did help us narrow down where she's going next."

"I did?" Gerti asked.

"You did help in the investigation, and for that, I thank you," the man said, hints of the goofy grin coming back. Gerti felt a wave of relief wash over her as the inexplicable tension suddenly left the room. She wondered why she'd felt the anxiety—or even fear, if that was the right word. She didn't think it was actually fear, just the compounded stress of the day and a horrible set of circumstances.

Oskar reached into his jacket pocket and pulled out a cell phone, wincing with pain as he did. He tapped the screen and pulled up a number, then dialed. She waited patiently, hoping that it would be over soon, so she could call CeCe, and maybe even Simon.

"Gertrude Pettingale," was all he said. He ended the call and returned the phone to his jacket pocket. He stood up, and

Gerti started to do the same, but he waved for her to return to her seat.

"Please, sit down," he said.

"But aren't we finished?"

"We are." He paused, licking his lips. "Almost finished. Have you noticed how the cold air makes your lips dry?"

Gerti scowled at the abrupt awkwardness of the question. She started to say that yes, she did notice her lips drying out in the wintertime, but he continued talking without waiting for her response.

"Every year since I was a little boy, it is the same. The winter comes, the cold arrives and I marvel at how my skin dries almost instantly in the winter wind." He began to walk around the table, toward Gerti, and she felt her heart beating faster and faster, with each step closer, and then he was right behind her, and she held her breath until he continued on without touching her.

"I come from a country where it gets very cold each year, and to me, it was always so fascinating, such an intricate and tender mystery of the universe, that the moisture was sucked dry from the air by winter itself." He stopped on the other side of the table, directly in front of Gerti, and she watched him warily.

"I don't understand what this has to do with my cards and passport being stolen," Gerti said, and made the move to stand up again.

"Please sit down," Oskar said, smiling. His voice was soft and gentle, and the smile on his face was warm.

"I'd really like to go home and get some rest," Gerti said. "I'm tired and I need to figure out what's going on with my friend in London, and I'd really just like to put this day behind me. I feel like you are trying to get me to say something about chapped lips, but—"

"No," Oskar said, "I'm not trying to get you to say anything; it's just something that I've been thinking about. The cold and dry air and mysteries. Like you, for example. You woke up this morning with no idea that fate and chance would turn against you before the day was done. I woke up with no foreknowledge of our meeting, yet here we are, together in this room. You had no idea that your last few moments of life would unravel in a tiny room underneath an airport, and I, again, did not know that your last breaths would be spent with me. Another mystery in a world full of mysteries."

Gerti stood up quickly, knocking her chair to the ground. She picked up her purse and crossed to the door. She kept her eyes trained on him.

"Sit down," he said. Gerti stopped walking and turned slowly, shaking her head.

"Listen, I don't know who you are or what you are talking about. Maybe you're having a breakdown, with the stress and everything, but I've got to go."

"Sit down, Ms. Pettingale," he said. She hesitated, but then returned to her seat slowly.

"See there!" He clapped his hands together with bang.

"Another mystery! Here I am, telling you very clearly that I intend to see you die in this room, and yet you sit down when I ask you to sit down. Now why is that? Is it because you think of me in some authority position, like the police or security, and for fear of disobeying an authority figure, you disregard not only your instincts, but knowledge of what I just said? Or maybe you realize the futility of your situation? That if you sit here and try to play nice with me, that I will forget that I ever said that silly thing about you dying here, as just so much nonsense?"

His accent was very strong, and Gerti thought it must be Swedish. She looked at the door, only a few feet away, and knew that he was right. If he wanted to kill her, he could and would. She couldn't believe what she was thinking, couldn't believe how fast the situation had turned from awkward to horrifying. She wanted nothing more than to get out of the room and away from this psycho.

Screw Rome, and CeCe and Heathrow International, she wanted to be in her bed at home, preferably with Simon there and his arms around her, and their covers pulled up to their chins to protect against cold air.

Oskar reached into the pocket on his pants and pulled out a small metal case. He set it on the table and opened it, revealing a tiny hypodermic needle and a small vial of yellowish liquid.

"Please," she said, "I didn't do anything."

The man unscrewed the vial and placed the needle through the rubber stopper. He slowly filled the needle until there was only a few drops left in the vial. When he was sure that there were no air bubbles inside the syringe, he set the tiny bottle on the table and walked behind Gerti. He ran his fingers through her hair, leaned forward and breathed in deeply.

"I love the smell of apple scented shampoo. It reminds me of picking apples as a child," he said, his fingers now groping at her neck, feeling along the tender muscles and bones. His face was close to her ear, and she could feel his warm breath on her skin, softly contrasting with the rough calluses on his hands and fingers.

"Sir, please," she said, crying now, "I just want to go home. I have money, do you want money? I can pay, just give me a phone, and I'll pay!"

He stood behind her, needle in one hand, the other hand running through her hair. He cleared his throat, and spoke softly and gently, in a voice that was closer to that of a university professor than a crazed killer.

"Are you familiar with the word: utilitarian?" he asked.

She shook her head, afraid that if she opened her mouth, she would break down into more of a blubbering mess than she already was. She sat with her back straight, fighting the urge to cringe beneath his touch, his fingers now caressing the skin under her jaw. Her mind screamed to stand up and fight, to yell and shout until someone came running to her rescue, but it was all just so insane. It couldn't be happening, and especially not to her. She was an independent woman, divorced and living on her own terms, and these things happened in movies, not to her. The thoughts flitted through her mind in a panic, and several seconds passed before she realized that he was once again talking.

"—part of the greater good, and that is your privilege." Oskar spoke, his fingers now massaging her scalp, his manicured nails gently rubbing against her skin and hair, and she felt like screaming and throwing up, but he kept talking.

"You see, sometimes one has to die in order to save many. You look through history, even your country's recent history and you know that this is a hard truth, a cold truth, but a truth nonetheless. Your military kills innocent people as collaterals in a greater picture, to save many from their extremist brothers. Every day, someone who has done no harm, who is not involved, has to die, in order to create balance and harmony in the world, to prevent the sick psychopaths of society, the underbelly of all that is filthy and unwholesome, from exacting their goals on more innocents. They are heroes, those that die for the greater good, whether or not that realization sets in before their life slips away. They are heroes. And tonight, that person is you. You are the hero that will save many."

He eyed the needle, and held it close to her skin, holding the point on her neck just below her ear. "It will be painful, yes, but nothing that countless people have not gone through before. You will die knowing that you have not only served your country, but mankind, securing your immortality as a heroine in the war against terrorism."

Gerti listened to this and nearly jerked at the catch phrase she'd heard for more than a decade, spoken now with such frequency that it was diluted and nearly meaningless to most people outside of political circles. To hear it coming from this man—the man who was about to kill her, who had probably killed countless others, who was now lecturing her on the war against terrorism—it didn't make sense, but her mind was too full of adrenaline and panic and fear to register much more than the seeming inconsistency.

"Please," she said again, the sound of her voice fading into a whimper. "Please don't kill me. I'm not a terrorist, and I don't want to be a hero."

"They'll find you here in this room after a cardiac arrest, maybe caused by the stress, but certainly nothing out of the ordinary," he said, ignoring her pleas.

And it was that—the thought of some airport security guard, finding her dead and slumped on the cold metal table, the thought of Simon hearing the news and never knowing what had happened, that finally mobilized her.

Her scream finally found its voice, and the sound was ragged and hoarse. She thrust her entire body into the man's torso and jumped to her feet in the same motion. He jerked away from her, as if expecting her to have made this move, but he wasn't quick enough. Her head collided with his nose and chin, and she pressed the full weight of her body into his chest and injured shoulder. He screamed in pain and stumbled backwards. She left her purse and phone on the table and darted for the door. Oskar recovered quickly, but the wound in his chest was seeping blood through his shirt. He grabbed the metal chair in which she'd been sitting, and threw it at her feet, nearly knocking her to the ground.

She felt an explosion of pain at the same time that she heard a cracking of bone. She stumbled, but kept her balance, lunging for the door. She pulled the handle and swung it open, crashing into a security guard who was blocking the doorway.

The woman was big, not nearly as big as the man, though she had some meat on her. The guard's eyes widened when she saw Gerti, and her mouth gaped in surprise. Gerti fell forward into the woman's arms, screaming and crying hysterically. The woman made no effort to hold onto Gerti, and even tried to back away from her, as if she were a crazy woman.

"He's going to kill me; we've got to get out of here!" Gerti screamed.

The security guard pushed Gerti back into the room and drew her gun, pointing it at the big man, who was standing by the table and wiping a trickle of blood from the corner of his mouth. He was breathing heavily, his large chest and shoulders rising slowly with each breath. His eyes fell on the woman's name badge, which read "Lt. White."

"Stop right there!" Lt. White yelled, her service weapon in both hands and trained on the man's chest. Her eyes darted from the big man to Gerti, and then back again, taking in the situation.

Oskar sighed as if bored by the whole thing. He set the needle on the table and considered the situation. It was then that he noticed the blood on his shirt. He touched crimson area gingerly and shook his head, as if annoyed.

"Guess the easy way is out of the question," he said, sounding disappointed. "She'll have bruises now, and those will have to be explained. Which is good, because I wasn't much looking forward to the clean and *heroic* end that I was ordered to provide for Ms. Pettingale."

Gerti backed away from the man who'd tried to kill her. She couldn't stop thinking about the feel of his hands in her hair, and wondered why on earth she'd let it go on for so long. Gerti's whole body shook as the seconds passed, her heart pounding in her ears.

The woman stood silently for several more seconds and then lowered her gun, pushing the safety switch to the "on" position. She whistled as she returned the gun to the holster on her hip, clipping the small leather strap over the handle so it would stay in place. Gerti watched this with disbelief and rising fear, praying once again that it was all a dream.

"Whew-ee, man, you guys scared the livin' daylights outta me," she said, her voice loud and obnoxious. The man opened the tiny metal canister and replaced the needle he'd been about to stick into Gerti's neck.

"So, what are we—" Lt. White said. She nodded toward the growing splotch of red on his chest and said, "what happened to you? She do this?"

"I was shot," he grumbled as he removed another, smaller syringe from inside his jacket.

"Are you kidding me? How are you up and around?"

"For one, the bullet passed right through." He held up the syringe before sticking it in his arm. "And then there's epinephrine."

"I don't care what ya'll shooting up in your veins, you need to get off your feet and rest."

Oskar cringed at the woman's loud accent, visibly annoyed.

"Please stop talking," Oskar said, his voice lowered. "Any credibility you have as a security guard dies the moment you open your mouth, so please stop talking. Where they find you people, I'll never know."

Gerti's heart sank as the security guard obeyed him. She felt the blood and built-up adrenaline rush from her face and limbs, and could feel despair creeping in as the realization set.

"As I said before, the easy way out of this situation is now out of the question."

He pulled a gun from a holster at the small of his back and fired two shots into Lt. White. Gerti screamed, sliding up the wall and back into a standing position. Her hands were shaking, her face white. The sound of the gunshots and then Gerti's screams was deafening in the small room, but even then Oskar didn't think it would draw anyone's attention. They were underneath the airport, and with all the commotion topside, no one would be paying attention.

Gerti watched the man cross the room to the fallen security guard. He pulled a pair of latex gloves from a small leather compartment on Lt. White's belt and pulled one of the gloves onto his right hand. He took hold of her gun and put it in Lt. White's hand, aiming the barrel at Gerti.

"No ..." Gerti said, but the gunshot cut off any other sound.

He watched her fall to the floor with much the same fascination that he had when marveling at the cold, dry air that parched his lips. Gerti Pettingale, so alive the moment before, but weak and unwilling to survive.

Oskar stood and pulled his phone from his front pocket. He found the correct app on the touch screen and waited a few seconds for it to load while he knelt beside Gerti's lifeless body. Once the software was ready for input, he took Gerti's hand and was about to place her four fingers on the screen, when he paused. Blood dripped from the middle two fingers. He sighed and removed a handkerchief from his coat pocket, which he used to clean the blood as best he could. He put the handkerchief back in his pocket and placed her four fingers on the screen of his phone. A green grid lit the screen for several seconds, capturing her prints. He dropped her hand and punched a few keys buttons. There was a soft beeping sound and the word "Transmitting ..." appeared on the screen. He dialed a telephone number and held the phone to his ear. He heard a connecting click and began speaking without waiting for a greeting.

"Transmitting prints now. Assign the prints to the Morales shooting earlier this evening. Subject is dead, along with a field tech, a Lt. White. Subject was travelling abroad, not currently married. Establish a story about a possible drug connection in Europe and leak it to the media."

"Lt. White is dead?" the man on the other end sounded young. "She was assigned as backup."

"She's dead because too many people are involved," Oskar said. "Run the story of the police shooting tonight and direct all attention away from the escapee."

"Did you get any leads regarding her whereabouts?"

"We know she used Gerti Pettingale's name to purchase the tickets. If you run a cross check on the passengers who departed, we'll find her. Doesn't matter how many tickets she bought, she could only use one."

"I'll run the search now, and it should only take a few moments, if you'd like to wait."

Oskar did not respond, only stood and stepped over Lt. White to leave the room. He thought briefly about any fingerprints that he'd left behind, but his fingerprints would yield nothing in an investigation. He was a ghost. Anonymous.

"We have a Gertrude Pettingale who departed on Flight 191 to Hartford, Connecticut."

"That's her. Has her plane landed?" Oskar turned down a side hall and used an access card to pass through a set of heavy doors marked "Security Personnel Only."

"Lands in twenty minutes."

"Send a bulletin to that airplane only, have them check passports and tickets before they land. She'll use her stolen identity, of course, and it will give her the false sense of security that her trail is cold. She'll have no idea that we know exactly where she is."

"But sir, after landing, she can go anywhere."

"Not anywhere." Oskar said. He couldn't help but smile a little as he climbed into the security elevator that would take him topside to the airport. Just before the signal cut out from his phone, he finished.

"She's going home."

He put the phone into his pocket. He would follow Mae, but first he had some unfinished business.

Chapter Twenty-Three

Paper and ink, and tall trees towered over the forest floor, which was blanketed with fallen autumn leaves. The white and grey branches were almost bare but still had bunches of red and orange and yellow leaves. An occasional breeze would whip through the branches and rustle the leaves, causing some to float downward, while others clung stubbornly.

The air was cold and biting, but not so cold that it smelled of snow, and it had the spicy scent of smoke wafting from fireplaces not far off.

He took her by the hand and together they walked along the winding trail through the trees and fallen leaves. Logs lay on the ground, and some jutted out over the pathway, with darkening green moss growing on the damp, dead wood. The smell was earthy and inviting, a comforting smell for a reason she couldn't place.

Mae remembered the sounds of their feet crossing through the leaves, the whisp, whisp, whisp as they walked, the crackle of autumn breeze through leaves and nearly bare branches, the trickling of a stream.

Beneath those sounds of October, there was faint music. Mae turned toward the sound and listened. The music was unmistakable, but too soft and quiet to make out any melody. Yet it harmonized with the natural sounds, and the kaleidoscope of color all around.

The colors were like a melting box of crayons. She looked up through the trees and saw the clear azure sky overhead, the crisp autumn blue. Thin tendrils of brilliant white clouds reached across the sky, and a raven lifted on a gust of wind and glided away.

They came to a ridge that opened up over the valley, and as far she could see were rolling waves of mist and color.

"It's beautiful," she said and he squeezed her hand. A small red leaf with tiny splotches of yellow lifted up off the forest floor. The leaf floated and stood in place several inches in the air before being swept away by the cool autumn breeze.

"Do you think the others will be along soon?" she asked. They turned and saw the trail behind them empty. They could see several hundred meters behind them through the quiet trees and meadows.

"I think we have a few moments," he said and pulled her along the pathway. She took off running, kicking up black dirt and leaves in her wake, laughing. He ran after her, and when they got to the clearing, she turned and wrapped both arms around his neck. He leaned forward and kissed her gently on the lips. When he pulled away, she looked up at him with her big green eyes and smiled. They heard the sounds of laughter and talking as the rest of their group made their way to the trail. The oohs and aahs followed next, as the group stood on the ridge that overlooked the rolling hills.

"We don't have much time," he whispered and kissed her again on the corner of her mouth. They tightened their embrace, not wanting the moment to end. Another leaf, this one a rusted orange color, lifted up in the windless air and fluttered. Three more leaves followed, like droplets of water trickling over the edge of a dried waterfall, but in this case, with the droplets falling up, rather than down. If the girl had been paying attention to the woods and the floating leaves, she would have smelled and recognized a faint electric odor to the air, like the static smell of air in a clothes dryer. But she didn't notice, wouldn't have noticed any smells but the smell of him and his face, and the taste of his kiss.

As the kiss grew deeper and their embrace tighter, more leaves lifted and swirled, no longer fluttering and floating, but whirling around the couple in a warm cyclone. The soft music swelled in the distance as rocks and twigs lifted and trees swayed, but neither noticed anything but the taste of each other on their lips and the smell of her hair and the feel of his hands against the back of her neck, their bodies close. The trees creaked and groaned as the cyclone of swirling leaves and forest expanded outward for several meters, whirling through the branches and boulders. In the wooded canyon below, the thatches of fog and mist began to lift upward in droves, like rain falling to the sky.

She pulled away first, looking up into his eyes and then snuggling into the crook of his shoulder. They stood and held each other until the trees and leaves began to fade and the smell of the cool autumn air and the blue sky melted into the past. The feeling of his embrace was the last to go, the tender touch of his lips on hers.

And then she was in the dark, dank cabin in the woods, the dirty snow in drifts against the outside walls, the dead trees creaking and groaning in the brisk winter wind. The chair was leaning backward over the bathtub and she was choking, dying. The rope cut into her wrists as she struggled to get free.

Then the gunshot, so loud and final, blasted through the cabin, and she was running through the forest. The crack of the ice underfoot, the freezing water. But he still followed—right behind her and breathing down her neck. She tried to get away, but his fingers grasped at her hair and pulled her to the ground. And then he was standing over her like a black specter.

The grey wolf.

He lifted his boot and placed it on her throat and she could feel the mud and dirt caked into its sole as he pressed harder and harder on her neck. She couldn't breathe, and she struggled to get away, writhing beneath this man's weight and choking for air.

The expression on his face was wild and dirty, a thin hint of a smile on his lips as he pressed his boot down, down into her neck, the police officer named Morales.

Chapter Twenty-Four

Mae sat back in her chair with a gasp, waking from the memory dream with a start. She touched a painful line on the side of her face and felt the indent from where she'd been leaning against the window.

His name was Adam, and she hadn't thought about him for a very long time, so she was surprised that her dreams had wandered back to him. Adam was the boy she'd first loved growing up, the boy who'd first held her hand, the first boy she'd kissed. She remembered that mountain ridge, overlooking October. The same butterflies she felt when their lips had touched, when she'd tasted and smelled him, fluttered now.

His boot on her throat.

The dream was tainted and dark. The feeling of first loves faded, replaced with the dark memories of that night.

"You alright?" the guy sitting next to her asked. She looked over, startled to see someone there. When she'd fallen asleep, the plane was still almost completely empty and they'd been parked next to the airport. Now, she felt the faint vibrations of the airplane as it cut through the sky. The seats were filled with people reading, watching movies on their tiny screens, or sleeping. One of the men sleeping, his head leaned back against the seat and his mouth gaping, looked as though he'd just stepped out of a board meeting. His white shirt was clean and pressed, his tie was straight and perfectly dimpled, and he was still wearing his suit coat. The contrast between what he was wearing and his slack jaw caused Mae's eyes to linger a moment too long, and the guy sitting next to her chuckled.

"He was drooling earlier, and talking in his sleep," the guy said. "If I'd known that you were so entertained by sleeping businessmen, I would have woken you up."

Mae chuckled, but then realized that she may have been drooling herself. She instinctively touched the corners of her mouth and was dismayed to feel a bit of moisture there. She wiped at her cheek and neck, suddenly very embarrassed to be sitting next to this guy. He noticed her movements and laughed.

"Don't worry, you didn't drool that much." He reached over and pulled a few strands of hair away from her cheek. "Looks like you did get a little in your hair though," he said and then whispered, "and I promise not to tell anyone what you told me while you were sleeping."

She looked away and blushed. Mae probably should have been worried about anything she might have said in her sleep, even though she was pretty sure that the guy was joking, but she was more embarrassed by the drool than anything. She glanced back at the guy and saw that he was cute, maybe a little older than her, but cute nonetheless.

"How long was I asleep?" Mae asked finally, after a few seconds. She ran her hand through her hair and rubbed at the sleep mark on her forehead.

"Well, you were asleep when I got on, and I'd say that we're going to land pretty soon," he said. "You must have been really tired, because the take off was a little rough, and they've been blaring on and on over the plane's PA system about the bad weather and how we need to be in our seats, blah, blah, blah."

"Can I get you anything, Miss?" The steward stood in the aisle and smiled patiently. The name tag on the lapel of his blue vest said that his name was Lenny. His smile was kind, but had that faint undertone of someone who'd been wearing the smile for a bit too long. Even the blonde highlights in his spiked hair looked tired.

"Um, no," Mae said, still trying to clear the sleepy cobwebs from her head. The steward nodded and went back to his seat in the forward cabin.

"Nice customer service," Mae muttered and reached into her bag for a mint or a stick of gum. When she remembered that she had next to nothing in her bag, except for a stolen passport and credit card, she sat back, a little embarrassed.

"Yeah, the airlines like to at least pretend that they're interested in the customers in first class, so they can charge up the wazoo." The guy rolled his eyes and turned back to the magazine in his hands.

Oh right, I bought first class, Mae remembered and felt a tinge of guilt for spending so much on Ms. Pettingale's credit card. It was a multi-destination ticket, with the first stop in Hartford, Connecticut, and then flights to Boston, and New York City, even though she had no plans to continue flying. She thought it was a clever ruse at first, but anyone who'd caught onto the fact that she'd borrowed Gertrude Pettingale's identity would also see whether she'd checked into each of her flights. Still, it was enough to muddy the waters—hopefully long enough to disappear completely.

Gotta dump the card and passport, though, in a place where they will never be found. It would not be good to be caught with something that would surely draw attention to her. Even the passport and card, if found, would probably point them in the right direction.

Her heart raced at the thought and she felt a wave of panic wash over her. They would always be hunting, she had to remember that.

But she calmed herself, forcing deep breaths. She'd successfully made it out of O'Hare, and to the best of her knowledge, no one knew where she was. She wanted to keep it that way.

She glanced sideways as casually as she could and studied the guy sitting next to her. He had messy, jet-black hair that was a little too long, and he was wearing dark blue jeans and a white collared shirt. He had on a sports coat with patches on the elbows—a style that Mae thought was long gone, but was alive and well in the seat next to her.

He was skinny, but not so skinny that he looked like a starving bean pole. From the looks of him, even sitting down, he seemed to be tall. He was broad in the shoulders and his face had a hard, chiseled quality that was very alluring. Yet, his grey eyes, even as they scanned over the magazine, had a coldness that she didn't like. Or maybe it wasn't coldness, but apathy. Either way, she'd seen too many eyes like that in her life, especially in recent years, and with the coldness always came something bad. He crossed his legs and she saw that he was wearing dark leather boating shoes and white socks.

"You like what you see?" he asked, lowering the magazine to his lap.

"Um." She looked away, hiding her blush. It had been a long time since she'd talked to a guy that didn't want her dead, much less one who was definitely attractive.

"It's okay," he said. "I'm used to it."

It took her a moment to register what he'd said, and when it clicked, she turned with an incredulous scowl on her face.

"Excuse me?" She couldn't help herself. The guy just sat there with a smug smile. She stared at him a moment and then shook her head in disgust, wanting to slug him. "Used to what?"

"To girls checking me out."

He grinned a lopsided smile and she almost melted inside. He was attractive, for sure, but he knew it and that self-assured confidence made her squirm.

"You're a creep," she said, almost choking on the words. It was like looking at a beautiful painting and telling the artist that it was a piece of garbage.

The guy just smiled as if he hadn't heard what she'd said.

"And I wasn't checking you out."

"Hey," he said, spreading his arms in mock sincerity, "I'm just saying that I'm okay with that. I'm okay with being checked out. In other words, and just so you're comfortable with it, feel free to check me out."

She made a face and rolled her eyes, looking outside the window at the dark clouds in the night sky. Her face burned.

"You've got white socks on, that's all I was looking at. Your socks don't go with your shoes, but of course you would know that."

She tried to make her voice as scathing as possible, but it came out more like a whine. She blushed further and bit her upper lip. White socks? What was she thinking?

"I just happen to like white socks—or, rather, they were the only pair of socks on sale in the hotel marketplace."

He thought for a moment, but Mae could tell the guy was just making fun of her. He said, "I guess I lost my other socks—the ones you would have approved of and liked. Of course, I may not have packed the socks you would have approved of, or maybe I just took them off somewhere and didn't remember to put them back on. Bowling alley, maybe, or an ice skating rink. You know, I never like to wear my own socks with those rented shoes, just too grimy and icky—the ick factor is too much for me, so come to think of it, I probably didn't take them off at the bowling alley or ice skating rink. But hey, at least there I would have had socks that you approve of."

The guy just went on and on, and Mae was more annoyed with every word that spilled from his mouth.

"Listen, I don't care about your socks, or you, or anything you have to say. Please, just leave me alone."

"Oh. Okay," he said. "Ouch."

The plane dipped through the clouds, and twinkling lights lined the ground below. She was almost home. Mae could almost taste the familiar air and felt a burst of excitement. It'd been nearly ten years since she'd left those twinkling lights behind and she'd thought about them ever since. She'd been just a girl then, when she'd sat at the window and stared at the lights as they climbed higher and higher into the sky and away from everything she'd known.

Everyone she'd known. For a second, she wondered if she'd made the wrong decision in coming back, but it was probably the last place they would look for her. And they would be looking, just as sure as day.

She was born and raised in a small town named Great Barrington in western Massachusetts. It was nestled along the Housatonic River with the Berkshire Mountains rising to the east. Snow would blanket the ground there this time of year, and the thought of walking down Main Street while it snowed and the yellow street lights glowed in the cold sent a tickle of excitement down her back. Mae could almost smell the clean, cool winter, spiced with fireplace smoke, and the tickle grew.

It had been so many years and she could hardly wait. She was going home, and the excitement was enough to drive away the feelings of terror that had been so prevalent in her life these last few hours—as well as the onset of irritation that'd come in the last few minutes.

"So if you weren't checking me out, then what?" he interrupted her thoughts.

"Are you serious?" Mae couldn't believe the nerve of this guy. She no longer felt even the slightest bit embarrassed.

"Flight attendants, please prepare for landing," The pilot said over the PA system.

"Listen, I don't want to start a whole thing." He raised his hands as if being eminently reasonable. She rolled her eyes and looked out the window. The wings of the airplane were cutting through clouds in the dark sky, like a knife through cotton batting.

"You need to fasten your seatbelt," he said.

"I wasn't checking you out," she said too quickly, before realizing what he'd said. The guy grinned, showing perfectly straight and stainless teeth.

"You're the one talking about it, and that is just a-okay."

"You just need to get over yourself," Mae shot back, taking the ends of her seatbelt and slamming them together. The buckles didn't click the first time, so she tried it again with no success.

"I think you just slide the two ends together ..." He demonstrated with his seatbelt, that stupid grin still plastered on his face.

"Just shut up," Mae said in a harsh whisper, finally snapping the belt into place and shifting her body away from him. She leaned against the window and sighed, her breath misting the window before quickly fading. Her cheeks burned, and she hated sitting next to this guy.

"Leave me alone, please."

He raised his hands again, exasperated, and flipped open his magazine to the article he'd been reading. Mae felt the tug on her insides as the plane descended toward the runway, hitting a few bumps of weather as it dropped from the sky. Outside the window, the snowflakes whipped by as little white streaks. The plane jostled to one side, and Mae gripped the armrest.

"You scared?" the guy asked, and then smiled politely—like a waiter presenting her with a crusty crème brulee after a lobster dinner. He stuck out his hand and she noticed that his nails were almost perfectly trimmed and that his shirt had French cuffs with silver cuff links.

"Listen, I'm sorry that we got off on the wrong foot here—and let's just admit that the wrong foot was mistakenly clothed in a white sock that didn't match." He grinned.

"My name is Ryan Coffee," he said. "Coffee, like the drink. You know, the lifeblood of America, America runs on Dunkin,' the drill. To be honest, I hate the stuff, but sometimes you've got to just live up to your name, right? I like mine with loads of cream and sweetener, like the peppermint mocha. Tastes like Christmas in a cup."

She hesitated a moment, and then took his hand. The mention of coffee brought back thoughts of the poor woman in the coffee shop at the airport and the warm cup of wasted Americano. Not wasted, per se, but she longed for another sip.

Several seconds passed before she realized that he was waiting expectantly for her to respond, their hands still pumping in a handshake that had awkwardly gone on too long.

"I like your name, it reminds me of coffee." Her voice trailed off as she realized just how stupid it sounded. She laughed, and pulled her hand away, but the movement was somehow just as awkward as the never-ending handshake. He kept his hand in the air for a few seconds, his cuff links glinting in the dim light of the cabin. They seemed to have what looked like tiny rabbits engraved in the side. The closer she looked, the more she saw of the intricate design. Tiny, winged dragons offset the rabbits in a pattern, bursts of flame or smoke coming from their snouts.

He saw her looking, and he rolled his eyes, pulling the cuffs of his jacket over the links.

"Yeah, those," he said and pulled his hands away. He placed his hands in his lap, and then fidgeted, folding his arms and then unfolding them.

"They're really nice," Mae said. "A lot of detail for something so small."

She couldn't be sure, but his cheeks were slightly flushed. He sighed and shook his head at the same time, as if she was the most exasperating thing on the planet.

"My dad gave them to me," he said. "We had this big hoop-la in Chicago, him I mean, and he wanted me there."

Mae touched her old Timex watch without realizing it. Her thoughts drifted back to the day she'd turned twelve, to the red velvet sheet cake that her mom had picked up from the only bakery in town. She'd been very happy to get the watch, and so proud to wear it around school. As a kid, she'd felt very sophisticated with that watch, but now, she felt foolish.

"What does your dad do?" Mae said when she realized that he was waiting for her to say something.

"For work?"

"Yeah."

"Oh ..." Ryan exhaled. "I don't know. He's an investor, you know, one of those hedge-fund guys who preys on the weak-minded folks of America who like to use their credit cards a little too much. Essentially, he buys and sells debt, leverages other people's mistakes and regrets, and makes a boatload."

"Is that what you do?"

"No." He laughed. "No, I didn't follow in Pop's footsteps, much to his dismay."

"So what do you do?"

He smiled a little devilishly.

"I like to drive cars."

"Like race cars?"

"Kind of," he said, and smiled that smile again.

"Oh, cool," Mae said.

They sat in silence for a few moments. Ryan took a sip from a bottle of water he had shoved into the back seat pocket, and pulled out a folded package of peanuts that the flight crew had apparently handed out earlier. He palmed a few honey-roasted nuts and slid them into his mouth. Mae watched his jaw move, admiring his chiseled features with a day's worth of stubble on his cheek.

"And you?" he asked when he'd swallowed the nuts.

"Oh." She stared at her fingernails, still dirty from her little jaunt in the woods.

"My dad's dead," she blurted.

Ryan paused, taken back by her quick response.

"I was asking your name," he said, "but I'm sorry to hear that about your dad."

"I'm Mae."

"Mae." He smiled and nodded approvingly. "Just Mae?"

"Mae Edwards, no middle name or anything," she said.

"Okay. Like April showers bringing May flowers, eh?"

Mae felt a chill as he said that, remembering Morales. She grinned nervously and tried to appear normal, even though she was screaming underneath the calm.

The plane suddenly leveled out and then started climbing back into the sky. Both Mae and Ryan felt the change in direction and looked toward the front of the plane, where everything seemed normal. Mae felt a twinge of panic returning and prayed that the plane would land safely, and that she could get away from the airport. She knew that they had probably figured out that she'd left on an airplane and were now sending their feelers out to the various planes that had taken off in the last few hours. She didn't know the full extent of power that they had, but thus far, they'd been quite resourceful in tracking her down.

"Excuse me, ladies and gentlemen," a voice said over the plane's PA system. "This is your captain speaking. We will have a short delay in the air—should last only a few minutes, but the runways are a little overcrowded at the moment. Again, should only be a few minutes, and we'll have you safely on the ground in no time."

"You see, you're not the most annoying thing that has happened to me on this flight," Ryan said, nodding toward the cockpit. "Apparently we have a bunch of incompetents who can't fly this plane, or a bunch of dumb nuts that can't organize a landing pattern—so get ready, we might just see this big bird burst into flames when it touches down, rolling end over end, and crushing everyone inside of it."

"Oh!" an older woman said from across the aisle. She was dressed in an extremely loud purple pant suit with a matching purple and gold giraffe pinned to the lapel of her jacket. Her white hair was styled into loose curls that stuck every which-way out of her scalp. Her makeup was applied in thick gobs, reddish-purple blush and bold crimson lipstick. She glared at Ryan over a set of thick-framed reading glasses with a gaze that would melt ice.

"Ma'am." Ryan bowed his head ever so slightly, not even close to being phased. The tilt of his head reminded Mae of a how a cowboy would greet an elderly lady sitting on a stool outside the market in an old-west mining town. He was trying to be funny, probably for Mae's benefit, but she saw that same, self-assured smugness in his eyes.

When he turned back to Mae, he continued, "as I was saying, the plane, well, if they can even get it to the runway without the wings being ripped off the body—"

"I think we got the idea," Mae said quickly. The old lady across the aisle looked pale, and either frightened or angry—Mae couldn't tell which. Her body was trembling, and her lips were pressed together in a thin line. The old lady seemed ready to jump up and start throwing punches. The last thing Mae needed right then, was more attention drawn to her. She watched the steward and stewardess at the front of the plane unbuckle their seatbelts and stand. They looked confused, as if they didn't know how to handle the delay. The steward pulled a telephone handset from a little compartment near a storage bin and spoke into the mouthpiece. Mae watched his lips, but lip-reading was a skill in which she was drastically underdeveloped.

"I wonder what's going on," she said, more to herself. Ryan looked up from his magazine and shrugged.

"Probably they tagged some terrorist and want to make sure they ID the freak before they bag 'em. But then again, the longer we're in the air, the more time the terrorist freak has to praise his god and ignite his skivvies."

A man dressed in a blue suit stood up from somewhere behind her and approached the front of the plane. He pulled something Mae couldn't see from the front pocket of his jacket and showed it to the steward, who hung up the telephone receiver and looked with rapt attention at him.

"And there's an air marshal," Ryan whispered, leaning close enough to Mae that she could smell his cologne. "Probably just letting them know he's around and available if said skivvies terrorist drops his pants."

Sure enough, the marshal spoke to the flight crew for a moment before hitching up his pants like the sheriff who had just rolled into town, and returning to his seat. He glanced at Mae, and she quickly looked away, praying that the glance had been random.

"You really think there is something going on?"

"Yeah, I'm sure they got someone here who is tickling their fancy," Ryan said, his voice low as he watched the whole exchange and made no effort to hide it.

Mae felt sick to her stomach. "Why wouldn't they just land it?"

"I don't know," Ryan said. "Maybe they're taking a utilitarian approach to the whole terrorist thing until they're sure that whatever ... device ... got smuggled on the plane isn't going to blow up the whole freakin' airport."

Mae opened her mouth to say something, but thought better of it. She touched her backpack with her foot, knowing the iPod was there.

The door to the cockpit opened and a man stepped out. Mae couldn't tell if it was the captain or co-pilot, but she didn't think it mattered. He had a piece of paper in his hand, which he kept turned away from the passengers. The man called the stewardess and steward over to him, and they stood shoulder to shoulder with him as he pointed at the page.

The crew studied the page and then looked up at the passengers, scanning the faces of those that they could see from the front of the plane. Mae looked around to see if any of the other passengers were watching. Most were either staring dumbly into their laps or out the windows, or they were asleep, their heads leaning back against the grimy headrests. The few people that were awake glanced towards the front casually but didn't notice the flight crew staring back at them.

Mae sank lower in her seat and watched from the space between the two seats in front of her. What could they possibly have? Her name, social security number, maybe a picture. Her hunters would not release much information on her, for fear of inciting a panic. No, they would need to move within their own circles, to keep the information about her as close to the chest as possible.

She sat back up in her seat, pulled the in flight magazine from the seat pocket in front of her and began to flip the pages. Over the top of the magazine, she studied the flight crew. The steward studied the page, then looked up at her. Their eyes met for a moment before she turned away.

Mae looked at the magazine, but listened intently instead of reading. Over the whirr of the engines, she could make out the flight crew talking, but only heard snippets of their conversation.

"Not … draw attention … panic …"

"Passports …" the steward said, and then folded the piece of paper. He nodded at the two women, and both left the front cabin. Mae turned slightly and saw one of the women walk to the rear of the cabin and started talking to the passengers. The other stewardess started with the front rows of the main cabin, and people reached into their bags, producing their passports and boarding passes. The stewardess would look over the ID and ticket, and then smile warmly as if she was sorry to have bothered the passenger.

"Your passport and boarding pass, sir?" the steward asked Ryan, startling Mae. She'd been so busy watching the flight attendants in the rear of the airplane, that she hadn't noticed the steward working his way back through the first class section. The steward looked past Ryan and smiled at her, but his smile was tired and worn. Ryan leaned down into his bag—a leather attaché case—and pulled out his passport, grumbling all the way.

"What's going on?" Ryan demanded as the steward opened the passport and studied the picture there, and then compared the name with the name on the boarding pass. "You all saw my ticket and picture ID before we got on the plane and that was after spending an hour in the security line. This is just ridiculous. Why can't you just do this as we're leaving the plane?"

"We are taking some precautionary measures before we land," the steward said and handed the passport and ticket back to Ryan. He grunted and slid them into his bag.

"That's stupid."

"I'm sorry for the inconvenience, sir." The steward said, and then held out his hand to Mae.

"Take the lovely young lady you're harassing at this very moment," Ryan said. "You think she's some sort of terrorist? You think she's going to land herself a harem of virgins? I mean, look at her. She's as blonde-haired and blue—oh wait, those are green—but about as American as you can be."

With his mention of the word 'terrorist,' the old lady across the aisle paled. Mae saw this, and so did Ryan, who gestured in her direction.

"And the elderly here are getting restless and scared. Is this any way to treat the golden-aged passengers on your plane?"

The steward nodded at the old woman, giving her a look that tried to apologize for Ryan's behavior. Ryan was unconsciously distracting the steward from Mae, and for the first time, she was glad to be sitting next to the obnoxious and self-entitled punk. She pulled out her passport and ticket and handed it to the man, who took it and studied it carefully.

"You colored your hair," he said and smiled approvingly.

"Actually, the blond is my natural color—I went brown for awhile, and then just couldn't stand it."

"Okay, so we're going to swap hairstyling tips now? Great," Ryan said and rubbed his eyes. "You know, I've got an important meeting that I'm going to miss if you guys don't get your act together and let us off this monster."

"Well, I think it looks very nice," the steward said, doing his best to maintain the fake smile and ignore Ryan.

"I once bleached my hair with hydrogen peroxide, but it didn't turn out as good as hers. But then again, I wear white socks."

"Thank you, Ms. Pettingale," the steward said and handed the passport and ticket back to her. Ryan stopped talking and his eyebrows arched when he heard the name she'd just been called. He opened his mouth, his eyes questioning, but Mae shook her head ever so slightly. He paused, and then stared in his lap. At least it shut him up, Mae thought.

"Here you go, Miss," the steward said, motioning with the passport. She smiled and took it quickly to mask her shaking hands. The steward kept his eyes on her a moment longer, the briefest hesitation, before turning away. Mae watched him move on to the lady across the aisle, who still looked as though death were upon them all.

"Ms. Pettingale?" Ryan said. The confidence had faded and he no longer seemed as sure of himself as he had been throughout their entire encounter. He looked at her, looking more confused than anything.

"Please don't talk to me," Mae said. She felt horrible, knowing that he knew that she'd lied. She watched the look of hurt first come into his eyes, and then get moved aside as he shrugged with a half smile, opened his magazine and began to read again.

Mae sat in her chair for several seconds, then reached down into her bag and pulled out the small notebook containing her drawings. She closed her eyes and pictured the autumn ridge where she'd first been given a kiss. But this time it wasn't Adam who held her in his arms. No matter what she did, it was Ryan's face.

Paper and ink.

She uncapped her black felt-tip pen and touched the point to a blank page.

Chapter Twenty-Five

Morales opened his eyes and the world flooded back to him in one big gush. The room was dark except for a single white bulb that glowed from its fixture on the ceiling a few meters from where he lay. The air in the room smelled fresh, but had a faint chemical undercurrent, like a room that has just been cleaned and then aired with open windows.

He heard a rhythmic whoosh of air to his left, and a soft beeping. He tried to turn toward the sound but couldn't move his head. He lifted his fingers and touched the hard plastic brace that kept his neck and head in place. He moved his hand to where he could see it and saw a clear tube that entered a vein at his wrist, held in place by white medical tape. He tried to lift his other arm but found that it was also held immobile.

Morales closed his eyes and pushed the whooshing and beeping sounds from his mind, thinking back to the moments before waking in the hospital. He remembered the cabin in the woods, the snow falling all around him, and the biting cold in his toes and fingers.

Three gunshots, and the punctured glass—but of what? He thought hard, straining his mind to find and settle on the memory that seemed just out of reach. There was a road and rumbling sound in the distance, and the squeal of brakes.

The bus, Route B, Michigan Ave.

He saw the bus in his mind's eye, and the girl climbing aboard, and Eddie pumping three bullets into the front windshield of the bus. He heard the click of his Desert Eagle and the whispered gunshot that followed, saw Eddie sprawl onto his back, and the girl, the girl who'd managed to slip through his fingers like running water, and it all came flooding back to him. He remembered her in the airport, remembered her in the van. His stomach dropped all over again when he remembered her holding the gun under his chin and whispering threats with her snake-like hiss.

Bright lights, nurses, the sound of rushing feet over a tiled floor, the squeak of the gurney, the surgical masks and goggled eyes peering over him, all blurred together, and even though he tried, he could not remember anything specific following the girl's escape in the van.

She'd escaped again, he thought, and the taste of it was bitter in his mouth. She'd escaped and here he was, stuck in a bed and helpless. He opened his eyes and looked at the walls above him, settling on a round clock just inside his peripheral vision. Twenty-three minutes past two A.M. In the middle of the night, he thought, or hoped. If he'd slept through the night, then he'd have a much larger problem on his hands. The room was windowless, but it felt like the dead of night to him. Of course, there was no telling how long he'd been out.

He gingerly moved the fingers of his free hand from the brace around his neck to the wound in his shoulder. He touched the bandages that were taped there, whispering a curse under his breath. He left the wound and felt for the button that would have been placed next to his free hand. When he found it, he mashed the button and waited. After several seconds, the door to his room opened and a nurse entered.

"Sir?" the nurse said as she crossed to the machinery next to his bed and checked the data readouts. "What can I do for you?"

"What happened?" Morales said, being careful to sound genuine.

She studied him as if trying to figure out if he was serious.

"You were shot," she said, her eyes pitying, "and you've got some nasty bruises on your face."

"Where was I?" he touched his forehead and feigned a brief spout of dizziness. "I ... I don't remember much."

"And no one can blame you for that, sir," she said, concerned. "You were in a van just outside the airport, parked in the unloading lane. The airport security found you unconscious and bleeding. It was lucky that they found you when they did, or you might well have bled out."

"Alone?"

"No, they think that there was someone else who was shot, because of the blood—at least that's what I hear. Anyway, airport security didn't know you were a police officer until the station put out a notice that you went missing after investigating another matter. It isn't entirely clear, from what I've heard."

"Oh," he said, his mind reeling. "And is there anyone here from the police department?"

"Yes, sir," she said and wrapped a blood pressure band around his arm. Once the band was fastened, she pressed a button on the console next to his bed and the band began to inflate. "The chief of police set two officers outside your door for protection, in case the psycho who shot you up in the first place showed up to finish the job, and there are a few others, friends of yours I think, who are still here as well."

"That's good," Morales said, licking his dry and chapped lips. He wanted a cigarette like nothing else in the world, craved even the feel of it in his lips.

"Do you want me to let some of them come in for a visit?" she asked.

He shook his head, and thought about who might be at the hospital, waiting for his recovery.

The thought didn't sit well with him. As far as friends in uniform that he might have, they would have been few and far between. He'd been with the Chicago PD for two-and-half years, transferring into the force as a detective from the Miami PD, where he'd served South Florida for eleven years. This was, of course, fabrication, mixed with truth. Even though he was a decorated detective, he did very little police work, only enough to maintain the façade.

Morales reported to the Deputy Chief of Police, who took care of paperwork, making it seem as though Morales was a contributing member of the force. Morales had no idea to what extent the Deputy Chief was involved in his work with Il Contionum, but regardless of his role, he cleared the way for Morales to lay low and do his job. To that end, Morales knew few officers on the force. Most assumed that he worked for Internal Affairs, and for most, that was enough to give him a wide berth.

Even if there were cops waiting to see if he was okay, the chance was too great that at least one of them was not who they said they were. Of course, nothing could rally the brotherhood of police officers like a brother fallen to a gunshot, but the risk was too great. He was a sitting duck there on the hospital bed, unable to move.

"Am I going to be alright?" Morales asked. He tried to mask the rising anxiety in his voice, and it worked, coming off as timid and slightly pathetic. The nurse smiled sympathetically, and shook her head like a mother admiring her child who is just so cute.

"You'll be right as rain, but it'll take awhile," the nurse said. "The bullet passed through and missed everything that would have been cause for concern. I imagine that you'll be up on your feet in a few weeks, no more than that."

Morales sighed and wondered if he should just get up and walk out of the hospital himself. Sure, it might make things worse as far as his body was concerned, but he knew that there were people on the outside who would be impatient.

Very impatient, and wondering just where the girl had gone and how he'd let her slip away twice in one evening. He had to focus very hard on keeping the red rage at bay, to keep the anger from clouding his thoughts. He needed to be alert and ready for whoever was sent to take care of him in much the same way that he'd taken care of Eddie.

"Anything else I can do for you?" the nurse asked, and Morales shook his head. She smiled and left the room, closing the door and leaving him in semi-darkness. He lay on his bed and looked at the ceiling tiles above, listening to the soft beeps of the machines.

The telephone rang on the night table beside his bed, and he jumped, startled. A jolt of pain burst in his shoulder, and he cried out. The phone was placed within easy reach of his free hand, so he quickly lifted the receiver from its cradle and brought it to his ear.

"Hello?" he said, but the only sound in response was a thin line of static. With each second that passed, the feeling in his gut grew heavier. His heart raced, and the pounding in his head worsened. His mouth suddenly felt dry and tasted like the head of a match. He swallowed with difficulty and pressed the phone into his ear.

"Hello?" he said again, and forced the panic from rising. This time he heard a long release of air, like the sound of someone sighing heavily into the phone.

"Harrison? Is that you? Listen, I'll get the girl," Morales said. He hesitated, then slammed the phone in its cradle. He exhaled slowly through pursed lips and closed his eyes. He rubbed the fingers of his free hand against his eyelids. The caller had to be Harrison, the boss of this operation, calling to confirm that Morales was indeed still alive.

The door swung open, and a man quickly stepped inside and shut the door. He was dressed in a blue dress shirt with the sleeves rolled to just below the elbows. He had thinning hair that was a just a shade away from grey, and his belly, though not substantial, protruded from beneath his shirt. He peered at Morales with his back to the door, his chest moving up and down in rhythm with his quick breathing.

Morales, on the other hand, was holding his breath, hoping that the end would come quickly, but knowing that he might not have such luck. A few years before, while still working in Florida, he'd slipped into the bedroom of a very sick congressman. Much like Morales now, the congressman was bedridden, with tubes running in and out of his body. The man was just shy of 50 years old, according to Morales' intelligence report, and much too young to die. He was married with three children, two of them in college and the oldest in medical school. Like the congressman, the wife was a lawyer—they'd met and fallen in love in law school, and she was asleep on the sofa in the next room when Morales arrived.

None of that mattered to Morales when he came into the room and shook the man awake from his drug induced slumber. Shaking his shoulders didn't do much to rouse the man from grogginess, so Morales had broken open a small paper tube of smelling salts beneath the man's nose.

A few seconds after his eyes had opened and focused on Morales, he'd known what was coming. His eyes were wide, and he tried to scream out, but Morales held his hand over the man's mouth and leaned closer, whispering to him to keep his honor and not wake his wife, or she would have to die as well. That shut the congressman's mouth, and he watched, wide-eyed, as Morales inserted a syringe into the IV that ran into the man's wrist. He smiled at the congressman as he pressed the syringe and watched the potassium chloride solution first enter the IV, then drip into the man's bloodstream. It was the same solution used in lethal injections, but unlike state-condoned executions, the congressman's heart would stop without the benefit of a prior injection of pentobarbital and pancuronium bromide, drugs that made the person fall asleep before their heart was stopped, making the exit from this world much more peaceful.

It took about thirty seconds before the congressman went into cardiac arrest. The pain and panic spread out over his face, and his eyes shone with fear, but his gaze never faltered. Despite the flooding and flittering fear in his eyes, the congressman stared at Morales until the life slipped from his body. He kept his honor.

Morales stared back, smiling but devoid of emotion. Morales had not known why the man had to die, only that the orders had come, and he had obeyed.

When it was over, Morales reached forward and closed the eyes with his thumb. Even though the man's life was gone from those eyes, the fear had remained, and it was unsettling.

And now, Morales waited for the injection, or a silenced bullet to the brain that would end his own life. He'd always known that it would come to this. You didn't run with the wolves to die of old age in a retirement home. You ran for the thrills and chills, and when the end came—thrilling as it may be—it would always be harsh and too soon. He fingered the nurse call button, but knew that even if he did call the nurse, it would likely just get her killed as well. In the end, there wasn't much he could do to stop the inevitable.

Morales stared with a cool hardness in his eyes at the man leaning against the door. He was afraid, but would not let the fear invade his eyes. He promised himself that there would be no fear on the outside for this assassin to relish.

The man stepped into the light, crossing the room quickly and extending his hand. He lowered it quickly when he saw that Morales made no effort to return the gesture. A faint scent of cinnamon came with him as he pulled the nurse's call button away from Morales' reach. He stood before Morales, panting.

"I'm Paul Freemont," the man said. "And I think I know who shot you."

Chapter Twenty-Six

"Excuse me?" the man in the bed asked, and Paul hoped that it was the policeman who'd been shot. Of course, with the police officers guarding his door, chances were good that this was indeed Officer Morales. Paul's heart pounded, and he felt the adrenaline rushing through his body. One of the policemen was flirting with a nurse at the nurses station a few doors down from Morales', and the other officer had left briefly to use the john. When the officer had asked his partner to guard the door while he was away, the one flirting with the nurse had summarily dismissed him.

Paul didn't blame the guy. The nurse was cute and seemed to like the attention she was getting from the policeman. He'd been watching the scene unfold from a chair near the elevators, and when he saw one officer leave, and the other occupied with the nurse, he made his move. He pulled out his phone and pretended to be listening as he walked directly into Morales' room, not even getting a second glance from the police officer.

"I think I know who shot you," he said again. "Well, not exactly, but there has been some weird stuff going on that you may have gotten involved in."

"Who are you?" Morales tried to sit up, but the brace on his neck made it very difficult. He instead fingered the nurse call button, hesitating before pressing down. The expression on his face was weird, and Paul figured that Morales had been waiting for someone else, or was not sure if Paul was the person he was waiting for.

"Listen, I know you've been hurt this evening and are probably not wanting any visitors. I'm a friend though, a reporter—and this is off the record completely. I just need some information."

Morales let the nurse call button drop to the sheets, and his tensed body relaxed. He glanced at the phone and then back at Paul.

"How did you get in here?" he asked. "I thought my room was being guarded."

"There were some policemen guarding your room, yes, and they might be back, but I, ah, took some liberties to get in here."

"I can see that."

Paul stepped forward, getting a better view of Morales as he lay in the bed. He had some nasty bruises on the side of his face, a brace around his neck and bandages over his shoulder. Despite the heavy bandaging, he did not look as bad as Paul was expecting.

"So?" Morales said, a hint of impatience in his voice. "You've got information?"

"Yeah," Paul said. "I think I do."

"Well, let's hear it," Morales said. "The night is waning and I'd really like to get some sleep before I get any more visitors."

"You mind if I sit?" Paul asked. Morales shook his head, and Paul crossed to the officer's bedside and sat in the chair.

"I was on a bus this evening," Paul started, noticing that Morales stiffened slightly.

"I'm not going to tell you all the details as to why I was on the bus, but I rode the route several times this evening, and the route went nowhere near the airport where you were ..."

"Shot," Morales finished.

"Shot." Paul shifted nervously in his chair. He realized that as good as his idea had sounded in his head, it didn't make much sense for him to be here in this room with Morales. The more he thought about it, the more he wondered why he'd actually decided to come. There were coincidences yes, but maybe the logical leap from fact to fact was too great for the coincidence to be more than just that.

"I got off the bus a few hours ago, and this evening while watching the news, I saw that the very bus I'd been riding on was found near the airport, the driver shot dead."

Paul took a breath and paused to let this sink in.

"Now, I think that the shooting on that bus may be connected to your shooting somehow. I think that the shooter may have forced the driver to the airport, maybe to find you, or maybe for some other reason. After shooting you, I believe that he continued on the bus, away from the airport, where he shot the driver."

"This is all the information you've got?" Morales said, his eyebrow raised.

"I think there is a connection there, yes," Paul said.

"If the shooter hijacked a bus to take him to the airport, then why would he get back on the bus? The way I see it, if you're going to the airport, you're on the run."

"Unless he had business at the airport, something to pick up, or drop off, I don't know." Fatigue was setting in, and Paul was having a hard time keeping up with the story. Morales wasn't buying it, he could tell.

"So," Morales said, "assuming this guy had some sort of business to take care of at the airport—an assumption that would not usually fly, but I'll give your idea a whirl because I don't feel much like arguing. Assuming he takes care of his business, hops back on the hijacked bus that is patiently waiting, and then drives to the interstate."

"I'll admit that—"

"It doesn't make sense, Mister—"

"Freemont."

"Mr. Freemont, I appreciate your time and passion in coming to the hospital, but I'm going to have to ask you to leave."

Paul opened his mouth to say more, but hesitated. The calm look that had been on Morales' face throughout their conversation had been replaced. Morales' jaw was set, and the muscles in his cheeks clenched. His gaze was steely, and Paul could tell that he was finished talking. He stood up and made a move to the door, but then stopped.

What have I got to lose? he thought. Paul turned back to Morales, whose hardened look had not changed.

"I know about Miami," Paul said. "I know that what happened there, and what happened here tonight, are connected somehow. I know that you are somehow involved in all this, a cover-up or something, but I will find out the truth."

Morales flinched, and it was enough for Paul to know that his gamble had paid off.

"I don't know what you're talking about," Morales said.

"I think you do. I think you're hiding something, and I'm going to find out what it is." Paul turned for the second time to leave the room.

"Mr. Freemont," Morales said, but Paul didn't stop. The seed was planted, and he figured that if Morales knew something, or had been involved in whatever cover-up had happened, he would come to Paul.

Paul left the room quickly, and was happy to see that the policeman had not yet returned to guard Morales' door. He looked down the hall toward the nurses station and saw that it was empty.

Paul chuckled. Maybe things had progressed quickly between the cop and the nurse, and they'd decided to take advantage of an empty room.

The shadow on the polished linoleum floor of an approaching figure caught Paul's eye. The figure was rounding the corner from the hallway down where the first policeman had gone to use the restroom.

Paul hesitated, but for only a moment before ducking into the darkened room across the hallway from Morales' room, just in time to miss being seen by the approaching officer. His heart thudded loudly, and he had to force his breathing to be slow and steady.

Paul waited in the shadows for the policeman to appear, hoping that the officer would step in to check on Morales before setting up post outside the door. If the officer didn't go into the room, Paul realized that he may be stuck in the dark, empty room until the guards gave him another break. If he left the room now, no matter how confidently he strode past the guards, he'd look pretty suspicious.

The policeman's footsteps echoed down the hallway, getting closer, and Paul wondered why the area was suddenly so quiet. He held his breath as a shadow fell across the floor directly in front of Morales' room, and then the figure appeared, pausing before entering the room.

The man standing there wasn't the cop that had been guarding the door. Paul couldn't tell if the guy was even a cop. The man was very tall and had broad shoulders. He was wearing a suit and carrying a briefcase. To Paul, he looked kind of like a businessman, or a government agent of some sort, which was strange, given the hour.

Finally, the man turned the door handle and pushed open the door. He heard some stirrings in the room before the door closed, and Paul breathed a sigh of relief. He wasn't caught, at least not yet. There were still the policeman-guards to worry about.

He left the dark room and walked quickly down the hall, which was empty. It didn't strike him as too strange, as only the nurse at the nurse's station and the two policemen had been there before. There'd been some orderlies passing through, and maybe a janitor or two, but for the most part, the floor had been empty.

Paul pushed the "down" button to the elevator and waited. Something caught his eye near the nurses station, a small movement. He stepped to the side to get a better look at what it was, and then froze.

A hand and arm lay extended from behind the nurse's station, the fingers curled and twitching. The fingernails were painted a faded red, and a woman's tennis bracelet hung from the wrist. His heart leapt, and a sinking dread filled him as he rushed around desk. Both the nurse and the police officer were on the ground in a heap, blood pooled around their bodies. Both were clearly dead, the nurse's fingers twitching as the last of her reflexes drained from her body.

Chapter Twenty-Seven

Mae walked passed the flight crew and stepped off the plane. The cold Connecticut air enveloped her instantly, and she shivered, wrapping her arms around her chest. She reminded herself that no amount of cold should ever bother her again, after her excursion in the woods a few hours before. The memory of lying naked on the forest floor, having just climbed from the freezing waters of the partially frozen river, seemed a thousand years ago, but her body still ached from the violent shivering on the icy banks.

The cold air had a certain smell that was unique to New England, a fresh smell with notes of cedar and pine, and she grinned despite the cold. It was winter in Connecticut, and it'd been too long since she'd been home.

She walked quickly within the throng of other passengers getting off the plane. Ryan was ahead of her and hadn't turned once to see if she was following. Knowing him, or knowing what little she knew about him, Mae thought that he would continue walking away from her and out of her life, never looking back or giving her another thought. Mae would try to do the same, but wondered if it would be possible. She longed for someone to look at her the way he had looked at her, and maybe to hold her hand, and hold her body close to his and protect her. It was silly, she knew, but she couldn't help thinking about it just the same.

Ryan continued with the crowd and disappeared down the concourse that led to the baggage claim area. Aside from the passengers unloading from the airplane, there were a few others about. A janitor was emptying trash bins into a larger bin on wheels. Nearby, a father slept in an awkward position on the chairs, with a small girl who couldn't have been more than two years old, sprawled out over his chest, sound asleep. Mae watched the two sleep as she walked by, and she smiled a little at the sight. The girl, perhaps wakened by the sounds of the passengers, stirred and looked up at the people. Her bright blue eyes were sleepy, and she buried her face in her dad's shoulder to rub the sleep from her vision. She looked directly at Mae and smiled faintly before dropping back off to sleep. The dad opened just one eye to make sure that all was well, and Mae was glad that he was at least aware of his surroundings.

Instead of following the crowd, Mae turned and walked toward a pair of restrooms. She glanced over her shoulder and saw that no one was watching her go, and that made her happy. At least she'd made it this far without someone picking back up on her trail, and she hoped that the trail.

Mae walked into the restroom and slipped into a stall. She leaned forward and glanced under the rest of the stalls, glad to see that the bathroom was empty. She sat on the closed toilet, opened her bag and pulled out the borrowed passport and credit cards. Mae flipped through the passport and saw that Ms. Pettingale was well-traveled. The first four pages of the book were filled with stamps from countries throughout Europe, with a sprinkling of stamps from the Caribbean.

Mae rubbed the tip of her finger on the stamp belonging to France and smiled. One of the books that she'd loved as a little girl, still unable to read at the time, was a picture tour book of countries around the world. She would stare at the pictures throughout the book, fascinated by the different people, cultures and scenery in each picture. Of all the countries she toured through that book, the one country that she would always come back to was France. She had studied the pictures with an intense curiosity. She had loved the pictures of the Eiffel Tower, the Moulin Rouge, and the Arc de Triomphe, but the photographs that fascinated her most, that swept her imagination away to a vibrant world full of color and sweet smells, were the photographs of the rolling lavender fields in Provence. She would close her eyes and imagine running along the eternal rows of purple flowers, floating on the sweetly pungent aroma.

As she grew older, the fascination only blossomed. It became more than just a dream; going there rose to the top of her bucket list. Mae's mom had also never been to France, and they would often talk about taking that trip in the future, as they huddled in cheap motel rooms, scared for their lives but enjoying the small amount of comfort the dream brought.

Back then, and even now, Mae doubted that she would ever visit France and its tapestry of lavender.

The fluorescent lights flickered above, and Mae looked up and studied the ceiling. The light seemed to drip down from above, swirling downward, as if draining from the world. She watched the light flicker again, and she felt that same draining sensation in her body, as if her entire being was draining downward.

And then it struck her. Like a roaring wave in the ocean, it pummeled against her and squeezed her heart and insides, twisting and wrenching it, draining her entire self. She felt the weight of the entire world against her, of a million pounds of pressure pressing down on her. She dropped from the toilet seat to the floor, falling to her knees, and cried. She fell further, curling into a tight ball on the floor and clutching the passport. She thought about the lavender fields in France, of picking those purple strands of flowers with her mother, laughing and talking as they walked along the rows and rows of millions of flowers. She cried harder, choking on her own sobs.

"Mom ..." she sobbed, her voice shaking with tears. She thought about laying in the hundreds of hotel rooms over the years, always running, and her mom always there to protect her. Sitting in the tire swing in the backyard of their house, so long ago, riding the wind in the cool autumn light, the feel of her mom's hands on her back, pushing her through the air, the orange and yellow and red leaves filtering the bright sunlight through the branches.

And then her mom was on her knees in the cabin in the woods, and their eyes held each other for a moment, her mom pleading with Mae to run, to find some place safe, away from these hunters.

"Mom, please ..." Her cries were softer now, and she pled. She took that last look through the dirty glass of the cabin window, and the men were coming back into the room, and Mae was running into the dark forest. The gun shot that followed, distant and dark, a single shot in the living room of the cabin, ending everything that Mae knew and loved, and she was alone. Mae cried, holding the false passport to her breasts, holding onto nothing, and the world drained around her.

Paper and ink, she thought, but the line of black on white, on that fresh and clean piece of paper never came. She cried, and the world stayed closed, pressing down on Mae, until there were no tears left, and Mae just lay on the floor, crying.

After what seemed to be a very long time, she brought the passport to her face, her hands and fingers shaking, and she ripped out each page of the passport, and then tore each page into pieces. She wiped at the tears on her cheeks and eyes and pushed herself up from the floor.

She divided the pieces of paper into tiny piles and tightly wrapped each pile in a length of bathroom tissue before flushing them down the toilet, one at a time. When she was finished, she left the bathroom and dropped the remains of the passport, and each of the credit cards, into separate trash bins. She hated to see the source of money and the separate identity go, but she couldn't be found in Connecticut as Ms. Gertrude Pettingale.

She stood up on shaky footing and pushed the door to bathroom stall open. The door swung open on the wide mirror of the bathroom, and she saw Mae Edwards, alone now in the world. Her blond hair was tangled, her eyes red from crying, and all around, she looked pretty pathetic.

"Move ... before the devil catches you," she muttered, remembering the bus driver's words. Mae straightened her hair. She wiped again at her eyes, walking quickly to the bathroom sink. The water from the faucet trickled out into her cupped hands, and she washed her face and eyes, wiping the redness away.

She left the restroom and walked fast, joining the last of the passengers sleepily making their way down the concourse towards baggage claim.

Chapter Twenty-Eight

Morales watched the reporter leave his hospital room and pounded angrily on the mattress where he lay. The rage he'd tried so hard to squelch burst up from within, and all he saw was red.

Who did this Freemont think he was? Coming in here and spouting about Miami. The reporter knew nothing, and Morales vowed that Paul would be dead before morning. All it would take would be one phone call, and the snooping reporter would find himself six feet under. Morales intended to make it happen.

That sniveling, snooping bastard, Morales thought. Oh, he would be dead alright.

The handle on the door suddenly turned, and the door swung open again. Morales peered into the shadows, hoping it was the reporter. He'd kill him right here, with his bare hands, regardless of the neck brace and injuries.

"Detective Morales," a voice said, so quietly that it was almost impossible to make out what was said. The accent in the voice, however, was unmistakable.

"Oskar?" Morales asked, and the big man stepped into view. "Oskar, I'm glad you're okay."

The tall man didn't say anything, just approached Morales and placed his briefcase on the foot of Morales' bed.

"Oskar, how did you get free of the van? I expected that little whore to kill you dead," Morales said, "and with the media, good grief, I don't know how you did it."

"Stealth," Oskar said, repeating a word that Morales often used when they were on assignments. Morales noticed that Oskar was favoring his left side, where he'd been shot.

"Are you okay?" Morales asked.

"Fine," Oskar said, "and when the work is finished tonight, I will rest before finding the girl."

"What work, Oskar? She's gone, flew out before …" Morales' voice trailed off as he realized what was happening here. All along, he'd assumed that an unfamiliar assassin would be sent to his room to finish him off. For a brief moment, Morales had thought that Oskar had been sent to get him out of this mess.

"Oskar," Morales said, his voice low, but not pleading. Morales would not beg, not even at the end. "You don't have to do this."

"It is my new assignment, before finding the girl," Oskar said in his slow and deliberate English.

"There are cops in the hallway, Oskar," Morales said, "and I can help you find the girl. We'll get her together, we'll finish this together."

"You have failed, and failure is not acceptable to Harrison," Oskar said.

"I'm your boss, Oskar, not Harrison. I brought you into the fold."

"No longer," Oskar said, and clicked the briefcase open. The tall man removed a single syringe and a small bottle of clear liquid. Potassium chloride, the dose of which would cause a massive cardiac arrest. The same liquid he'd injected into the congressman's heart, so many years before.

Morales felt the first traces of fear, underlying the rage.

"Oskar," Morales said, "There is someone else who knows about our work. About Il Contionum's work. He's a reporter, and he knows too much. We must find him, and kill him."

"Will you die with honor?" Oskar said, ignoring him as he filled the syringe with the clear liquid and then tapped the plastic base to clear the remain air bubbles.

"Oskar."

"Will you die with honor, sir?"

Morales watched, those first tinges of fear transforming into a horror that was almost completely foreign to him. He'd watched the congressman die, watched the pain in his eyes, the muscles tensing as his body died. Even though the congressman hadn't screamed, Morales could see the excruciating torture as his body twisted and writhed and died.

When it was over, there was nothing, and it was that nothingness that caused the horror to overtake the anger, the terror to fill his mind and soul.

"Oskar," Morales said, but the tall man moved toward him, the syringe reflecting the low light in the hospital room.

The door suddenly swung open, banging into the wall with a loud thwack and knocking a bottle of hand sanitizer and a box of latex gloves to the floor. Both Morales and Oskar jerked toward the sound, Oskar pulling a silver pistol from inside his coat and raising it toward the intruder.

At first, Morales thought it must be one of the guards, maybe recovering from a blow to the head outside his door, but just as soon as he had that thought, he realized that Oskar would not have let any witnesses live. To all future onlookers of this scene, Morales would have been finished off by the same assassin who'd started the job. The policemen guarding his room, and maybe even some nurses would have just been victims to an unexplained act of violence toward one of the city's cops. Morales knew this because that is what he would have done.

It wasn't the police guard who came barreling low into the room, but the reporter from before. Morales watched as Paul smashed into Oskar with the force of a linebacker, sending them both pummeling into the wall. Oskar fired two silenced shots, but they went wild, piercing the ceiling above Morale's head.

The lamp on the bedside table crashed to the floor, toppling the machine monitoring Morales' vitals to the ground, and Morales caught a glimpse of the syringe holding his death skittering beneath a small chest of drawers.

As the men struggled, Morales ripped the brace from his neck and shoulder, screaming in pain as a jolt of bright white agony ignited in his injured shoulder and thudded throughout his body.

Oskar and Paul were on the ground, thrashing. Oskar punched Paul in the side of his head, blood bursting from the reporter's ear, and shoved his forearm into his face. As Paul grunted and winced with the force of the blow, Oskar rolled over on top of him, tearing at the reporter's face with his fingers, the muscles in his hands and wrists and arms tensed and shuddering. Paul began to scream.

Morales swung his feet to the floor, feeling shaky and uneasy as he tried to stand. The world wobbled, and that throbbing, flashing white pain just wouldn't stop. He scanned the floor and found what he was looking for: Oskar's gun, the silencer still screwed to the barrel.

He took a step forward and stumbled to his knees, smacking his injured shoulder on the hard floor. The explosion of pain nearly sent him spiraling into unconsciousness, darkness bursting from the edges of his vision. He resisted the urge to give in to the darkness and thrust his body along the floor in a slow, agonizing slide toward the weapon. Finally his fingers grasped at the barrel, and he pulled it closer.

Paul was screaming in full bellow as he punched Oskar in the side and face and head. The bigger man didn't seem to notice, but moved his thumbs until they were over Paul's eyes before pushing down. Paul's scream was no longer from just pain, but from panic and the fear of losing his eyes. The pressure intensified and he bucked his body and punched, but Oskar didn't move, just pushed harder against his eyes, waiting for the pop when the sclera ruptured.

The whisper of a gunshot sounded, barely discernible among Paul's screams, and was quickly followed by a thud, as Oskar was thrown to the ground by the force of the bullet. Paul looked up, his eyes watering and his head pounding, to see Morales leveling the gun at him.

"Who are you, really?" Morales asked.

"I told you," Paul said through rasping gasps for air. "Paul—"

"How do you know about Miami?"

"Was ... was there," Paul said.

Morales tried to stand, but the drugs that'd been used on him during the recent surgery in his shoulder, and the thudding pain throughout his body, prohibited the movement and he nearly fell. He dropped the gun to his side as he realized that no matter how quiet and discreet Oskar had been in coming to his room, the ensuing fight was sure to get some attention.

"They're dead," Paul said, more of his voice coming through now. "The guy who was trying to kill you also killed the cops guarding your room. And the nurse, maybe others."

Morales wanted to kill the reporter right there, to put a bullet in him as he'd done with Oskar, but he needed Paul's help to get out of the room. If Oskar had been sent to finish Morales, surely they would send another.

"I need your help." Morales said as he pulled himself to a standing position by the bed. "We've got to get out of here."

"But the police will be here, and they'll see that your attacker is dead." Paul was getting up now too, being careful to avoid Oskar's corpse. "If we run, it might look like we're guilty."

"I'm going to tell you something right now, and you've got to listen carefully," Morales said. "Whoever sent this man to kill me will send someone else. If any word gets out that you were here, and the word *will* get out, then you're a dead man too. These people, they're very powerful. Now I need you to get my things for me, and help me out of here. We'll have to take the stairs to the garage. The elevator is too risky."

"But you just got shot, you need to rest," Paul said. He pointed to Morales' shoulder, where blood was seeping through the bandage.

"I'll rest later," Morales nearly shouted. "We've got to get out of here now!"

Chapter Twenty-Nine

Before Mae even rounded the corner in the hallway that led to baggage claim and the exit, she could smell the roasted aroma of freshly ground coffee. Mae inhaled deeply and savored the smell, wishing she'd held onto Ms. Pettingale's credit card for 10 minutes more. She snaked her hand into her pocket and felt for any spare change, even though she knew nothing was there.

As she approached the little coffee stand, advertising the local Green Mountain blends, she felt a wave of fatigue rush over her, and the smell of the coffee wasn't just enticing, but one of necessity. It was always like that—no matter how rested she was, the smell of coffee always made her feel tired, like she needed that quick boost of energy to take another step. And if there was ever a time when she might have actually needed the caffeine for those additional steps, it was now. She felt sluggish and tried to think of when she'd last had a good night's sleep. The nap on the plane hadn't counted, because for her, sleep on an airplane was never refreshing. Surely, the last good night of sleep had come before the few days in the cabin, and even then, the rest had been almost frenzied, pocked with paranoia and the sense that there was someone always just outside, waiting to break in.

Mae stopped in front of the counter and read over the various types of coffee that were printed on the chalkboard above the register. Two employees bustled about as quickly as possible for it being in the middle of the night. The woman, a heavyset hipster in black skinny jeans, a knit cap on her nappy hair, and black-rimmed holes in her ears, was busy emptying and cleaning carafes. She directed the other employee at certain tasks—a teenager who looked tired and bored, as if this job were his father's idea, and his father's only. When the boy saw her standing in front of the counter, he looked relieved to escape the menial tasks of closing shop to help a customer. He stood at the register, swaying on his feet. The expression of relief in his eyes quickly gave way to the same tired and bored expression that'd been there before. He had a fresh bout of acne on his forehead and around his nose. Thin-rimmed glasses covered his eyes, and his longish hair was parted but strewn messily about. He waited patiently by the register, shifting from one foot to the other, shrugging every few seconds.

"Can I help you?" he finally asked.

"I don't think so," Mae said with a wan smile. She turned her attention back to the chalkboard, and the description of a type of toasted marshmallow latte that she'd never heard of. It was a curious flavor, but not one that she would ever try. She hated all the sugar and milk and flavors that people poured into coffee to hide the pungent but woody flavor of roasted beans.

The cashier suddenly looked more than confused.

"I'm just looking, thank you," she said. The kid looked away and sighed, watching another group of people enter the baggage claim area from another concourse.

"Well," the kid said after a few more moments, "if you're not going to get anything, I've got to start cleaning up. I get off at 2:30—late shift, you know, and I want to leave as soon as we close…"

His voice trailed off, but he didn't move from his post behind the register.

"Seriously, you're making this kid so nervous, it's making me nervous," a familiar voice said from behind her. She turned, trying to snap out of her daze—she couldn't get over how tired she felt—and saw Ryan sitting at a table toward the rear of the café area, thumbing through the same magazine he'd been looking at on the airplane. The magazine was looking more and more like a prop to Mae, something Ryan didn't read, but held onto for the sake of holding something.

Mae just stared at him and tried not to look at his perfect grey eyes, cold as they were. She forced her gaze away from his face, and from him in general, turning back to the sign above the café's counter.

"You'd think I was Dr. Kemp's good friend Griffin, with that look you're giving me."

"I don't understand," Mae said, her mind finally catching up with the situation. Jeeze, she was tired—the weight of the last few days coming down on her like a grand piano on the Road Runner in those old cartoons.

"H.G. Wells, come on …" Ryan gave her a look of disbelief and shook his head. He approached the teenage cashier and placed his wallet on the counter.

"I'll have what she's having."

"She isn't having anything," the teenager said with cocked eyebrows. Ryan was clearly the only one who seemed to be thinking at normal speeds at the moment.

"I thought you'd already gone from here," Mae said, and Ryan turned from the counter. Mae saw the coldness still in his eyes, but there was another expression that wasn't there before. He looked curious, but also mildly concerned. He didn't want to talk about it right there in the open room coffee shop, but he did want to talk. He cocked his head sideways to the menu, as if to say, "Hurry up already, order before we give this poor kid an aneurism."

"Double Americano," she said with a faint smile, and sat down at the table where Ryan had been waiting for her.

"And she's not messing around," Ryan said, turning back to the cashier. "If I had a double right now, I'd be bouncing around like a hyperactive pinball. I'll just have a cup of your darkest roast."

The kid, who seemed to be relieved that the awkwardness of the last few minutes was over, punched a few buttons on his register, and Ryan paid for the drinks. As Mae sat, her eyelids grew heavier by the second and her brain seemed to be shutting her body down on its own accord, despite her desperate efforts to stay awake. She blinked rapidly and stretched her aching muscles, wondering what good the nap on the airplane had done, with this creeping fatigue setting in. After a few seconds, the desire to lay her head on the table and slip into the void was too much for her, and she stood up.

A row of television monitors caught her attention, all tuned to CNN, where a man with a strong jaw and immaculate hair was speaking seriously into the camera. It wasn't the man who caught Mae's expression, as almost all news anchors looked the same to her—it was what he was talking about.

"—shooting at Chicago O'Hare International Airport, with the shooter still at large ..." A video shot from a roving helicopter appeared on the screen, showing the road that wound around the airport completely blocked by ambulances and police cars. The news anchor's voice came in over the image.

"Police are saying that the shooting took place in an unmarked police van just outside the airport. The van was parked in the unloading zone, but airport security apparently recognized the tags as belonging to the Chicago PD."

"Again, this begs the question, Charles, do we need more restrictions on firearms? Time and time again, we are seeing these public shootings by psychopaths who are able to get a gun with no problems whatsoever. We've got these psychos gunning down children in schools and movie theaters, and now cops at airports."

"That's a good point, Sally, and a question that will likely be debated with fervor as this police shooting unfolds. For those viewers just joining us, Detective Robert Morales of the Chicago PD was shot tonight in an unmarked van outside O'Hare International. The shooter is still at large, causing all flights to be grounded until further notice."

An image of the police officer that Mae had shot flashed up on the screen. The detective was sitting in front of an American flag and looked noble as he posed for his official photo. The expression on Morales' face was serious, but he had a faint smile that Mae knew was charming. She also knew that anyone looking at this picture right now would instantly empathize with the fallen peace officer—a man of duty and courage who'd been gunned down by a lunatic.

Of course, all those people looking at his picture now did not know the truth about this man. They had not seen the spittle flying from his mouth as he raged and slammed his fist into the wall next to her head, again and again, and then when her mother was finally dead, how he had knelt over her and relished the last few seconds of her life like a wine connoisseur contemplating the after notes of a rather fine La Tâche. They did not know of his relentless pursuit, and his willingness to brutally kill anyone in his way. Even Mae doubted that she knew the true extent of this man who was really a monster in human skin, who felt no remorse for taking a life.

Now, looking at his picture on the bank of television screens, amid the drone of the anchor's voice, Mae wished that she'd killed him in much the same way that he'd killed her mother. The thought that he would live another day, and now as a near-martyr hero made her feel like throwing up.

"Please sit down," Ryan said, crossing over to her table with the two cups. "You're making me nervous now. You're like a monkey on speed."

Mae closed her eyes and forced the image of the killer detective from her mind, and concentrated again on the situation at hand. She wasn't out of it yet, not until she ditched Ryan and got on her way. Sure, he was cute—the sound of his voice and his smile, and the way he studied her with a curious affection—but she couldn't afford to get close to anyone, now that her mom was gone. Because when you're close to someone, or worse yet, when you love someone, there is a breaking point. The loved one became a leverage point that someone like Morales could use to make her do anything that he wanted. With no one special in her life, at least not anymore, there would be no leverage. Never again.

When she opened her eyes, the thoughts of Morales were pushed away, and she smiled.

"Did you just call me a monkey?" she said, not sure whether she should be offended by his comment or not. He was smiling at her though, a crooked and goofy half grin that made her feel giddy.

"On speed," he confirmed and held the warm cup out to her.

Mae took the offered cup of coffee and sipped at the bitter drink, instantly feeling relieved. She sat back down at the table, holding the cup in both hands. She bent forward and breathed the earthy aroma, allowing even the smell to calm her nerves.

Ryan turned to the bank of television screens and motioned with this cup.

"Crazy, huh?" he said. "And to think that we almost got stuck in that mess."

"I know, right?"

"I was watching that for a few minutes while I waited for you, seems like we got out of the Chicago at the perfect moment—and they're thinking that whoever shot the cop was either getting on an airplane, or just getting off." He stopped talking for a few seconds while he placed his cup on the table and set a handful of creamers and sugar packets into a little pile next to his cup.

He nodded, as if to agree with his own thoughts, and said, "Which is probably why those stooges were checking passports."

"Yeah, probably."

Ryan fell quiet again, and Mae was relieved that he didn't continue that line of thinking. Instead, he began to slowly unpeel the wrappers from cups of cream and pour them into his drink. Once the cream was in, he ripped opened four sugar packets at the same time and dumped them all into the cup.

Mae almost gagged at the thought of so much sugar and cream, but she kept it to herself. He caught Mae watching him and grinned again.

"You're probably thinking that this is a lot of sugar and cream, and you'd be right."

Mae nodded and took another sip of her drink, relishing the warmth and feeling more alert and awake with every tiny swallow.

"Truth is, I'm not a huge fan of the coffee flavor, which again, given my last name, is a bit ironic. I much prefer the taste of the cream and sugar that you add to the coffee—especially around this time of year, you know with all the flavored creamers and such."

Mae nodded again, and took another sip. She took her coffee black, as she'd always done, from the moment she'd snuck a drink from her father's cup as a child.

They sat in silence for a few moments, Ryan staring into his cup and Mae looking at the few people who were still waiting for their suitcases. Janitors and security guards mingled about, but mostly the airport was empty. Mae held off the surge of panic at again being in such lonely surroundings, but she doubted that anyone had noticed her.

Except for Ryan. She peered at him from the corner of her eye and wondered why he was taking such an interest in her. Mae knew that she was pretty, but also knew that she wasn't drop dead gorgeous.

Ryan, on the other hand, was drop dead gorgeous—at least in her book, and she didn't think her book would be too far from the common female consensus. He was strong and confident, thin and muscular, but not so much so that it was distracting from his cool and even features. Again, she was drawn to his eyes, which were like looking into the dark grey waters at the base of a glacier, deep and cold, yet somehow curious and inviting.

She didn't think that he was among those hunting her. If he was, she likely would have been taken from the airplane before any passengers were able to get up out of their seats, and before there was any chance that she could escape again. Her knowledge of the hunters was limited—but she knew that they did not like loose ends, and loose ends were tied up quickly. She never would have made it out the airplane doors if they had known she was on that flight. And they almost found out, too, she thought, certain that it was Il Contionum, and maybe Morales himself who ordered the flight attendants to check passports. If Morales was still alive, that is.

"So, you're Ms. Pettingale," Ryan said slowly, turning the coffee cup with his thumbs and forefingers. "I'll be honest, I kind of like the other you name you gave me. Pettingale sounds a bit stuffy to me. Kind of like the hoity-toity people my parents run around with."

"I'm sorry about that," she said and placed her own cup, now only half full, on the table before them.

A few seconds of silence passed—the awkward kind that seem to go on and on forever.

"Are you going to tell me why?"

"Why what?"

"Why you gave me a fake name." He shrugged and looked genuinely hurt. "I mean, what's it to you? I'm a nobody, just some schmoe on the airplane trying to start up conversation with my seatmate—"

"Seatmate?" she said, with a burst of chuckles. Ryan exhaled and looked into his lap, seeming to be a little embarrassed. Mae stopped chuckling and studied Ryan. She saw that he wasn't embarrassed, but instead getting angry.

Not angry, no, Mae thought, frustrated and upset. He's a logical guy, and he's been thinking about the lie she told since the flight attendant had studied her borrowed passport and read her borrowed name allowed. Ryan was upset, and he kept spinning the coffee cup in his hands as he thought hard. For some reason, his cuff links caught Mae's attention again, and she thought that he probably wasn't used to not getting what he wanted.

"You know what I mean," he said, and made an effort to shrug. The movement was probably intended to ease the growing tension, but the stiffness of the motion only emphasized his frustration. "All I'm asking is why you had to lie to me? What difference would it make? Now I know that you probably don't care about me in the least, and I get that. I understand that you don't know me, and that you don't owe me anything, least of all the truth. But your name, I mean, I could look it up in the phone book, or Facebook, or whatever and at least know your name. Now, you might not want to know me, I mean, you're a beautiful girl and you've probably got a boyfriend, and I get that. You don't want me to know who you are, so I don't go trying to look you up on Facebook."

"I ..." Mae bit her lower lip and crossed her arms across her chest. She felt the bandage on her shoulder beneath the sweater and grimaced slightly with the pain of her touch.

"I had to lie." Her voice was soft, but firm. "And I can't explain it, but even my name is ... well, let's just say that you wouldn't be able to look me up in the phone book, and what's Facebook?"

She grinned with that last question, and it cut through the tension. All this time she'd been thinking about his smile, rare and charming that it was, and she'd forgotten about her own smile, which seemed to have a similar melting effect on Ryan.

"Well, do you?"

"Do I what?"

"Have a boyfriend?"

Mae laughed and brushed some hair from her face. She took another drink and avoided his gaze. Finally, she shook her head.

"No," she said, "no boyfriends to speak of."

"Then why?"

"I could just as easily turn this around, you know. I'm just some girl on an airplane who you'll never see again, a girl who is not even half as pretty as any of the women you could have, and you know it—"

"You're wrong about that," he said, and Mae saw that he wasn't joking.

"So why do you care so much?" she asked. "Why didn't you just walk off the plane, and into the crowd like everyone else?"

"Because you're a mystery."

"And you're an enigma," she said. He placed the cup of coffee on the table and clasped his hands between his knees. He looked at the ground, and then massaged the back of his neck.

"Alright," he said. "I get it."

He stood up and stuck out his hand for her to shake.

"Ms. Pettingale, it's been a pleasure." The smile was sincere, but Mae ignored it. She couldn't do this again, couldn't get close to anyone else. She couldn't …

He waited a moment longer, watching her avoid his eyes, and then turned away.

"My real name is Mae," she said. "I never lied to you."

He stopped walking and turned to look at her. His smile was back, but it was tentative. Even this smile caused a flurry of butterflies to take flight in her stomach.

"Really?"

"Really." She pointed to the chair across from her and motioned him to come back. From the corner of her eye, Mae noticed the cashier kid watching this exchange with an even dumber expression of confusion than he'd had before.

"So, Mae …" he said, and hesitated.

"I don't want any more questions right now, I just want to talk."

"About what?"

"How about H. G. Wells?" she asked. He was about to say something in return when she suddenly cocked her head to the side, listening.

"How about where you're going tonight?" Ryan said.

"Tonight?" she asked, and then looked away. She was embarrassed not because he'd guessed that she had nowhere to go, but that she'd not yet planned that far in advance.

"Let me put you up in a hotel," he said. "I know a good one down in West Hartford."

She laughed nervously, and then shook her head.

"It's okay, really."

"I'm not going to ask you why you don't have a place to go, and I'm not going to even think about it that much, but it's weird, and you need a place to sleep."

"I don't know," she said. "I mean, we kind of just met."

"Whoa." He spread his hands defensively. "Listen, I'm not suggesting we hop under the covers together, geeze. You think I'm some kind of a man-slut? No. I'll drop you off. Or, rather, my driver will drop you off. Totally legit."

Mae wondered if this was how most girls went missing. An attractive guy invites you into his car, and then chop suey.

Good grief I'm paranoid, she thought, but then quickly reminded herself of how quickly Morales had closed in at the cabin and then found her again after she'd escaped.

What could it hurt?

Ryan smiled at her and shook his head. "No touchie, I promise. I'm not a creep like that."

"Okay," she said.

He smiled at her and gathered up the trash on the table before him.

"Let's go then, I'm starting to get tired, and I live in the opposite direction from Hartford."

Mae started to respond, but heard a familiar name before she registered who said it, and couldn't recall why it sounded familiar to her.

Nick Ambrose.

"Busy night in Chicago tonight," the Anchor said, "with the airport shooting of Detective Robert Morales. Now, we're getting reports of another shooting near the airport, which may be related."

"Thank you, Charlie." The scene cut to a shot of a pretty blond woman, bundled up in a thick winter parka and standing in front of a section of freeway that had been blocked off with flares and yellow crime scene tape.

"I'm here near a new crime scene that may be related to the O'Hare shooting earlier this afternoon. A city bus was found parked along the interstate near the airport. The driver, Nick Ambrose, was found on the bus, shot to death."

Mae watched, and blood drained from her face.

Chapter Thirty

Paul's head pounded, and he felt like a weight had been attached to the backs of his eyes, trembling and throbbing with each thud in his head. Morales was hanging onto him, and they were making their way down the stairs to the hospital parking garage. Paul carried the assassin's briefcase in his free hand. Back in the room, Morales had insisted that they take the brief case and the assassin's cell phone with them. Morales had taken the phone and clutched it close to his body, while Paul had slammed the briefcase shut and carried it in his free hand. Morales had kept the gun, tucking it into the bandage beneath his shoulder. The gun fit snugly, like in a shoulder holster, hidden from view.

It wasn't until they'd made it down a few flights of stairs that Paul started to wonder what could be in the briefcase or on the assassin's phone that would be of value to Morales. He considered that there may have been information about Morales, but mostly, the briefcase would have incriminated the assassin, not Morales. Unless there was something in there that Morales needed to keep hidden, something that would incriminate Morales as well.

But how would Morales have known what was in the briefcase? If he had known, then maybe he'd known who the assassin was, and maybe, just maybe, Morales' motive for shooting the assassin was more than just self-preservation.

They heard shouts from the floors above as the corpses of the policeman and nurse were being discovered. In the distance, police sirens wailed.

"We've got to move faster," Morales whispered, breathing heavily. The increase in activity seemed to have made him woozier than before, more dependent on Paul to carry him.

"I'm going as fast as I can," Paul said, struggling under Morales' nearly dead weight. "I don't think the stairs go all the way to the garage. We'll need to transfer over to the elevator, maybe the service elevator?"

The thudding behind his eyeballs grew worse, and his vision was tinted in dark red. With each step, the reddening worsened, and the pounding in his head intensified. They reached a landing for the eighth floor, and Paul stopped.

"We have to keep going," Morales said. "Any minute now, they're going to close off the stairways and any exits to the hospital. There will be no way out of here, and you'll be stuck with me."

"I'm going to pass out," Paul said through heavy breathing. "I've got to stop."

He set Morales down on the bottom few steps, then had an idea. He opened the door to the eighth floor, which was quiet and mostly empty. A nurse was walking down the hallway in the opposite direction, engrossed in her charts. She paused for a few seconds, then disappeared into a room. Paul slipped through the door and started down the hallway, looking into the rooms as he passed them. Finally, he spotted what he was looking for. Paul grabbed the wheelchair that was folded up and propped near the door. He carried it back to the stairway and opened it up. Morales looked at him skeptically, but climbed to the chair.

"Give me the briefcase," Morales said. Paul gave it to him, and he set it on his lap, placing the cell phone on top. Paul backed through the doorway, pulling Morales through the door, then swiveling him around toward the elevator.

At that moment, the nurse stepped out of the room, and Paul froze. She was marking something off on her chart. She lowered the file folder, rubbed her eyes and tucked a loose strand of hair behind her ear before starting down the hallway, again in the opposite direction. She paused at the next room, flipping through the pages on her chart and then stepping into the room.

She's doing her rounds, Paul realized, and gave a sigh of relief. Had she looked in their direction, she would have spotted the blood and immediately known that something was not right.

Paul quickly pushed the chair down the hallway toward the elevator, praying that the nurse would not come out of the room and that no one else would spot them.

The chair was a blessing, not just because it saved Paul from having to help the policeman walk, but it supported him as well. His body was stiffening by the second, and the pulsing throb in his head was not getting any better.

They finally reached the elevator, and Paul pressed the button marked P2, the level on which he was parked. The door dinged open, and they joined several other people in the elevator. Paul nodded to a doctor who barely noticed them, and the rest of the people either stared straight ahead or looked away, ignoring Paul and Morales.

Oh this new age of terrorism, Paul thought. If you see something, say something. At the moment, he was grateful that no one cared to actually *see*.

But am I *seeing*? Paul wondered. He tried to cut through the pounding in his head, to think about what had actually happened. His thoughts were hazy, and he found it difficult to think, his mind returning in horror to the thought of what would have happened if the assassin had been successful in pressing his thumbs into his eyes until they'd popped. He cringed, and shook his head to clear the idea.

What am I supposed to see? He knew that Morales was connected to the attack in Miami. Morales' reaction when Paul had mentioned Miami was enough of a confirmation. The police officer at least knew something about it, Paul was sure.

But the assassin had come to the hospital to kill Morales and any witnesses who might have gotten in the way. Paul thought about the risks of murdering someone—a police detective at that—in a hospital filled with people, witnesses, and armed guards. There was also the problem with exits—not many in the hospital.

The risk must have been outweighed by the need for Morales to be dead.

Gradually, the people on the elevator got off, most on the main floor where there was a coffee shop still open, and Paul was left alone with Morales. The door finally dinged open on P2, and Paul slowly pushed Morales into the parking garage. The garage was empty of people, as he'd expected at this time of night, and his car was parked close to the elevator. Paul pushed Morales to the car and opened the front door. Then he stopped, considering his next words carefully.

Before Paul could open his mouth, the cell phone on top of the briefcase began to vibrate. Both Paul and Morales glanced down and saw that the number was RESTRICTED. Morales answered the phone and held it to his ear without saying anything.

"Is it done?" a man said, his voice low and deep, but loud enough for Paul to hear what was being said. Morales clenched the phone, the knuckles on his fingers turning white.

"Oskar?" the man asked.

"It's done," Morales said, and then smiled a wicked grin. "Oskar is dead, Harrison, and you've got yourself a merry little mess to clean up at the hospital."

"Morales?" There was fear in the other man's voice. "We follow protocol, you know that. We did what we had to do in the situation. The girl escaped, and you—"

"If you ever send someone to kill me again," Morales interrupted, "It will be last thing you do."

The voice on the other end said nothing that Paul could hear.

"Oskar had the latest information on the girl's whereabouts?"

Again, Paul could hear no response, but Morales absently touched the briefcase. Paul wondered if the girl they were speaking of was the contact he'd been planning to meet the evening before on the bus. But his contact hadn't sounded like a girl. He felt a sinking sensation as he remembered his contact's paranoia, her certainty that the people hunting her were far more powerful than he could possibly have understood, and that they would find her and kill her. Paul was suddenly very aware of the danger in this situation, and the image of Morales pointing the gun at him suddenly made sense. Morales would have killed him, but needed him to get out of the hospital. Paul had willingly done so, and had brought Morales to his car. His usefulness was about to expire.

"Good. Morales said, interrupting Paul's thoughts, "the girl is mine,".

Morales ended the call just as another car pulled onto the second level of the garage and parked next to Paul's car. Both Paul and Morales watched as a woman climbed from the driver's seat. She was wearing surgical scrubs beneath a heavy leather coat and carrying a luxurious, but well-used, purse at her side. Paul guessed she was a doctor, and would have tried to get her attention if he didn't believe that Morales would kill her just as quickly. Paul had to get the gun. If he could somehow get the gun, he thought he could get the upper hand in the situation. He didn't know how much Morales had recovered from the drugs used in his surgery, but a quick jab to his shoulder was sure to debilitate him if needed.

The doctor walked to the elevator, her footsteps echoing softly in the silent garage. She didn't pay much attention to Paul and Morales. The seconds dragged, ticking like the detonator on a bomb, as they waited until she was inside the elevator and the door was completely closed.

"Who's the girl?" Paul asked at the same time that Morales reached for the gun under his arm with lightning speed. Paul saw this and flipped the wheelchair, spilling Morales, the briefcase and phone on the ground. Morales screamed as he fell on his shoulder, but rolled to his back with incredible speed, firing two shots at Paul as he rolled. The first bullet went wild, but the second punched a hole in the fender above the front tire on Paul's car. Paul ducked to the ground, moving on his hands and knees around to the other side of the car.

Morales shot again, this time aiming at Paul underneath the car, and this bullet caught Paul in the knee, shattering the bone and spraying blood. Paul screamed as the agony exploded through his body, but adrenaline kicked in, and he moved as fast as he could, dragging the bloodied leg behind him.

Keep movin' before the devil gets ya.

Who had said that? Was it Nick, the bus driver who was now dead? He couldn't remember, his mind empty of everything but survival. He reached the side of the car opposite Morales, and pulled himself into a sitting position, his back to the tire. He didn't think Morales had a clear shot, but it wouldn't take long for the cop to move into a position in which he could finish Paul.

Keep movin'

His leg was bleeding, his pants completely soaked in blood, and Paul couldn't look at his leg. He wanted to scream, to bite down on his fist and scream, but Morales would kill him.

Distantly, as if a million miles away, he heard the elevator doors ding open. In the same instant he made the decision to move, hoping that Morales would be distracted for at least a fraction of a second.

Before the devil gets ya.

He moved, rolling over his dead leg and pulling himself up on his good leg. He pulled himself along the car, seeing the same doctor who'd just left the garage a moment before exit the elevator, returning to her car as if she'd forgotten something.

A look of confusion, and then downright terror, crossed her face. She screamed and ducked away just as a bullet struck the concrete to her left. Paul was around the side of the car, his bleeding leg scraping across the concrete behind him and leaving a trail of blood. Morales had his back to him and was getting to his feet as Paul tackled him from behind. He threw his entire weight into the tackle, coming down on Morales and driving his head into the concrete.

Paul saw his chance and took it, punching as hard as he could at the widening circle of blood on Morales' bandaged shoulder. Morales screamed for just a second before the pain over took him and he lost consciousness.

Before the devil gets ya.

Paul had maybe seconds before Morales woke up, so he had to move.

Move, move move, he thought, the mantra running over and over in his head. Before the devil gets ya. He snatched the fallen briefcase and it fell open, papers fluttering free and scattering across the grey concrete. He shoved a few back into the case and slammed it shut. He didn't have time to grab more. He had to move before Morales woke up. Even in a dazed state, Morales would overtake him, and he'd be dead.

Paul crawled towards the elevator. The doctor was in there now, crouched in the corner and crying.

"Hold the elevator!" Paul screamed. "Please!" He half crawled, half dragged his body to the open door. The woman hesitated, then stuck her leg between the closing doors. His leg was numb now, the throb a dull ache, and the daze was settling over him.

He reached the elevator, and the doctor helped him inside. The doors were closing again, and they both saw Morales lifting his head from the concrete.

The doctor noticed Paul's bleeding leg and her fears slipped away as habit took over. She ripped the belt from his waist and wrapped it just above Paul's knee. Paul was fading quickly, the adrenaline rushing out of his body as quickly as it had rushed in, shock taking its place.

The doors opened on the lobby. Several people nearby saw the bloody mess and the screaming began.

No more than two minutes went by before the SWAT team arrived, called in response to the shootings of the police officers and nurse, and the missing detective, Robert Morales.

Half the team went upstairs, and the other half went to the garage. When they got to Parking Level 2, all they found was the trail of blood from Paul's leg.

Morales was gone.

Chapter Thirty-One

The car, a black and sleek Mercedes, arrived to collect Mae and Ryan from the airport. She was amazed at how quickly it had come after his phone call, but deep fatigue was setting in too quickly for her suspicions to be aroused.

"You can take the backseat, all to yourself," Ryan said, holding the door open for her. "No funny business."

"I can't pay for a hotel." Mae said, sleep already invading her words. Ryan just smiled at her and shook his head. She climbed inside the car and leaned her head against the cold glass of the passenger window and felt the sleep overtake her. The urge to shut her eyes and allow the world to drip away into nothing was powerful—too powerful to resist.

Who was Ryan, really? she wondered, and then the all important question: could she trust him?

As it had done since she was only a child, her mind naturally went to that place with paper and ink. As always, it started with a single line, drawn down the middle of the page. As she slept, her muscles twitched with the memory of the way the pen felt in her fingers, and her hands moved with the swift and smooth movements of putting ink to the clean white page.

Paper and ink, here and now, she dreamt. Her dream was as natural as it had ever been, and the movements of her hands and muscles flowed from her body as if it were made to draw these lines and open the door to reality.

As always, the line appeared on the page, a split in reality, and the world opened before her. The ink was black, but as the world opened, light and color flooded through, like a door opening from a dark interior to the bright day outside, or eyelids opening after a deep sleep. The colors swept in from the black line of ink, and the picture before her took shape with every etch of ink on the blank paper.

The world opened on a darkened city street in the wake of spring. Trees lined the streets with buds of pink blossoms opening, a sepia tone in the yellow light of the street lamps. The ground was damp from an evening rain storm, and the smell of the water coming off the cobblestones sent a ripple of pleasure through her body. She whirled in the night, her feet tapping against the ground and splashing through the puddles. She crossed to the bridge and looked down into the churning river. She didn't think of the river that'd held her in its grasp only hours before, but admired the deep blue of the water with flickering yellow light reflecting off like faraway stars in the deep blue of a night sky.

The air was still cool, but warm enough to be a respite from the harsh winter, and it touched her skin and whispered through her hair. She closed her eyes and felt the moist breeze on her face and tasted the remnants of rain.

She looked around and saw that she was alone, except for a group of people sitting outside a café down the street. Men and women, and even the waiters and waitresses, pulled chairs and tables together, and they laughed at each other's jokes and stories, and swayed to the jazz music that melted through the night. Not a single person looked her way, as their party was in full swing, and it was here and now and nowhere else.

She sat at a table, not minding the cold, wet seat. She sat and watched the party play on down the street and listened to the faint bursts of horn and percussion. She watched the windows in the buildings above the street, some dark or covered with curtains, others glowing with yellow lights. A string of drying purple lavender hangs above one window, with a child's play clothes hanging from a clothesline above another.

Footsteps echod along the stone street and brick buildings, and she hears them laughing before they turn the bend and approach the bridge. She smiles when she sees them, the boy with a jacket and scarf, his arms around the girl's shoulders. Their laughing breaths make short bursts of mist in the night air, and her smile grows.

Her notebook is open on the table before her, never mind the wet tabletop, and she draws. First the black line from top to bottom, then the bridge that spans the river, with its cobblestone surface and ancient stone railings.

She draws the boy and girl. They are speaking melodic words that she doesn't understand, but she wants to understand. She is telling him that she loves him, and he her, and their words are soft and belong only to them, and she asks him, "What is this love, that makes me love? Ce que l'amour est cet amour?"

He touches his forehead to hers and she steps up on the tips of her toes to kiss his chin, and his cheek, the corner of his mouth, and then his lips. She doesn't understand, but she wants to understand.

They stood on a bridge, not too far from where she sat drawing and wishing and hoping. They stood on the bridge that overlooked a river that cut through the center of an old city. The boy held the girl's hand, and she laughed, and he laughed.

Mae put the pen down, and the picture was done. She watched the worn wooden benches and the potted plants and the clapboard signs that were put away for the night. Nothing moved, nothing floated upward in the air, not even the petals on the fading flowers that sat in a window box just outside the nearest shop.

That was good. Her mind was clear and focused on the boy and the girl. She smiled, and with the pen on the paper, paper and ink, the world closed to her, and she slept.

Chapter Thirty-Two

Detective Morales exited the hospital parking garage and began driving fast. His head and body ached, but he didn't care. He screamed as he drove, pounding his fist into the steering wheel and the dashboard. The red rage was turning black.

Morales had minutes to disappear before all police cars would be on the lookout for the reporter's car.

He swore, spittle spewing from his mouth.

A few miles from the hospital, he pulled into a residential neighborhood, turned down a few streets, and pulled into the driveway of a darkened house. He turned off the car and waited to see if any lights would turn on inside the house, but none did.

Morales dialed a number from memory and waited until he heard that the connection was made.

"I need a car, at current location, and disposal of current vehicle," Morales said, and waited while the operator on the other end tracked his phone.

"Estimated time of arrival is 23 minutes."

"Great." Morales hung up the phone and closed his eyes. He concentrated on calming the anger, but could only think about how had it all gone so wrong tonight. Every step of the way he'd been thwarted, and the failure tasted bad in his mouth.

He picked up some of the crumpled papers that had fallen from the briefcase, papers he'd grabbed from the floor of the garage as he escaped. He was glad to see that most of the information was marked out. That stupid, meddling journalist wouldn't get far, but Morales had decided to kill the reporter regardless.

Near the bottom of the stack of papers, Morales came across some information on Mae's current whereabouts. Turns out that a woman at the airport had filed a complaint that her passport and credit cards were stolen, a woman named Gertrude Pettingale, who had been on her way to visit her boyfriend in California.

A second ticket had been purchased for Ms. Pettingale, a multi-destination ticket with its first stop in Hartford, Connecticut.

"Ah," Morales said, feeling a bit elated at the news. "So you're going home."

He thought for a moment, recalling names and faces in his mind. It didn't take long. He opened his phone again and dialed a number that would connect him with a different operator, one who handled the directory of sleeper cells. When the connection was made, he requested the number of a particular cell, one who'd been sleeping for some time now. The operator patched him through, and the dial tone rang.

Morales waited for three rings before the other end was picked up.

"Hello?" The young man on the other end didn't know exactly who was calling him so late in the night, only that it was his employer. He also would have known that the call would not have been made unless his employer had some urgent business for him.

"The girl," Morales said.

"I understand." The young man's voice fresher now and more alert.

"I'll need a report as soon as possible," Morales said.

"Yes, sir."

Morales ended the call and smiled. Finally, Mae had played into their hands, as they'd known she would do eventually. He leaned his seat back a few inches and shut his eyes to sleep for a few minutes before his replacement car arrived. Oh Mae flowers, April showers, he thought as he drifted off to sleep, how stupid you are. And soon you'll be dead.

Chapter Thirty-Three

Mae's eyes fluttered open and closed when she heard talking, but she fought the urge to just stay asleep,. She wondered if Ryan and the driver were talking, but the conversation sounded more one-sided. Finally, she pushed the sleep away for just long enough to hear Ryan talking into his cell phone.

"Yes, sir," he said, and then the call had ended. She sleepily wondered what that had been about, so late at night.

She leaned against the window, watching the snow falling beneath the yellow streetlights, and for the first time in many years she felt warm and safe, like she'd felt as a child snuggling beneath heavy blankets with blizzards raging outside. They passed farmhouses among the rolling hills, and even though the windows were closed, the smell of chimney smoke spiced the air. She remembered quiet moments on cold winter nights, laughing and eating popcorn, the crackling wood in the fireplace, and howling wind outside.

They will never stop hunting you, her mother had said so long ago. Move, before the devil catches you, the bus driver had said, but he had died protecting her. Now Ryan would be killed. They had found her and they would shoot him as they carried her away.

She turned and looked up through the car's moon roof, sleep once again taking her.

They will never stop hunting you. The words echoed from far away, warning her of something that wasn't quite right, and Mae thought she smelled Ryan's cologne, a spicy sweet smell that made her heart flutter.

Mae stared up at the dark winter sky, the twinkling stars, and snow falling.

Part Four
Aftermath

Chapter Thirty-Four

Heather stared at her computer screen and watched the progress of the clean-up and emergency crews. She couldn't watch what was happening with a camera, of course, but she monitored the radio frequencies and cell phone triangulation, and the streaming data became almost as good as an image.

She hated it when people died during the games, but at least three of the players had gotten out alive. She had to remind herself that these people did what they did because they wanted to. She told herself again and again that while she was the one who organized the games, she saw a way for a lot of people to make money and improve the world at the same time, the players in this game had been playing for a long time before she showed up on the scene.

But the guilt persisted. She studied the flowing data stream and saw that Sam was already in the ambulance, being taken to a nearby hospital. At least he was alive, she thought, knowing that he had a wife and a new baby at home. The wife--she thought her name was Dani, but couldn't remember--would of course have no idea where her husband was, or how he'd been so hurt.

Those were the rules. But just like everyone else who played the game, Sam's wife benefited from the risk and Sam's injuries in the games. Hazard pay, after all.

She hit a few keys on her keyboard and pulled up the Lit Dragon payment account and sent payments to each of the players. Heather checked her own account to make sure that money had been deposited into her account as well.

She leaned her head on her keyboard and breathed deeply, allowing the stress to flow out of her. After a few moments, she turned back to her computer and navigated to the VPN portal that routed her computer through seventeen different countries, then plunged into the Deep Web where she felt most at home. She got lost in that space between computers, amidst the data that was unsearchable by normal means, not paying attention to the time. Several hours passed before she even thought about going to bed. She was tired and had to teach a class early the next morning.

Heather's computer suddenly emitted a soft chirp, and the message bar on the bottom of her screen began to flash a burnt orange color. She moused over the flashing bar, and saw that she'd received a message from DukE_of_DarkNEss_83.

    u there?

Heather tapped the message and a window appeared on her screen. She clicked the box and typed:

    Yep.

DukE_of_DarkNEss_83
How was the event this evening?
Any casualties?

ANONX^17
One dead. Sucks.

DukE_of_DarkNEss_83
Sucks. r u okay?

Heather looked out the window of her third floor apartment at the boring courtyard beyond. A playground stood alone in the darkness, a swing gently rocking back and forth in the night breeze. She wished for the sounds of kids playing outside; it was too quiet at the moment. She didn't want to think about the player who had died, and had spent the last few hours doing her best to drop it from her mind.

And now, the Duke of Darkness wanted to talk about it. She didn't blame him, and supposed that most good guys wanted to listen and take care of their friends. In truth, the Duke was one of those good guys, really the total opposite of darkness. He was a single guy in grad school at a university out west, and one of the more talented hackers that Heather had ever met in the digital universe. Of course, she'd never seen the guy, didn't even know his real name (although that wouldn't have been terribly difficult to find) but she imagined him to be a smallish guy with narrow shoulders, always draped in a button-down shirt that was tucked into neatly pressed jeans. He would be wearing thick rimmed glasses, which framed his pale complexion. She pictured him sitting alone in his apartment, sipping hot chocolate as he worked his magic. And magic was the right word for what the Duke did. He ran a website with a group of fellow socially-minded hackers, called Wiki-Bust. They used their incredible combined talent to bypass whatever firewalls or protections stood in their way, uncovering whatever they determined to be unsavory to society and posting it for the world to see. Their most recent bust was the bribing of an Italian judge in an internationally-known murder case. And they didn't stop with the bribery; they also exposed the judge's ties with crooked politicians, and the European drug trade. The Duke and the hackers at Wiki-Bust were ruthless, but always objective in who they exposed. They ousted tumors on society, individuals who threatened the common good.

DukE_of_DarkNEss_83

still there?

ANONX^17

Yeah. I'm fine, just thinking.

DukE_of_DarkNEss_83

So...

ANONX^17

Yeah?

DukE_of_DarkNEss_83

Just how crazy did things get with your game this evening?

ANONX^17

What do you mean? Someone died, another in the hospital.

>DukE_of_DarkNEss_83
>no cops?
>ANONX^17
>No. why

Heather moved her chair closer and stared at the screen. It wasn't like the Duke to be so dodgy about things. Something was clearly going on.

>DukE_of_DarkNEss_83
>the drivers were in the Windy City, right?
>ANONX^17
>yep whats going on?
>DukE_of_DarkNEss_83
>u see the news?

Heather had a web crawler working all major news outlets which would immediately tell her if certain key words were mentioned. It was part of her job to ensure that the Lit Dragons stayed in the shadows, but she couldn't focus all of her attention on every news source. So far, nothing had matched the criteria enough to alert her about the games that evening.

She opened her browser and saw that things had indeed been heating up in Chicago that evening, so much so that she was surprised she hadn't notice before. The murder of a bus driver, a shooting at O'Hare and then later in the hospital. All flights grounded, and an active manhunt for a cop killer.

What was going on?

She ran some searches, scanning headlines and police reports, becoming engrossed again in the data. Heather didn't notice the new message from the Duke for several seconds, and when she did, she had already seen the name of the *Gazette* reporter, Paul Freemont. She recognized his name, but couldn't remember from where.

     DukE_of_DarkNEss_83

```
We did some sniffing around
when things started heating up,
tapping into police and
emergency frequencies, police
records, even call logs for the
city buses. u saw the bus
driver got shot, right?
```

     ANONX^17

```
Yeah.
```

     DukE_of_DarkNEss_83

```
Take a look at these.
```

A message popped up with a link to a secure viewer. She clicked, and the image of two PDFs appeared, compared side-by-side. She scanned the image and saw that they were police incident reports. They detailed the shooting of a police officer, the same she'd seen in the news a few seconds before. The second report was for a woman with a name she didn't recognize. Gertrude Pettingale was also shot, in a manner that was almost identical to the police officer.

In fact, after a few seconds of flitting between the images, she saw that the description of the incident in both reports was identical. A few seconds later, she confirmed that everything on the report was identical except for the names.

What is this?

Another message with another link appeared on her screen. She clicked the link and a single image appeared in the window. The police report bearing Ms. Pettingale's name was now different. The description of the shooting was partly deleted, and it looked like a new description was being inputted to the form. She toggled between the previous images and this new one, and saw that the birth dates and physical descriptions had changed, but the report number was still identical.

DukE_of_DarkNEss_83
u catch it.

ANONX^17
they're the same.

DukE_of_DarkNEss_83
one of the guys here just
happened to be looking at the
officer's police report when he
noticed that it was being
changed. He took a few screen
shots and forwarded them over.
This was a couple of hours ago.
There is no longer any record
of an Officer Robert Morales
being shot, or even being on
the Chicago pd.

ANONX^17
just like that

DukE_of_DarkNEss_83
just like that, he's gone.
thin air kind of stuff. but
this gertude pettinggale does
exist and was shot at the
airport tonight. her body was
discovered by airport personnel
after the police incident
report was edited.

Heather began to tap her fingers on her desk impatiently. It wasn't like the Duke to string her along like this, and she could tell that it was leading up to something. The anxiety and near panic she'd felt during the games was compounded. The sound of her heartbeat was in her ears, and her fingers felt numb and fidgety. Heather took a sip of her tea and tried to force its calming effects on her body.

DukE_of_DarkNEss_83
thats not all. turns out that
gertrude didn't die at all, but
left on a flight out of Chicago
to hartford.

ANONX^17
Did some one steal her passport
after she was killed?

DukE_of_DarkNEss_83

Thats what we thought at first, but we don't think so. One of my guys confirmed that there was a body recovered matching the general description of getrude pettingale. We also tapped airport security footage of the woman posing as Ms. Pettingale. We ran her image through facial recognition and confirmed that the woman acting as Pettingale is definitely not her. Pettingale is dead, just like the report says.

ANONX^17

But why the switch?

· DukE_of_DarkNEss_83

With the shooting at the airport, NDA is monitoring all calls in and out of the surrounding area. We figured that whoever changed the police report would also monitor NDA transcripts. sure enough, someone else was in system, deleting data.

ANONX^17

Bot?

DukE_of_DarkNEss_83

No, I think human. The searches and alterations were too subjective for a bot, and the data wasn't deleted, just changed. Like the police report. You delete something, and there's an empty space, but if the data is just altered, the changes hide in plain sight.

ANONX^17

reminds me of

DukE_of_DarkNEss_83

Miami. I know, and just wait. we recovered some cell phone transcripts before they were changed. check the attached.

The Duke sent another link containing a compressed folder. She clicked on the folder and a number of PDFs automatically extracted onto her screen. She scanned the documents in seconds and felt a chill on the back of her neck.

DukE_of_DarkNEss_83

did you see it? they've cropped up again.

As soon as he typed the message, Heather saw it.

Il Contionum. It was the name of an entity that, for all intents and purposes, didn't exist. The Contionum was a ghost, and neither Heather nor the Duke knew who they were or what they did, only that they were powerful enough to erase data that couldn't be erased, to fully disappear in a digital world when it was impossible to disappear. The few times the name had shown up had been associated with unmitigated disasters.

The attack in Miami, hundreds dead. The collapse of a bridge in New Orleans during a category 5 hurricane, preventing thousands from evacuating and causing the deaths of hundreds. The disappearance of an airplane off the coast of Portugal (with 173 people aboard), into thin air.

Of course, there could have been more mentions of the Contionum, but any information was slippery and tended to disappear almost as soon as it appeared.

```
              ANONX^17
I see them.
          DukE_of_DarkNEss_83
This is the first solid lead we
have on this group.
```

Heather saw a name that was familiar, but she couldn't put her finger on it. She was sure that she'd heard it before, but couldn't quite remember when and where.

```
              ANONX^17
Do you recognize the name Paul
Freemont?
```

DukE_of_DarkNEss_83
He was the reporter in Miami... but ur probably remembering his name from the news tonight. he almost got himself killed in the hospital. original police report says he was claiming to be helping a police officer who'd been shot, who had then tried to kill him. I'll give you one guess as to who the police officer was.

ANONX^17
Morales. When the Miami thing went down, Freemont wouldn't shut up. is anyone listening to him now?

DukE_of_DarkNEss_83
as far as we can tell, no. the report on the incident says he's in shock from loss of blood. maybe the report was changed, but if it was, the changes happened before we pulled the report.

ANONX^17

what is going on?

DukE_of_DarkNEss_83

i don't know. but whatever it is, its happening fast. we stumbled on this stuff by luck, really, and if we hadn't, the cover up would have been complete.

ANONX^17

like Miami.

DukE_of_DarkNEss_83

like Miami.

Heather continued to scan. There were multiple references to a girl, and whoever had been speaking about her was doing very well at not mentioning her name. But almost all the calls listed on the transcript mentioned the girl at least once. She was the focus of most of the conversations, and although she couldn't read emotion into any of the written transcripts, Heather thought that the almost constant back and forth about "the girl" was frantic.

ANONX^17

Who's the girl?

DukE_of_DarkNEss_83

We don't know, but we're working on it now. keep reading tho. She seems to have been part of this group for a very long time. We'll find her, and it won't take long. its not looking good.

ANONX^17

Why?

DukE_of_DarkNEss_83

Keep reading. They're not just looking for her. they want her dead.

Chapter Thirty-Five

Several weeks passed with Paul in a haze induced by pain killers and a constant fear that gnawed at him during his waking hours, turning his dreams to nightmares. When he was awake, every shadow was Officer Morales returning to finish the job. And while he slept, he was running from an unseen force of darkness that never stopped hunting him. Paul was fully aware that he was dabbling at the edges of insanity, but he felt like there wasn't anything he could do. The insanity was inevitable, an undercurrent that already existed in his mind, ready to burst free.

Morales' bullet had nicked the bone in Paul's leg, sending splinters of bone into his muscles and bloodstream. After removing the bullet, the surgeons spent the better part of week digging through his legs to remove the fragments of bone, during which time Paul slipped in and out of consciousness. He dreamt of his ex-wife and riding bikes with her through the hills of the mountain town in which he grew up. When the dreams went bad, as they so often did, he dreamt of running through underground parking garages, dodging shadows and bullets. He dreamt of pain and fear and paranoia.

After his surgeries, Paul was kept in the hospital (just down the hall from where Morales had been holed up), until he was able to walk with a cane. He hated the physical therapy and thought the therapist was the devil incarnate, but he worked hard. Although the doctors and therapists were convinced he would once again be able to walk without a cane, some day far in the future, they told him that his leg would be permanently damaged. Paul would walk, but never run. It was an injury he would carry with him for the rest of his life. So far, the mental damage seemed worse than the leg, and Paul couldn't decide which was worse to carry on as baggage.

Dennis was Paul's only visitor, and he came every few days to sit next to Paul's bed and give updates on the daily on goings at the Gazette, and relayed the status on stories they were working on together. They never spoke about the night Paul was shot, or how it might relate to Paul's theories on what had happened in Miami. Paul did his best to not even think about that night, or Miami, or anything else that would get him shot again. He wanted to put that night and his theories to rest, once and for all. It was this investigation, this obsession, with the incident in Miami that had cost him his marriage and family, and now his leg and possibly his sanity.

On the day Paul was discharged from the hospital, the nurse brought a shoebox sized plastic container into his room.

At the moment, Paul was sitting up in his bed, watching reruns of Frasier on the old television. He smiled at the nurse as she entered, and then cocked an eyebrow when he noticed the container she was carrying. She set it on his bed and started pulling items, laying them on the mattress by his feet.

"These are the items you had on your person when you arrived at the hospital," she said and then pointed to a pile of neatly folded rags.

"Your clothes are here. They were cut from your body so they aren't much use as clothes anymore, and we couldn't get the blood stains out. But some people get upset when they hear we threw away their ruined clothes, so here you go. They're clean, just stained and ragged."

Paul chuckled despite the sick feeling that rose in his gut at the sight of the blood splatters. His blood, or Morales'? He wondered, but then decided he didn't want to know.

"You can toss the clothes. I can't think of why I'd want to keep them," his voice quavered despite his efforts to remain steady.

"That's what I thought," the nurse said and set aside the bundle. "We've also got your keys here, wallet, some chap stick, and a flash drive."

"Well thank you for hanging on to this stuff," Paul smiled warmly at the nurse, who blushed. She was a younger woman with a pretty face, despite the stress lines and creases that were developing. As she blushed, he could see past the hardened exterior that was necessary for a nurse in Chicago, and he saw playfulness that was very attractive.

"To be honest, I don't know if I would have missed these things until I got to my car and needed my keys, or the store and needed my wallet."

"Most people forget about the stuff they came in with, which is understandable especially when you get shot."

"Yeah, well that's certainly true."

"We also have your briefcase," she said and lifted the small leather case to the bed, which he hadn't seen her bring into the room. Paul could see the dried smears of blood and water on side, staining the leather. A chill ran down his spine and the place where he'd been shot began to throb. In the commotion of the previous weeks, with the surgeries and therapy, he'd forgotten about Morales' briefcase. He stared at the nurse and the briefcase, remembering that night in more detail than he cared for. A flood of emotions swept over him and he felt the same fear and paranoia that he'd been working so hard to put behind him.

The nurse shifted from one foot to another, uncomfortable with his silence.

"The briefcase was jammed open when you were brought into the hospital, but we didn't open it," she said tentatively. "We had one of the tech guys who do maintenance in the hospital fix it, and it latches now. I hope you don't mind."

"No, I don't mind."

"Okay, well all your stuff is here. I've got your discharge papers, and you're all set. Do you have someone picking you up?"

"Yes," Paul said, but his mind was far away, thinking about the woman he was supposed to have met on that bus, at the beginning of all this—"

"Okay then," she said, cutting through the silence. "It's been nice to know you, Mr. Fremont. I wish you a swift recovery, and hope you stay out of trouble in the future. You know, and not get shot."

The corners of her mouth turned up coyly in that same playful smile he'd found so charming only a few minutes before. When he didn't return the smile, or even acknowledge her goodbye, she nodded and left the room, leaving Paul to his thoughts.

***

Dennis picked Paul up from the hospital and they drove in near silence to the hotel where Paul kept a room. Dennis pulled up to the curb and held out his hand for Paul to shake.

"Buddy, glad to see you on your feet. I'll be glad to have you back at work here soon too."

"Not on my feet yet," Paul grumbled and nudged the plain metal cane his therapist had give him.

"You know what I mean."

Paul opened the door and was hit with an icy blast of wind. He shivered, realizing that it had been several weeks since he'd been outside in the cold. Even so, he was getting sick of this winter.

"I think I'm moving to Florida," Paul said and climbed out of the car, grunting as he swung his leg onto the icy sidewalk.

"When are you going to get a real apartment like a normal person?" Dennis asked. "You might feel better if you had a home to go home to."

"I like the turn down service," Paul shrugged. He gathered his tiny bundle of things, and the brief case, and stood on the sidewalk, leaning heavily on his cane.

"Coming into work tomorrow?"

"I don't know. Probably not."

"I'll let the editor know then," Dennis said, sighing. "Take care, Paul."

"You too. Thanks for the ride."

Paul closed the car door and watched as Dennis drove away. For the first time in several weeks, Paul felt very alone. He didn't want to think about the briefcase nor what was inside, wanted to toss them into the trash can on his way back inside, but on the other hand, he couldn't stop thinking about it. The briefcase seemed important to Morales, so he figured there had to be something worthwhile in there.

He walked toward the entrance of the Hotel Monoco, eyeing the trash can as he passed.

Throw it away, get rid of it, his mind screamed. The part of his mind that didn't want to be involved anymore. The part that didn't want to be shot and killed.

Maybe just one look, he thought. Not going to get involved, just one look, and then be done with this whole mess and move on with his life.

***

Paul's room was exactly as he'd left it. Stacks of papers and research covered most surfaces. A half empty bottle of Wild Turkey on the counter in the kitchenette, standing next to an unopened full bottle. His bed was neatly made, and his clothes had been hung in the closet.

He set his things on the table and opened the brief case. The papers were a jumbled mess inside, some wrinkled and bent, and most stained with drops of blood. Paul took the papers and stacked them on the table. He examined the now empty briefcase for any hidden zippers or pockets on the cloth interior, but didn't find anything.

Paul turned back to the papers, straightened the stack, and stared at the first blood-splattered piece of paper. The first page was an email, the sender and recipient's addresses encrypted. The subject line simply read GODMEN. Most of the text in the body of the email was smeared and unreadable. He could make out only a few words and phrases, none of which made any sense. Paul took a deep breath, then stood and poured himself a glass of the bourbon.

Paul stood at the floor to ceiling window in the room and sipped as he looked out over the city and the lake beyond. Lights were beginning to twinkle in the twilight, and dark grey clouds churned over the water. He was cold just looking, but the Wild Turkey was warming his body.

After several minutes, he finished off his drink, poured another, and returned to the table and the stack of papers. He turned to the second page in the stack, which was crumpled and creased through the middle of the page, both vertically and horizontally. The page was blank except for a single line of text across the top, and a handwritten note along the bottom.

On the top of the page, it read:

$$41° \ 51' \ N \ / \ 87° \ 56' \ W$$

In the bottom right hand corner, someone had jotted in messy handwriting:

MICHIGAN AV R B

The top line of text was obviously the latitude and longitude of a location. He opened his laptop and entered the coordinates into the search browser. His search pulled up a number of websites that would convert the latitude and longitude into an address. He clicked on the first website, and a map appeared across his screen, a little red pin pointing to a place just outside of Chicago.

Okay, this was interesting, Paul thought. He sipped again at his bourbon, enjoying the burn and allowing it to calm his nerves. He clicked on a magnifying glass on the bottom of the screen and zoomed in on the map. As details became more apparent, he saw that the pin identified an area of forest preserve in DuPage County.

Paul stared at the screen, trying to think of how this would fit with what had happened that night. Why would Morales be interested in these specific coordinates? As far as he could tell, this was a wide expanse of forest.

Morales had been looking for a girl who'd escaped from somewhere. Paul didn't get any more details than that, but was it possible that she could have been hiding in the forest? Paul absently reached into his pocket for a piece of cinnamon candy, but it was empty. He made a mental note to pick up more fireballs the next time he was at the store.

He stood with his glass of bourbon and walked to the window, thinking back on that night for anything else that Morales had said that would give him a clue as to why those coordinates were in Morales' briefcase.

Paul watched the traffic on the streets below, absently following cars as they turned and stopped at lights. A city bus stopped a few blocks away, and people climbed on and off.

He stared at the bus, and it all came back to him to suddenly, he almost dropped his glass of bourbon. Paul couldn't believe it had taken even this long for the connection. On that night several weeks ago, he was supposed to meet a woman on the bus.

ROUTE B MICHIGAN AVENUE.

He went back to the table and stared at the scribble on the bottom of the paper. It was the same bus route.

The woman he was supposed to meet was going to shed some light on the bombing in Miami. She had sought him out, not the other way around. Paul remembered her inexplicable fear, but at the same time, her assurance that she would meet him on the bus.

It was dark and storming when Paul had ridden the bus, so he couldn't remember exactly where the route had taken him, but he seemed to remember being in the middle of nowhere during parts of the ride. He wondered if the bus had driven by Morales' coordinates. Paul wasn't sure but it seemed possible.

With his heart thumping, he returned to his laptop and pulled up the city bus routes. It took a few minutes of searching, but he finally found Route B Michigan Avenue, and the road was near the forest preserve. Not directly next to, but close enough.

Paul was getting excited now. He set his glass on the table, only a few drops of bourbon remaining.

It all made sense. He was supposed to meet the woman on the bus. The same bus that was near the coordinates that Morales was interested in. A few hours later, the bus driver is found shot on his own bus, near the airport and Morales is found shot in the back of a van, and then taken to a hospital.

It was all connected, he thought. Had to be.

But there was something missing.

Was the woman Paul was going to meet the same girl Morales was looking for? He didn't think so. Morales was specific when he called her a girl, and Paul was sure that it was an older woman he'd talked to on the phone. Not elderly, but older. Regardless, there seemed to be a connection.

He stood, pacing his little room with the metal cane and ignoring the throbbing pain in his leg. Paul was sure there was a connection, but everything seemed just out of focus. He saw the big picture, but not the details.

The coordinates. Whatever had been at the coordinates was important enough to draw Morales' attention, and maybe there was something left. Some detail or clue to bring the picture into focus.

But he'd been shot and almost killed for getting too involved, his mind screamed at him. He was fully aware that just minutes before, he'd been ready to ignore the briefcase and chuck in the trash. But now...

He needed to see what was at the coordinates. Paul considered calling the cops with the coordinates and his theories, but then again, Morales was a cop. He couldn't risk it with the police, but he needed to see what in the forest was so important.

Then Paul had a thought and returned to his computer. He opened his web browser to a map of the forest preserve. He clicked a button that changed the illustrated map to a satellite view. Paul knew that the satellite images were not updated regularly, but he hoped there might be something on the current image to shed some light as to why the coordinates were important. He zoomed in on the image and began scrolling through the forested area.

After the first thirty minutes, he stood and poured himself another glass of Wild Turkey. So far, he'd seen nothing but forest and trees, and the occasional hiking trail or access road. He was discouraged and his excitement from before was warring off.

Maybe the coordinates were for a meeting place, or a drop-off or pick-up point. In that case, he thought, there wasn't going to be anything for him to find on the satellite images.

Paul was getting tired, and the bourbon was working its dark magic. His leg hurt and he wanted to pop a few pills and go to sleep. He gave himself just ten more minutes of scouring the satellite imagery before he would call it quits.

Maybe there was simply nothing for him to see--just like his pipe dream conspiracy theory on the attack in Miami. Maybe he was once again barking up the wrong tree.

And then something caught Paul's eye. A rectangular structure set several miles into the forest preserve, surrounding by a small clearing. A thin access road led from the cabin and wound its way through the forest and exited to the county highway that boarded the preserve.

He toggled to the other tab in his web browser and examined the map containing highlighted route for Route B Michigan Avenue. Sure enough, the city bus drove right by the access road.

It probably meant nothing, and Paul forced himself not to get too excited. It was, after all, just a cabin in the woods.

But maybe... just maybe there was something at the cabin that would connect all these dots.

Paul stood, ignoring the raging pain in his leg. He hobbled to the large window and stared out at the city. It was full dark now, and the winter storm had arrived at the shores of the lake. He couldn't go now, in the dark and with the impending storm. But in the morning, he would call a cab and make the trek out to the forest.

It's probably nothing, he thought, just a lonely cabin in the woods.

But maybe not.

Paul watched the first flakes from the winter storm flutter toward the twinkling lights of the city below and smiled.

To Be Continued...

ABOUT THE AUTHOR

Derrick Hibbard is the author of the best selling *Fast Track* Series, *This Side of Eden,* and *Impish.*

Be sure to visit Derrick Hibbard on his blog, Facebook and Twitter for the free, private newsletter and get instant access to
exclusive extras and treats, including novels, novellas, stories, and more.

For more information visit:
https://www.facebook.com/derrickhibbard.author
derrickhibbard.blogspot.com
twitter.com/derrickhibbard
http://derrickhibbard.tumblr.com/

Also By Derrick Hibbard

Snow Falling

Book Two in the Snow Swept Trilogy. As Mae's false sense of security and her feelings for Ryan grow, her past threatens to destroy everything.

Snow Pyre

Book Three in the Snow Swept Trilogy. The survivors of the attack by Il Contionum regroup and embark on an impossible mission to rescue Mae, and finally uncover the truth.

THIS SIDE OF EDEN

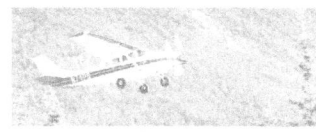

A love story

Derrick Hibbard

Bestselling Author of
The Double Stroller Handgrenade

This Side of Eden

A small plane crashes in the icy waters of a lake set in the heart of Alaska.

A father and his two-year-old daughter are stranded alone in the wilderness with no food, no supplies, and no hope of rescue.

This is their story...

The Double Stroller Hand Grenade

Peter Wilcox is a bright-eyed and fluffy-tailed new attorney, who witnesses the "hit" of the managing partner in his law firm. Because of this inadvertent run-in and supposed link with the mafia, Peter can't find another job anywhere and is forced to tend his kids full-time while his wife, Alison, brings home the bacon. Peter hates the new job: His young kids are a whirlwind of destruction wherever they go, and he and Alison seem to be growing further and further apart as she works long hours.

As it turns out, Alison is not an interior designer, as Peter was led to believe, but is the assassin who killed Peter's boss—a fact that Peter is none-too-happy about. Things really get crazy when Alison's Mafioso peers decide that she is better off dead. What follows is a hilarious romp, as the emasculated Peter has to deal with a super-cool-femme-fatale of a wife, while he and his two kids are mercilessly thrust into a world of gangsters and professional hit men.

IMPISH

IMPISH is the story of a young lawyer named Travis, who accidently sells his soul to Satan in exchange for financial gain and some luck with the women.

The devil is a little too backed up with attorneys, so Travis is instead assigned an Imp to help him with his endeavors, and Hell literally breaks loose. What follows is a hilarious—at times outrageous—adventure as Travis and his Imp try to break free from the clutches of eternal damnation.

Law School Fast Track: Essential Habits for Law School Success

For a law student, numerous and massive reading assignments loom from the very first day -- with no let-up until final exams -- and with zero feedback until those finals. Law students wonder where to begin, how to begin, and what to do each day.

Law School Fast Track is short, fast, inexpensive, and easy-to-read. It is written to help law students starting on day one with one thousand pages of assigned cases. Its immediate suggestions, examples, and tips focus on the first week of law school, emphasizing the importance of establishing and maintaining good habits.

Law School Fast Track will help form good habits before and during the first week of law school. For example, during the first week a student will decide where to study, how long to study, how to brief a law case, what to do with class notes, how to outline, and when to start outlining, among many other demands.

Law School Fast Track will cut right to the most important issues: essential habits for law school. Better success, easier study, and higher grades and graduations prospects.

College Fast Track: Essential Habits for Less Stress and More Success in College

College Fast Track is concise, easy-to-read, and written in an approachable, peer tone with today's college student in mind. Its message is one of building good study and personal habits, achieving greater academic success while enjoying a better, less-stressful college experience. College Fast Track focuses on immediately usable habits. Its goal is to help students improve in measurable ways, and in ways that provide greater—not less—time for enjoyment: success and less stress! Once college begins, however, the reading load is enormous (and parties beckon), thus "extra-curricular" reading is unappealing. Unlike other books on college, this book is not over-laden with details about mundane issues. Instead, College Fast Track cuts right to the most important issues. Better success, easier study, and higher grades and graduation prospects.

Made in United States
North Haven, CT
15 September 2023